just one year

ALSO BY GAYLE FORMAN

Sisters in Sanity

If I Stay

Where She Went

Just One Day

just one year

GAYLE FORMAN

DUTTON BOOKS
AN IMPRINT OF PENGUIN GROUP (USA)

DUTTON BOOKS
Published by the Penguin Group
Penguin Group (USA) LLC
375 Hudson Street
New York, New York 10014

USA * Canada * UK * Ireland * Australia
New Zealand * India * South Africa * China

penguin.com
A Penguin Random House Company

LIBRARY OF CONGRESS CATALOGING-IN-PUBLICATION DATA
Forman, Gayle.
Just one year / by Gayle Forman.
pages cm
Sequel to: Just one day.
Summary: "After spending an amazing day and night with a nameless girl in Paris, Willem
embarks on his own transformative journey to find her once again"—Provided by publisher.
ISBN 978-0-525-42592-2 (hardback)
[1. Voyages and travels—Fiction. 2. Self-actualization (Psychology)—Fiction. 3. Love—Fiction.]
I. Title.
PZ7.F75876Jw 2013
[Fic]—dc23
2013022976

Printed in the United States of America

1   3   5   7   9   10   8   6   4   2

Designed by Danielle Delaney
Set in Sabon LT Std

FOR MARJORIE, TAMARA,
AND LIBBA

Double, double, toil and trouble . . .

WHEN I WAS AT HOME, I WAS IN A BETTER PLACE:
BUT TRAVELLERS MUST BE CONTENT.

From William Shakespeare's *As You Like It*

PART ONE

One Year

One

*I*t's the dream I always have: I'm on a plane, high above the clouds. The plane starts to descend, and I have this sudden panic because I just know that I'm on the wrong plane, am traveling to the wrong place. It's never clear where I'm landing—in a war zone, in the midst of an epidemic, in the wrong century—only that it's somewhere I shouldn't be. Sometimes I try to ask the person next to me where we are going, but I can never quite see a face, can never quite hear an answer. I wake in a disoriented sweat to the sound of the landing gear dropping, to the echo of my heart beating. It usually takes me a few moments to find my bearings, to locate where it is I am—an apartment in Prague, a hostel in Cairo—but even once that's been established, the sense of being lost lingers.

I think I'm having the dream now. Just as always, I lift

the shade to peer at the clouds. I feel the hydraulic lurch of the engines, the thrust downward, the pressure in my ears, the ignition of panic. I turn to the faceless person next to me—only this time I get the feeling it's not a stranger. It's someone I know. Someone I'm traveling with. And that fills me with such intense relief. We can't *both* have gotten on the wrong plane.

"Do you know where we're going?" I ask. I lean closer. I'm just about there, just about to see a face, just about to get an answer, just about to find out where it is I'm going—

And then I hear sirens.

I first noticed the sirens in Dubrovnik. I was traveling with a guy I'd met in Albania, when we heard a siren go by. It sounded like the kind they have in American action movies, and the guy I was traveling with commented on how each country had its own siren sound. "It's helpful because if you forget where you are, you can always close your eyes, let the sirens tell you," he told me. I'd been gone a year by then, and it had taken me a few minutes to summon the sound of the sirens at home. They were musical almost, a down-up-down-up la, *la*, la, *la*, like someone absentmindedly, but cheerfully, humming.

That's not what *this* siren is. It is monotonous, a *nyeah-nyeah, nyeah-nyeah*, like the bleating of electric sheep. It doesn't become louder or fainter as it comes closer or gets farther away; it's just a wall of wailing. Much as I try, I cannot locate this siren, have no idea where I am.

I only know that I am not home.

I open my eyes. There is bright light everywhere, from overhead, but also from my own eyes: tiny pinprick explosions that hurt like hell. I close my eyes.

Kai. The guy I traveled with from Tirana to Dubrovnik was called Kai. We drank weak Croatian pilsner on the ramparts of the city and then laughed as we pissed into the Adriatic. His name was Kai. He was from Finland.

The sirens blare. I still don't know where I am.

The sirens stop. I hear a door opening, I feel water on my skin. A shifting of my body. I sense it is better to keep my eyes closed. None of this is anything I want to witness.

But then my eyes are forced open, and there's another light, harsh and painful, like the time I spent too long looking at a solar eclipse. Saba warned me not to, but some things are impossible to tear yourself away from. After, I had a headache for hours. Eclipse migraine. That's what they called it on the news. Lots of people got them from staring at the sun. I know that, too. But I still don't know where I am.

There are voices now, as if echoing out from a tunnel. I can hear them, but I cannot make out what they're saying.

"Comment vous appelez-vous?" someone asks in a language I know is not mine but that I somehow understand. *What is your name?*

"Can you tell us your name?" The question again in another language, also not my own.

"Willem de Ruiter." This time it's my voice. My name.

"Good." It is a man's voice. It switches back to the other

language. French. It says that I got my own name right, and I wonder how it is he knows this. For a second I think it is Bram speaking, but even as muddled as I am, I realize this is not possible. Bram never did learn French.

"Willem, we are going to sit you up now."

The back of my bed—*I think I'm on a bed*—tilts forward. I try to open my eyes again. Everything is blurry, but I can make out bright lights overhead, scuffed walls, a metal table.

"Willem, you are in the hospital," the man says.

Yes, I was just sussing that part out. It would also explain my shirt being covered in blood, if not the shirt itself, which is not mine. It is gray and says SOS in red lettering. What does SOS mean? Whose shirt is this? And whose blood is on it?

I look around. I see the man—a doctor?—in the lab coat, the nurse next to him, holding out an ice compress for me to take. I touch my cheek. The skin is hot and swollen. My finger comes away with more blood. That answers one question.

"You are in Paris," the doctor says. "Do you know where Paris is?"

I am eating tagine at a Moroccan restaurant in Montorgueil with Yael and Bram. I am passing the hat after a performance with the German acrobats in Montmartre. I am thrashing, sweaty, at a Mollier Than Molly show at Divan du Monde with Céline. And I'm running, running through the Barbès market, a girl's hand in mine.

Which girl?

"In France," I manage to answer. My tongue feels thick as a wool sock.

"Can you remember what happened?" the doctor asks.

I hear boots and taste blood. There is a pool of it in my mouth. I don't know what to do with it, so I swallow.

"It appears you were in a fight," the doctor continues. "You will need to make a report to the police. But first you will need sutures for your face, and we must take a scan of your head to make sure there is no subdural hematoma. Are you on holiday here?"

Black hair. Soft breath. A gnawing feeling that I've misplaced something valuable. I pat my pocket.

"My things?" I ask.

"They found your bag and its contents scattered at the scene. Your passport was still inside. So was your wallet."

He hands it to me. I look at the billfold. There are more than a hundred euros inside, though I seem to recall having a lot more. My identity card is missing.

"We also found this." He shows me a small black book. "There is still quite a bit of money in your wallet, no? It doesn't suggest a robbery, unless you fought off your attackers." He frowns, I assume at the apparent foolishness of this maneuver.

Did I do that? A low fog sits overhead, like the mist coming off the canals in the morning that I used to watch and will to burn off. I was always cold. Yael said it was because though I looked Dutch, her Mediterranean blood was swimming in me. I remember that, remember the scratchy wool blanket I would wrap myself in to stay warm. And though

I now know where I am, I don't know why I'm here. I'm not supposed to be in Paris. I'm supposed to be in Holland. Maybe that explains that niggling feeling.

Burn off. Burn off, I will the fog. But it is as stubborn as the Dutch fog. Or maybe my will is as weak as the winter sun. Either way, it doesn't burn off.

"Do you know the date?" the doctor asks.

I try to think, but dates float by like leaves in a gutter. But this is nothing new. I know that I never know the date. I don't need to. I shake my head.

"Do you know what month it is?"

Augustus. Août. No, English. "August."

"Day of the week?"

Donderdag, something in my head says. Thursday. "Thursday?" I try.

"Friday," the doctor corrects, and the gnawing feeling grows stronger. Perhaps I am supposed to be somewhere on Friday.

The intercom buzzes. The doctor picks it up, talks for a minute, hangs up, turns to me. "Radiology will be here in thirty minutes." Then he begins talking to me about *commotions cérébrales* or concussions and temporary short-term memory loss and cats and scans and none of it is making a lot of sense.

"Is there someone we can call?" he asks. And I feel like there is, but for the life of me, I can't think who. Bram is gone and Saba is gone and Yael might as well be. Who else is there?

The nausea hits, fast, like a wave I had my back to. And then there's puke all over my bloodied shirt. The nurse is quick with the basin, but not quick enough. She gives me a towel to clean myself with. The doctor is saying something about nausea and concussions. There are tears in my eyes. I never did learn to throw up without crying.

The nurse mops my face with another towel. "Oh, I missed a spot," she says with a tender smile. "There, on your watch."

On my wrist is a watch, bright and gold. It's not mine. For the quickest moment, I see it on a girl's wrist. I travel up the hand to a slender arm, a strong shoulder, a swan's neck. When I get to the face, I expect it to be blank, like the faces in the dream. But it's not.

Black hair. Pale skin. Warm eyes.

I look at the watch again. The crystal is cracked but it's still ticking. It reads nine. I begin to suspect what it is I've forgotten.

I try to sit up. The world turns to soup.

The doctor pushes me back onto the bed, a hand on my shoulder. "You are agitated because you are confused. This is all temporary, but we will need to take the CT scan to make sure there is no bleeding on the brain. While we wait, we can attend to your facial lacerations. First I will give you something to make the area numb."

The nurse swabs off my cheek with something orange. "Do not worry. This won't stain."

It doesn't stain; it just stings.

"I think I should go now," I say when the sutures are done.

The doctor laughs. And for a second I see white skin

covered in white dust, but warmer underneath. A white room. A throbbing in my cheek.

"Someone is waiting for me." I don't know who, but I know it's true.

"Who is waiting for you?" the doctor asks.

"I don't remember," I admit.

"Mr. de Ruiter. You must have a CT scan. And, after, I would like to keep you for observation until your mental clarity returns. Until you know who it is who waits for you."

Neck. Skin. Lips. Her fragile-strong hand over my heart. I touch my hand to my chest, over the green scrub shirt the nurse gave me after they cut off my bloody shirt to check for broken ribs. And the name, it's almost right there.

Orderlies come to wheel me to a different floor. I'm loaded into a metal tube that clatters around my head. Maybe it's the noise, but inside the tube, the fog begins to burn off. But there is no sunshine behind it, only a dull, leaden sky as the fragments click together. "I need to go. Now!" I shout from the tube.

There's silence. Then the click of the intercom. "Please hold still," a disembodied voice orders in French.

I am wheeled back downstairs to wait. It is past twelve o'clock.

I wait more. I remember hospitals, remember exactly why I hate them.

I wait more. I am adrenaline slammed into inertia: a fast car stuck in traffic. I take a coin out of my pocket and do the

trick Saba taught me as a little boy. It works. I calm down,
and when I do, more of the missing pieces slot into place. We
came together to Paris. We *are* together in Paris. I feel her
hand gentle on my side, as she rode on the back of the bicycle.
I feel her not-so-gentle hand on my side, as we held each other
tight. Last night. In a white room.

The white room. She is in the white room, waiting for me.

I look around. Hospital rooms are never white like people
believe. They are beige, taupe, mauve: neutral tones meant to
soothe heartbreak. What I wouldn't give to be in an actual
white room right now.

Later, the doctor comes back in. He is smiling. "Good news!
There is no subdural bleeding. Only a concussion. How is
your memory?"

"Better."

"Good. We will wait for the police. They will take your
statement and then I can release you to your friend. But you
must take it very easy. I will give you an instruction sheet for
care, but it is in French. Perhaps someone can translate it, or
we can find you one in English or Dutch online."

"*Ce ne sera pas nécessaire*," I say.

"Ahh, you speak French?" he asks in French.

I nod. "It came back to me."

"Good. Everything else will, too."

"So I can go?"

"Someone must come for you! And you have to make a
report to the police."

Police. It will be hours. And I have nothing to tell them, really. I take the coin back out and play it across my knuckle. "No police!"

The doctor follows the coin as it flips across my hand. "Do you have problems with the police?" he asks.

"No. It's not that. I have to find someone," I say. The coin clatters to the floor.

The doctor picks it up and hands it to me. "Find who?"

Perhaps it's the casual way he asked; my bruised brain doesn't have time to scramble it before spitting it out. Or perhaps the fog is lifting now, and leaving a terrific headache behind. But there it is, a name, on my lips, like I say it all the time.

"*Lulu.*"

"Ahh, Lulu. *Très bien!*" The doctor claps his hands together. "Let us call this Lulu. She can come get you. Or we can bring her to you."

It is too much to explain that I don't know where Lulu is. Only that she's in the white room and she's waiting for me and she's been waiting for a long time. And I have this terrible feeling, and it's not just because I'm in a hospital where things are routinely lost, but because of something else.

"I have to go," I insist. "If I don't go now, it could be too late."

The doctor looks at the clock on the wall. "It is not yet two o'clock. Not late at all."

"It might be too late for me." *Might be.* As if whatever is going to happen hasn't already happened.

The doctor looks at me for a long minute. Then he shakes

his head. "It is better to wait. A few more hours, your memory will return, and you will find her."

"I don't have a few hours!"

I wonder if he can keep me here against my will. I wonder if at this moment I even have a will. But something pulls me forward, through the mist and the pain. "I have to go," I insist. "Now."

The doctor looks at me and sighs. "*D'accord.*" He hands me a sheaf of papers, tells me I am to rest for the next two days, clean my wound every day, the sutures will dissolve. Then he hands me a small card. "This is the police inspector. I will tell him to expect your call tomorrow."

I nod.

"You have somewhere to go?" he asks.

Céline's club. I recite the address. The Métro stop. These I remember easily. These I can find.

"Okay," the doctor says. "Go to the billing office to check out, and then you may go."

"Thank you."

He touches me on the shoulder, reminds me to take it easy. "I am sorry Paris brought you such misfortune."

I turn to face him. He's wearing a name tag and the blurriness in my vision has subsided so I can focus on it. DOCTEUR ROBINET, it reads. And while my vision is okay, the day is still muddy, but I get this feeling about it. A hazy feeling of something—not quite happiness, but solidness, stepping on earth after being at sea for too long—fills me up. It tells me that whoever this Lulu is, something happened between us in Paris, something that was the opposite of misfortune.

Two

At the billing office, I fill out a few thousand forms. There are problems when they ask for an address. I don't have one. I haven't for such a long time. But they won't let me leave until I supply one. At first, I think to give them Marjolein, my family's attorney. She's who Yael has deal with all her important mail, and whom, I realize too late, I was supposed to meet with today—or was it tomorrow? Or yesterday now?—in Amsterdam. But if a hospital bill goes to Marjolein, then all of this goes straight back to Yael, and I don't want to explain it to her. I don't want to *not* explain it, either, in the more likely event she never asks about it.

"Can I give you a friend's address?" I ask the clerk.

"I don't care if you give me the Queen of England's address so long as we have somewhere to mail the bill," she says.

I can give them Broodje's address in Utrecht. "One moment," I say.

"Take your time, *mon chéri*."

I lean on the counter and rifle through my address book, flipping through the last year of accumulated acquaintances. There are countless names of people I don't remember, names I didn't remember even before I got this nasty bump on my head. There's a message to *Remember the caves in Matala*. I do remember the caves, and the girl who wrote the message, but not why I'm supposed to remember them.

I find Robert-Jan's address right at the front. I read it to the clerk, and as I close the book it falls open to one of the last pages. There's all this unfamiliar writing, and at first I think my eyesight must really be messed up, but then I realize it's just that the words are not English or Dutch but Chinese.

And for a second, I'm not here in this hospital, but I'm on a boat, with her, and she's writing in my notebook. I remember. She spoke Chinese. She showed it to me. I turn the page, and there's this.

There's no translation next to it, but I somehow know what that character means.

Double happiness.

I see the character here in the book. And I see it larger, on a sign. Double happiness. Is that where she is?

"Is there maybe a Chinese restaurant or store nearby?" I ask the clerk.

She scratches her hair with a pencil and consults a colleague. They start to argue about the best place to eat.

"No," I explain. "Not to eat. I'm looking for this." I show them the character in my book.

They look at each other and shrug.

"A Chinatown?" I ask.

"In the thirteenth arrondissement," one replies.

"Where's that?"

"Left Bank."

"Would an ambulance have brought me here from there?" I ask.

"No, of course not," she answers.

"There's a smaller one in Belleville," the other clerk offers.

"It is a few kilometers from here, not far," the first clerk explains and tells me how to get to the Métro.

I put on my rucksack, and leave.

I don't get far. My rucksack feels like it's full of wet cement. When I left Holland two years ago, I carried a big pack with many more things. But then it got stolen and I never replaced it, instead making do with a smaller bag. Over time, the rucksacks kept getting smaller and smaller, because there's so little a person actually needs. These days, all I keep is a few changes of clothes, some books, some toiletries, but now even that feels like too much. When I go down the stairs into the Métro, the bag bounces with each step, and pain knifes deep into me.

"Bruised, not broken," Dr. Robinet told me before I left. I thought he was talking about my spirit, but he'd been referring to my ribs.

On the Métro platform, I pull everything out of the rucksack except for my passport, wallet, address book, and toothbrush. When the train comes, I leave the rest on the platform. I'm lighter now, but it's not any easier.

The Belleville Chinatown begins right after the Métro stop. I try to match the signs from her character in my book, but there are so many signs and the neon lettering looks nothing like those soft ink lines she wrote. I ask around for double happiness. I have no idea if I'm asking for a place, a person, a food, a state of mind. The Chinese people look frightened of me and no one answers, and I begin to wonder if maybe I'm not really speaking French, only imagining I do. Finally one of them, an old man with grizzled hands clutching an ornate cane, stares at me and then says, "You are a long way from double happiness."

I am about to ask what he means, where it is, but then I catch a glimpse of my reflection in a shop window, my eye swelling purple, the bandage on my face seeping blood. I understand he isn't talking about a place.

But then I do glimpse familiar letters. Not the double happiness character, but the SOS letters from the mysterious T-shirt I was wearing earlier at the hospital. I see it now on another T-shirt, worn by a guy my age with jagged hair and an armful of metal cuffs. Maybe he's connected to double happiness somehow.

It winds me to catch up with him, a half block away. When I tap him on the shoulder, he turns around and steps back. I point to his shirt. I'm about to ask him what it means when he asks me in French, "What happened to you?"

"Skinheads," I reply in English. It's the same word all over. I explain in French that I was wearing a T-shirt like his before.

"Ahh," he says, nodding. "The racists hate Sous ou Sur. They are very anti-fascist."

I nod, though I remember now why they beat me up, and I'm pretty certain it had little to do with my T-shirt.

"Can you help me?" I ask.

"I think you need a doctor, my friend."

I shake my head. That's not what I need.

"What do you want?" the guy asks me.

"I'm looking for a place around here with a sign like this."

"What is it?"

"Double happiness."

"What's that?"

"I'm not sure."

"What is it you're looking for?"

"Maybe a store. Restaurant. Club. I don't know, really."

"You don't know shit, do you?"

"I know that I don't know shit. That counts for something." I point to the egg on my head. "Things got scrambled."

He peers at my head. "You should have that looked at."

"I already did." I point to the bandage covering the stitches on my cheek.

"Shouldn't you be resting or something?"

"Later. After I find it. The double happiness."

"What's so important about this double happiness?"

I see her then, not just see her, but *feel* her, soft breath against my cheek as she whispered something to me just as I was falling asleep last night. I didn't hear what she said. I only remember I was happy. To be in that white room. "Lulu," I say.

"Oh. A girl. I'm on my way to see *my* girl." He pulls out his phone and texts something. "But she can wait; they always do!" He grins at me, showing off a set of defiantly crooked teeth.

He's right. They do. Even when I didn't know they would, even when I'd been gone a long time, the girls, they waited. I never cared one way or another.

We take off, walking up and down the narrow blocks, the air thick with the smell of stewed organs. I feel like I'm running to keep up with him, and the exertion sets my stomach churning again.

"You don't look so pretty, friend," he tells me right as I retch bile into the gutter. He looks vaguely alarmed. "Are you sure you don't want a doctor?"

I shake my head, wipe my mouth, my eyes.

"Okay. I think maybe I should take you to meet my girl, Toshi. She works in this area, so she might know this double happiness place."

I follow him a few blocks. I'm still trying to find the double happiness sign, but it's even harder now because I got some sick on my address book and the ink's smeared. Also, there are black spots dancing before my eyes making it hard to see where the pavement really is.

When we finally stop, I almost cry in relief. Because we've found it, the double happiness place. Everything is familiar. The steel door, the red scaffolding, the distorted portraits, even the faded name on the facade, Ganterie, after the glove factory it must have once been. This is the place.

Toshi comes to the door, a tiny black girl with tight dreadlocks, and I want to hug her for delivering me to the white room. I want to march straight to the white room and lie down next to Lulu, to have everything feel right again.

I try to say this, but I can't. I can't even really get my legs to move because the ground beneath me has turned liquid and wavy. Toshi and my samaritan, whose name is Pierre, are arguing in French. She wants to call the police and Pierre says they have to help me find double happiness.

It's okay, I want to tell him. *I've found it.* This is the place. But I can't quite make the words come out straight. "Lulu," I manage to say. "Is she here?"

A few more people crowd around the door. "Lulu," I say again. "I left Lulu here."

"Here?" Pierre asks. He turns to Toshi and points to his head and then to my head.

I keep repeating her name: *Lulu, Lulu.* And then I stop but her name continues, like in an echo chamber, like my pleas are traveling deep into the building and will bring her back from wherever it is she's gone.

When the crowd parts, I think it really has worked. That my words dredged her up, returned her to me. That the one time I wanted one to wait, one did.

A girl steps out from the crowd. "*Oui, Lulu, c'est moi,*" she says delicately.

But that's not Lulu. Lulu was willowy with black hair and eyes as dark. This girl is a petite china doll, and blonde. She is not Lulu. Only then do I remember that Lulu is not Lulu either. Lulu was the name I gave her. I don't know her real name.

The crowd stares at me. I hear myself babbling about needing to find Lulu. The other Lulu. I left her in the white room.

They look at me with odd expressions on their faces and then Toshi pulls out her mobile phone. I hear her talking; she is requesting an ambulance. It takes me a minute to realize it's for me.

"No," I tell her. "I already have been to the hospital."

"I would hate to see you before," Wrong Lulu says. "Were you in an accident?"

"He got beaten up by skinheads," Pierre tells her.

But Wrong Lulu is right. Accident—how I found her. Accident—how I lost her. You have to give the universe credit, the way it evens things out like that.

Three

I take a taxi to Céline's club. The fare eats into the last of my money but it doesn't matter. I just need enough to get back to Amsterdam, and I already have a train ticket. On the short ride over, I nod off in the backseat and it's only when we pull up outside La Ruelle that I remember we left Lulu's suitcase here.

The bar is dark and empty, but the door is unlocked. I hobble down to Céline's office. It's dark inside there, too, only the grayish glow of her computer monitor lighting her face. At first, when she looks up and sees me, she smiles that smile of hers, like a lion waking from a nap, refreshed but hungry. Then I click on the light.

"Mon dieu!" she exclaims. "What did she do to you?"

"Was she here? Lulu?"

Céline rolls her eyes. "Yes. Yesterday. With you."

"Since then?"

"What happened to your face?"

"Where is the suitcase?"

"In the storage room, where we left it. What happened to you?"

"Give me the keys."

Céline narrows her eyes with one of her looks, but she opens a desk drawer and tosses me the keys. I unlock the door, and there's the suitcase. She hasn't come back for it, and for a moment I feel happy because it means she must still be here. Still be in Paris, looking for me.

But then I think about what the woman from Ganterie said, the one who came downstairs after my vision went all black and Toshi threatened again to call an ambulance and I begged for a taxi instead. This woman said that she saw a girl race out of the doors when she unlocked them this morning. "I called after her to come back, but she just ran away," she told me, in French.

Lulu didn't speak French. And she didn't know her way around Paris. She didn't know how to get to the train station last night. She didn't know how to get to the club, either. She wouldn't know where her suitcase is. She wouldn't know where I was—even *if* she wanted to find me.

I take the suitcase, search for a luggage tag, and find nothing: not a name tag or an airplane baggage claim. I try to open it, but it's locked. I pause for all of a second before yanking off the flimsy padlock. As soon as I open the bag, I'm hit with the familiar. Not the contents—clothes and souvenirs I've never seen before—but the smell. I pick up a neatly folded T-shirt, put it to my face, and inhale.

"What are you doing?" Céline asks, suddenly appearing in the doorway.

I slam the door shut in her face and continue going through Lulu's things. There are souvenirs, including one of those wind-up clocks like one we looked at together at one of the stalls on the Seine, some plug adapters, chargers, toiletries, but nothing that tracks back to her. There is a sheet of paper in a plastic bag, and I pick that up, hopeful, but it only contains an inventory of sorts.

Tucked underneath a sweater is a travel journal. I finger the cover. I was on a train to Warsaw more than a year ago when my rucksack got nicked. I had my passport, money, and address book on me, so all the thieves got was a half-broken backpack with a bunch of dirty clothes, an old camera, and a diary inside of it. They had probably just thrown everything away once they'd realized there was nothing to sell. Maybe they got twenty euros for the camera, though it was worth a lot more to me. As for the diary, worthless; I prayed they tossed it. I couldn't bear the idea of anyone reading it. It was the only time in the last two years I'd considered going home. I didn't. But when I bought new things, I didn't replace the diary.

I wonder what Lulu would think of me reading her journal. I try to imagine how I'd have felt had she read all my raw rantings about Bram and Yael from my stolen journal. When I do, it's not the usual embarrassment or shame or the disgust that washes over me. Instead, it's something quiet, familiar. Something like relief.

I open her journal, flipping through the pages, knowing I shouldn't. But I'm looking for a way to contact to her, though maybe, I'm just looking for more of her. A different way to breathe her in.

But I find no scent of her. Not a single name or address: not hers, not anyone's she met. There are only a few vague entries, nothing telling, nothing Lulu.

I flip to the end of the journal. The spine is stiff and cracks. Behind the back cover is a deck of postcards. I search them for addresses, but they're blank.

I reach for a pen on one of the shelves and start writing my name, phone number, email address, and Broodje's address for good measure, on each of the postcards. I write myself into Rome, Vienna, Prague, Edinburgh. London. All the while, I'm wondering why. *Keep in touch.* It's like a mantra on the road. This act you do. But it rarely happens. You meet people, you part ways, sometimes you cross paths again. Mostly, you don't.

The last postcard is of William Shakespeare from Stratford-upon-Avon. I'd told her to skip *Hamlet* and come see us instead. I'd told her the night was too nice for tragedy. I should have known better than to say a thing like that.

I flip Shakespeare over. "Please," I begin. I'm about to write something else: *Please get in touch. Please let me explain. Please tell me who you are.* But my cheek is throbbing and my vision has gone all soft-focus again and I'm exhausted and weighted with regret. So I bookend the "please" with that regret. "I'm sorry," I write.

I tuck all the postcards back in the bag and then back in the journal. I zip up the suitcase and put it back in the corner. I shut the door.

Four

The last time I was in Céline's flat, more than a year ago, she hurled a vase of dead flowers at my head. I'd been staying with her about a month, and I told her it was time for me to move on. It had been unseasonably warm and I'd stayed unusually long. But then the weather had turned cold and I felt the claustrophobia return. Céline accused me of being a fair-weather boyfriend, and she wasn't entirely wrong about the weather, but I'd never actually been her boyfriend, never promised to stay. There was screaming, curses, then the vase sailing through the air, missing my head but smashing into the faded blue wall. I tried to help with the mess before I left, but she refused to let me.

I don't think either of us expected me ever to set foot in here again. I don't think we ever thought we'd see each other again. But then I bumped into her at La Ruelle a few months later. She had recently been made booking manager, and she seemed happy enough to see me. She gave me free drinks all night and invited me down to her office to show me the roster of bands she had scheduled in the coming months. I went with her, even though I was pretty certain that the calendar was not what she wanted to show me, and sure enough, as soon as we got to the office, she locked the door, and never turned on her computer.

There was an unspoken agreement that I'd never go back to her flat. I had a place to stay, anyway, and I was leaving the next morning. After that, I saw her whenever I came through Paris. Always at the club, in the office, with the door locked.

So I think we are both surprised when I ask if I can stay at her place.

"Really? You want to?"

"If you don't mind. You can give me the keys and meet me later. I know you have to work. I'll leave tomorrow."

"Stay as long as you like. Let me come with you. I can help you."

My fingers absently touch the watch, still on my wrist. "You don't have to. I just need to rest."

Céline sees the watch. "Is that hers?" she asks.

I run my finger along the cracked crystal.

"Are you going to keep it?" she asks, her tone gone sour.

I nod. Céline starts to protest, but I hold up my hand to stop her. I barely have the energy to stand. But I am keeping this watch.

Céline rolls her eyes, but she also shuts down her computer and helps me up the stairs. She calls out to Modou, who is now digging around behind the bar, that she is taking me home for the night.

"What happened to your friend?" Modou asks, popping back up.

I turn back toward him. The lights are dim and Céline's arm is around me for support. I can hardly see him. "Tell her I'm sorry. Her suitcase is in the closet. If she comes back. Tell her that." I want to tell him to make sure she looks at the postcards, but Céline is yanking me out the door. Outside, I was expecting darkness, but, no, it's still daytime. Days like these go on for years. It's the ones you want to last that slip away—one, two, three—in seconds.

The watermark from where the vase smashed into the wall is still there. So are the piles of books, magazines, CDs, and precarious towers of vinyl records. The picture windows, which she never bothers to cover, even at night, are wide open, letting in the endless, endless daytime.

Céline gives me a glass of water, and at last I take the painkillers Dr. Robinet gave me before I left the hospital. He advised me to take them *before* the pain came on, and to keep taking them until it subsided. But I was afraid taking them earlier would dull whatever wits I had left about me.

The instructions on the bottle say one pill every six hours. I take three.

"Lift up your hands," Céline instructs. And it's like yesterday, when she was making me change my clothes and Lulu walked in on us, and I'd thought it cute that she tried to hide her jealousy. And then Modou had kissed her and I'd had to hide mine.

I can't lift my arms over my head, so Céline helps me off with the hospital scrubs. She stares at my chest a long time. She shakes her head.

"What?"

She clucks her tongue. "She should not have left you like this."

I start to explain that she didn't leave me like this, not knowingly. Céline dismisses me with a wave of her hands. "No matter. You are here now. Go into the bathroom and clean yourself up. I will cook something."

"You?"

"Do not laugh. I can make eggs. Or soup."

"Don't trouble yourself. I have no appetite."

"Then I will make you a bath."

She draws me a bath. I hear it running and think of rain, which has stopped. I feel the drugs starting to work, the soft tentacles of sleep slowly tugging me under. Céline's bed is like a throne and I collapse onto it, thinking of my airplane dream earlier today and how it felt slightly different from the usual nightmare. Right before I fall asleep, one of my lines—Sebastian's lines—from *Twelfth Night* pops into my head: "If it be thus to dream, still let me sleep!"

At first, I think I'm dreaming again. Not the airplane dream, a different one, a good one. A hand trailing up and down my back, slipping lower, lower. She kept her hand on my heart. All morning as we slept on that hard floor. This hand tickles toward my waist and then goes lower. *Bruised, not broken*, the doctor said. In my sleep, I feel my strength returning.

My own hand finds her warm body, so soft, so inviting. I slip my hand between her legs. She groans.

"*Je savais que tu reviendrais.*"

And then it's the nightmare all over again. Wrong place. Wrong person. Wrong plane. I jolt up in bed, push her away so hard she tumbles to the floor.

"What are you doing?" I shout at Céline.

She stands up, unapologetically naked in glow of the streetlight. "You are in *my* bed," she points out.

"You're supposed to be taking care of me," I say. This sounds all the more pathetic because we both know I don't want her to.

"I thought I was," she says, attempting a smile. She sits down on the edge of the bed, pats the sheet next to her. "You don't have to do anything but lie back and relax."

I am wearing nothing but my boxers. When did I take off my jeans? I see them folded neatly on the floor, along with the shirt from the hospital. I reach for the shirt. My muscles protest. I stand up. They howl.

"What are you doing?" Céline asks.

"Leaving," I say, panting with the exertion. I'm not entirely sure I can get out of here, but I know I cannot stay.

"Now? It is late." She looks incredulous. Until I step in my jeans. It is a painstakingly slow process, and it gives her time to digest the fact that I am, in fact, going. I can see what will happen: the reprise of the last time I was here. A stream of cursing, in French. I am a prick. I have humiliated her.

"I offered you my bed, me, and you push me out. Literally." She is laughing, not because it's funny but because it's inconceivable.

"I'm sorry about that."

"But you came to *me*. Yesterday. Again today. You *always* come back to me."

"It was only for a place to leave the suitcase," I explain. "It was for Lulu."

The look on her face is different from what it was last time, when she threw the vase at me, after I told her it was time for me to go. That was fury. This is fury before it's had time to set, raw and bloody. How foolish it was to visit Céline. We could've found another place for that suitcase.

"Her?" Céline yells. "Her? She was just some girl. Nothing special! And look at you now! She left you like this. I am always the one you come running to, Willem. That means something."

I hadn't taken Céline for one of the ones who wait. "I shouldn't have come here. I won't do it again," I promise. I gather the rest of my things and hobble out of her flat, down the stairs to the street.

A police car flies by, its lights flashing through the finally dark streets, its siren whining: *nyeah-nyeah, nyeah-nyeah.*

Paris.

Not home.

I need to get home.

Five

SEPTEMBER
Amsterdam

Marjolein's office is in a narrow canal house off of the Brouwersgracht, the inside of it all white and modern. Bram designed it, calling it one of his "vanity projects." But there was nothing vain about Bram; that was just his code for not getting paid.

Bram's day job was designing temporary crisis shelters for refugees, something he believed in but that didn't challenge his creative side. So he was always on the lookout for ways to exercise his modern sensibilities—like transforming a tired transport barge into a three-story glass, wood, and steel floating palace that was once described as "Bauhaus on the Gracht" in a design journal.

Sara, Marjolein's assistant, sits behind a clear Lucite table, a vase of white roses on the desk. When I come in, she gives me a nervous smile and slowly rises to take my coat. I lean in to kiss her hello. "Sorry I'm late," I apologize.

"You're *three weeks* late, Willem," she says, as she ushers me in, accepting a kiss but not eye contact.

I give my best rogue's grin, even though it pulls at the now-itchy wound on my cheek. "But worth waiting for?"

She doesn't answer. It was more than two years ago that Sara and I had our moment. I was spending a lot of time in this office then, and she was there, our family attorney's assistant. When it had first happened, I'd been besotted, Sara the older woman with the doleful eyes and the blue-painted bed. But it didn't last. It never does.

"Technically, I was only a few days late," I tell her now. "Marjolein's the one who delayed us by two weeks."

"Because she went on holiday," Sara says, strangely huffy. "Which she had purposely booked for after the closing."

"Willem." Marjolein towers in the doorway, naturally tall, and taller yet in the stiletto heels she always wears. She beckons me into her office where Bram's modern sensibility is everywhere. The messy papers and folders in precarious piles are Marjolein's contributions.

"So you threw me over for a girl," Marjolein says, shutting the door behind her.

I wonder how it is that Marjolein can possibly know this. She stares at me, clearly amused by something. "I called back, you know?"

On the train from London to Paris, I'd tried to text Marjolein about my delay, but my phone wouldn't get a signal and was about to die anyway, and for some reason, I didn't want to tell Lulu about any of it. So when I'd seen one of the

Belgian backpacker girls in the café, I'd borrowed her phone. I'd had to fumble in my backpack for Marjolein's number in my address book and had wound up spilling coffee all over me and the Belgian girl.

"She sounded pretty," Marjolein says, with a grin that is both mischievous and scolding at the same time.

"She was," I say.

"They always are," Marjolein says. "Well, come give us a kiss." I step forward to be kissed but before I do, she stops me. "What happened to your face?"

One upside to our meeting being postponed is that it's given the bruises time to fade. The sutures have dissolved, too. All that's left now of that day is a thick raised welt that I'd hoped would go unnoticed.

When I don't answer, Marjolein does. "Tangled with the wrong girl, eh? One with an angry boyfriend?" She gestures to the reception area. "Speaking of, Sara has a nice Italian bloke, so lay off. She moped for months after you left last time. I almost had to fire her."

I hold up my hands and feign innocence.

Marjolein rolls her eyes. "Was that really because of a girl?" She points to my cheek.

Put that way, the story skirts a little close to the truth. "Bicycle. Beer. Dangerous combination." I cheerfully mime falling off a bike.

"My God. Have you been gone so long you've forgotten how to drink and ride a bike?" she asks. "How can you even call yourself Dutch anymore? We got you back just in time."

"So it appears."

"Come. Let me get you a coffee. And I have some excellent chocolate hiding around here somewhere. And then we'll sign the papers."

She calls to Sara, who brings in two demitasses of coffee. Marjolein rifles around in her drawers until she pulls out a box of hard, chewy chocolates. I take one and let it melt on my tongue.

She starts explaining what I'm signing, though it doesn't matter because my signature is only required due to some bureaucratic formality. Yael never took Dutch citizenship, and Bram, who used to say, "God is in the details," when it came to the meticulousness of his designs, apparently held the opposite view when it came to his personal affairs.

All of which means my presence is necessary to finalize the sale and set up the various trusts. Marjolein prattles on as I sign and sign and sign again. Apparently Yael's not being Dutch, and no longer residing here or in Israel either, but floating around like some stateless refugee, is actually a big tax boon for her. She sold the boat for seven hundred and seventeen thousand euros, Marjolein explains. A chunk goes to the government, but a much larger sum goes to us. By the end of business day tomorrow, one hundred thousand euros will be deposited into my bank account.

As I sign, Marjolein keeps looking at me.

"What?" I ask.

"It's just I forgot how much you look like him."

I pause, the pen poised over another line of legalese. Bram always used to say that though Yael was the strongest woman in the world, somehow his mild mannered genes clobbered her dark Israeli stock.

"Sorry," Marjolein says, back to business. "Where have you been staying since you got back? With Daniel?"

Uncle Daniel? I haven't seen him since the funeral, and before that only a handful of times. He lives overseas and rents out his flat. Why would I stay there?

No, since I've been back it's almost been like I am still on the traveler circuit. I've stuck to the tight radius around the train station, near the budget youth hostels and the disappearing red-light district. Partly this was a matter of necessity. I wasn't sure I'd have enough money to last the few weeks, but somehow, my bank account hasn't hit zero. I could've gone to stay with old family friends, but I don't want anyone to know I'm back; I don't want to revisit any of those places. I certainly haven't gone anywhere near Nieuwe Prinsengracht.

"With a friend," I say vaguely.

Marjolein misreads it. "Oh, with *a friend*. I see."

I give a half-guilty smile. Leaving people to jumped conclusions is sometimes simpler than explaining a complicated truth.

"Be sure this friend doesn't have an angry boyfriend."

"I'll do my best," I say.

I finish signing the papers. "That's that then," she says. She opens her desk and pulls out a manila folder. "Here's some mail. I've arranged for anything that goes to the boat to be forwarded here until you give me a new address."

"It might be a while."

"That's okay. *I'm* not going anywhere." Marjolein opens a cabinet and pulls out a bottle of Scotch and two shot glasses. "You just became a man of means. This deserves a drink."

Bram used to joke that as far as Marjolein was concerned, every time the minute hand of the clock passed twelve, it was cause for a drink. But I accept the shot glass.

"What shall we toast?" she asks. "To new ventures? A new future."

I shake my head. "Let's drink to the accidents."

I see the shock in her face, and I realize belatedly that this sounds like I'm talking about what happened to Bram, though that wasn't so much an accident as a freak occurrence.

But that's not what I'm talking about. I'm talking about *our* accident. The one that created our family. Surely Marjolein must've heard the story. Bram loved to tell it. It was like a family origin myth, fairy tale, and lullaby all wrapped together:

Bram and Daniel, driving through Israel in a Fiat that broke down constantly. It was broken down one day outside of the seaside town of Netanya and Bram was trying to fix it, when a soldier, rifle slung over the shoulder, cigarette dangling, ambled over. "Scariest sight you could ever imagine," Bram would say, smiling at the memory.

Yael. Hitching her way back to her army base in Galilee after a weekend's leave spent in Netanya, at a friend's house, or maybe a guy's, anywhere but at the apartment she'd grown up in with Saba. The brothers were driving to Safed, and after she reconnected their radiator hose, they offered her a ride.

Bram gallantly offered her the front seat; after all, she'd fixed the car. But Yael, seeing the cramped backseat said, "Whoever's shortest should sit in back." She claimed to have meant herself, and to not have known which brother was taller, because Daniel had been in the passenger seat, rolling a joint with the Lebanese hash he'd bought off a surfer in Netanya.

But Bram had misunderstood, and so after a needless measuring decided Bram was taller by about three centimeters, Daniel took the back.

They drove the soldier back to her base. Before they parted ways, Bram gave her his address in Amsterdam.

A year and a half later, Yael finished her military service and, determined to put as much distance as she could between herself and everything she grew up with, took what little money she'd saved and began hitching her way north. She lasted four months and got all the way to Amsterdam before she ran out of money. So she knocked on a door. Bram opened it, and even though he hadn't seen her in all that time, and even though he didn't know why she was there, and even though it wasn't really his way, he surprised himself and he kissed her. "Like I'd been expecting her all that time," he'd say in a voice full of wonder.

"See how funny life is," Bram used to say as the epilogue to their epic love story. "If the car hadn't broken down just there, or if she'd run out of money in Copenhagen, or if Daniel were the taller one, none of this might ever have happened."

But I knew what he was really saying was: *Accidents. It's all about the accidents.*

Six

---

*T*wo days later, one hundred thousand euros appears in my bank account, as if by magic. But of course, it's not magic. It's been a long time since I was kicked off my economics course, but I've since come to understand that the universe operates on the same general equilibrium theory as markets. It never gives you something without making you pay for it somehow.

I buy a beat-up bike off a junkie and another change of clothes from the flea market. I may have money now, but I've grown used to living simply, to owning only what I can carry. And besides, I'm not staying long, so I may as well leave as few fingerprints as possible.

I wander up and down the Damrak looking at travel agencies, trying to decide where to go next: Palau. Tonga. Brazil. Once the options increase, settling on one becomes harder. Maybe I'll track down Uncle Daniel in Bangkok, or is it Bali now?

At one of the student agencies, a dark-haired girl behind the desk sees me peering at the ads. She catches my eye, smiles, and gestures for me to come inside.

"What are you looking for?" she asks in slightly accented Dutch. She sounds Eastern, maybe Romanian.

"Somewhere that isn't here."

"Can you be more specific?" she says, laughing a little.

"Somewhere warm, cheap, and far away." *Somewhere that with one hundred thousand euros, I can stay lost as long as I want to*, I think.

She laughs. "That describes about half the world. Let's narrow it down. Do you want beaches? There are some fantastic spots in Micronesia. Thailand is still quite cheap. If you're into a more chaotic cultural affair, India is fascinating."

I shake my head. "Not India."

"New Zealand? Australia? People are raving about Malawi in Central Africa. I'm hearing great things about Panama and Honduras, though they had that coup there. How long do you want to go for?"

"Indefinitely."

"Oh, then you might look into a round-the-world ticket. We have a few on special." She types away on her computer. "Here's one: Amsterdam, Nairobi, Dubai, Delhi, Singapore, Sydney, Los Angeles, Amsterdam."

"You have one that doesn't stop in Delhi?"

"You really don't want India, huh?"

I just smile.

"Okay. So what part of the world *do* you want to see?"

"I don't care. Anywhere will work, really, so long as it's warm, cheap, and far away. And not India. Why don't you pick for me?"

She laughs, like it's a joke. But I'm serious. I've been stuck in a kind of sluggish inertia since coming back, spending whole days in sad hostel beds waiting for my meeting with Marjolein. Whole days, lots of empty hours, holding a broken-but-still-ticking watch, wondering useless things about the girl whom it belongs to. It's all doing a bit of a number on my head. All the more reason for me to get back on the road.

She taps her fingers against her keyboard. "You have to help me out. For starters, where have you already been?"

"Here." I push my battered passport across the desk. "This has my history."

She opens it. "Oh it does, does it?" she says. Her voice has changed, from friendly to coy. She flips through the pages. "You get around, don't you?"

I'm tired. I don't want to do this dance, not right now. I just want to buy my airplane ticket and go. Once I'm out of here, away from Europe, somewhere warm and far, I'll get back to my old self.

She shrugs and returns to leafing through my passport. "Uh-oh. You know what? I can't book you anywhere yet."

"Why not?"

"Your passport's about to expire." She closes the passport and slides it back. "Do you have an identity card?"

"It got stolen."

"Did you file a report?"

I shake my head. Never did call the French police.

"Never mind. You need a passport for most of these places anyhow. You just have to get it renewed."

"How long will that take?"

"Not long. A few weeks. Go to City Hall for the forms." She rattles off some of the other paperwork I'll need, none of which I have here.

Suddenly I feel stuck, and I'm not sure how that happened. After managing for two entire years not to set foot in Holland? After going to some absurd lengths to bypass this small-but-central landmass—for instance convincing Tor, Guerrilla Will's dictatorial director, to forgo performing in Amsterdam and to hit Stockholm instead, with some half-baked story about the Swedes being the most Shakespeare-loving people in Europe outside the UK?

But then last spring Marjolein had finally cleared up Bram's messy estate and the deed of the houseboat transferred to Yael. Who celebrated by immediately putting the home he'd built for her up for sale. I shouldn't have been surprised, not at that point.

Still, to ask me to come and sign the papers? That took gall. *Chutzpah*, Saba would call it. I understood for Yael it was a matter of practicality. I was a train ride, she was a plane ride. It would only be a few days for me, a minor inconvenience.

Except I delayed for one day. And somehow, that's changed everything.

Seven

It occurs to me, belatedly, that maybe I should've called. Maybe last month, when I first got back. Certainly before now, before showing up at his house. But I didn't. And now it's too late. I'm just here. Hoping to make this as painless as possible.

At the house on Bloemstraat, someone has swapped out the old doorbell for one in the shape of an eyeball that stares reproachfully. This feels like a bad omen. Our correspondence, always irregular, has been nonexistent in the last few months. I can't remember the last time I emailed or texted him. Three months ago? Six months? It occurs to me, also belatedly, that he might not even live here anymore.

Except, somehow, I know he does. Because Broodje wouldn't have left without telling me. He wouldn't have done that.

Broodje and I met when we were eight. I caught him spying on our boat with a pair of binoculars. When I asked what he was doing, he explained that he wasn't spying on *us*. There'd been a rash of break-ins in our neighborhood, and his parents had been talking about leaving Amsterdam for somewhere safer. He preferred to stay put in his family's flat, so it was up to him to find the culprits. "That's very serious," I'd told him. "Yes, it is," he'd replied. "But I have this." Out of his bike basket he'd pulled the rest of his spy kit: decoder scope, noise-enhancing ear buds, night-vision goggles, which he'd let me try on. "If you need help finding the bad guys, I can be your partner," I'd offered. There were not many children in our neighborhood on the eastern edge of Amsterdam's center, no children at all on the adjacent houseboats on the Nieuwe Prinsengracht where our boat was moored, and I had no siblings. I spent much of my time kicking balls off the pier against the hull of the boat, losing most of them to the murky waters of the canals.

Broodje accepted my help, and we became partners. We spent hours casing the neighborhood, taking pictures of suspicious-looking people and vehicles, cracking the case. Until an old man saw us, and, thinking we were working with the criminals, called the police on us. The police found us crouched next to my neighbor's pier, looking through the binoculars at a suspicious van that seemed to appear regularly (because, we later found out, it belonged to the bakery around the corner). We were questioned and we both started crying, thinking we were going to jail. We stammered our explanations and crime-fighting strategies. The police listened, trying hard not to laugh, before taking us home and explaining everything to Broodje's parents. Before they left, one of the detectives gave each of us a card, winked, and said to call with any tips.

I threw away my card, but Broodje kept his. For years. I spotted it when we were twelve, tacked to the bulletin board in his bedroom in the suburbs where he wound up moving after all. "You still have this?" I'd asked him. He'd moved two years before and we didn't see each other frequently. Broodje had looked at the card, and then looked at me. "Don't you know, Willy?" he'd said. "I keep things."

A lanky guy in a PSV soccer jersey, his hair stiff with gel, opens the door. I feel my stomach plummet, because Broodje used to live here with two girls, both of whom he was constantly, and unsuccessfully, trying to sleep with, and a skinny guy named Ivo. But then the guy eyes spark open with recognition and I realize it's Henk, one of Broodje's friends from the University of Utrecht. "Is that you, Willem?" he asks, and before I can answer he's calling into the house, "Broodje, Willem's back."

I hear scrambling and the creak of the scuffed wood floorboards and then there he is, a head shorter and a shoulder wider than me, a disparity that used to prompt the old man on the houseboat next to ours to call us Spaghetti and Meatball, a moniker Broodje quite liked, because wasn't a meatball so much tastier than a noodle?

"Willy?" Broodje pauses for a half second before he

launches himself at me. "Willy! I thought you were dead!"

"Back from the dead," I say.

"Really?" His eyes are so round and so blue, like shiny coins. "When did you get back? How long are you here for? Are you hungry? I wish you'd told me you were coming, I would've made something. Well I can pull together a nice *borrelhapje*. Come in. Henk, look, Willy's back."

"I see that," Henk says, nodding.

"W," Broodje calls. "Willy's back."

I walk into the lounge. Before, it was relatively neat, with feminine touches around like flower-scented candles that Broodje used to pretend to dislike but would light even when the girls weren't home. Now, it smells of stale socks, old coffee, and spilled beer, and the only remnant of the girls is an old Picasso poster, askew in its frame above the mantel. "What happened to the girls?" I ask.

Broodje grins. "Leave it to Willy to ask about the girls first." He laughs. "They moved into their own flat last year, and Henk and W moved in. Ivo just left to do a course in Estonia."

"Latvia," Wouter, or W, corrects, coming down the stairs. He's even taller than me, with short, unintentionally spiky hair and an Adam's apple as big as a doorknob.

"Latvia," Broodje says.

"What happened to your face?" W asks. W never was one for social pleasantries.

I touch the scar. "I fell off my bike," I say. The lie I told Marjolein comes out automatically. I'm not sure why, except for a desire to put as much distance as possible between myself and that day.

"When did you get back?" W asks.

"Yeah, Willy," Broodje says, panting and pawing like a puppy. "How long ago?"

"A bit ago," I say, treading water between hurtful truth and balls-out lies. "I had to deal with some things in Amsterdam."

"I've been wondering where you were," Broodje says. "I tried calling you a while back but got a strange recording, and you're shit about email."

"I know. I lost my phone and all my contacts, and some Irish guy gave me his, including his SIM card. I thought I texted you the new number."

"Maybe you did. Anyhow, come in. Let me go see what I have to eat." He turns right into the galley kitchen. I hear drawers opening and closing.

Five minutes later Broodje returns with a tray of food and beers for all of us. "So tell us everything. The glamorous life of a roving actor. Is it a girl every night?"

"Jesus, Broodje, let the guy sit down," Henk says.

"Sorry. I live vicariously through him; it was like having a movie star in the house having him around. And, it's been a little dry these past few years."

"And by past few years, you mean twenty?" W says drolly.

"So you've been in Amsterdam?" Broodje asks. "How is your ma?"

"I wouldn't know," I say lightly. "She's in India."

"Still?" Broodje asks. "Or there and back?"

"Still. This whole time."

"Oh. I was in the old neighborhood recently and the boat

was all lit up and there was furniture inside, so I thought she might be back."

"Nope, they must've put furniture in there to make it look lived in, but it's not. Not by us, anyhow," I say, rolling up a piece of *cervelaat* and shoving it in my mouth. "It's been sold."

"You sold Bram's boat?" Broodje says incredulously.

"My mother sold it," I clarify.

"She must've made a boatload," Henk jokes.

I pause for a second, somehow unable to tell them that I did, too. Then W starts talking about a piece he read in *De Volkskrant* recently about Europeans paying top dollar for the old houseboats in Amsterdam, for the mooring rights, which are as valuable as the boats themselves.

"Not this boat. You should've seen it," Broodje says. "His father was an architect, so it was beautiful, three floors, balconies, glass everywhere." He looks wistful. "What did that magazine call it?"

"Bauhaus on the Gracht." A photographer had come and taken pictures of the boat, and us on it. When the magazine had come out, most of the shots had been of just the boat, but there had been one of Yael and Bram, framed by the picture window, the trees and canal reflecting like a mirror behind them. I'd been in the original of that shot but had been cropped out. Bram explained that they'd used this one because of the window and the reflection; it was a representation of the design, not our family. But I'd thought it had been a fairly accurate depiction of our family, too.

"I can't believe she sold it," Broodje says.

Some days I can't believe it and other days I can absolutely believe it. Yael is the sort to chew off her own hand if she needs to escape. She'd done it before.

The boys are all looking at me now, their faces blanking out with a kind of concern that I'm unaccustomed to after two years of anonymity.

"So, Holland-Turkey tonight," I begin.

The guys look at me for a moment. Then nod.

"I hope things go better for us," I say. "After the sad offerings during Euro Cup, I don't know if I can take it. Sneijder . . ." I shake my head.

Henk takes the bait first. "Are you kidding? Sneijder was the only striker who proved his mettle."

"No way!" Broodje interrupts. "Van Persie scored that beautiful goal against Germany."

Then W jumps in with math talk, something about regression toward the mean guaranteeing improvement after the last lousy year, and now there's nowhere to go but up, and I relax. There's a universal language of small talk. On the road, it's about travel: some unknown island, or a cheap hostel, a restaurant with a good fixed-price menu. With these guys, it's soccer.

"You gonna watch the game with us, Willy?" Broodje asks. "We were going to O'Leary's."

I didn't come to Utrecht for small talk or for soccer or for friendship. I came for paperwork. A quick visit to University College for some papers to get my passport. Once I get that, I'll go back to the travel agent, maybe ask her for a drink this time, and figure out where to go. Buy my ticket. Maybe take a trip to The Hague to pick up some visas, a visit to the travel clinic for some shots. A trip to the flea market for new clothes. A train to the airport. A thorough body search by immigration officials, because a lone man with a one-way ticket is always an object of suspicion. A long flight. Jetlag. Immigration. Customs. And then finally, that first step into a new place, that moment of exhilaration and disorientation, each feeding the other. That moment when anything can happen.

I have only one thing to do in Utrecht, but suddenly the rest of the things I'll need to accomplish to get myself out of here feels endless. Stranger yet, nothing about it excites me. Not even arriving somewhere new, which used to make all the hassle worthwhile. It all just seems exhausting. I can't summon the energy for the slog it'll take me to get out of here.

But O'Leary's? O'Leary's is right around the corner, not even a block away. That I can manage.

Eight

October turns cold and wet, as if we used up our quota of clear, hot days during the summer's heat wave. It's especially cold in my attic room on Bloemstraat, making me wonder if moving in had been the right call. Not that it had been a call. After I woke up on the downstairs sofa for the third morning in a row, having accomplished little during my days in Utrecht, Broodje had suggested I move into the attic room.

The offer was wasn't so much enticing as a *fait accompli*. I was already living here. Sometimes the wind blows you places you weren't expecting; sometimes it blows you away from those places, too.

The attic room is drafty, with windows that rattle in the wind. In the morning, I see my breath. Staying warm becomes my main vocation. On the road, I often spent whole days in libraries. You could always find magazines or books, and respite from the weather or whatever else needed escaping.

The Central University library offers all the same comforts: big sunny windows, comfortable couches, and a bank of computers I can use to browse the Internet. The last is a mixed blessing. On the road, my fellow travelers were obsessive about keeping up with email. I was the opposite. I hated checking in. I still do.

Yael's emails come like clockwork, once every two weeks. I think she must have it on her calendar, along with all the other chores. The notes never say much, which makes answering them next to impossible.

One came yesterday, a bit of fluff about taking a day off to go to a pilgrim festival in some village. She never tells me what she's taking a day off from, never elaborates about her actual work there, her day-to-day life, which is a bleary mystery, the contours filled in only by offhanded remarks from Marjolein. No, Yael's emails to me are all in a sort of postcard language. The perfect small talk, saying little, revealing less.

"Hoi Ma," I begin my reply. And then I stare at screen and try to think of what to say. I'm so conversant in every kind of small talk, but I find myself at a loss for words when it comes to my mother. When I was traveling, it was simpler because I could just send a sort of postcard. *In Romania now at one of the Black Sea resorts, but it's off season and quiet. Watched the fishermen for hours.* Although even those had addendums in my mind. How watching the fishermen one blustery morning reminded me of our family trip to Croatia when I was ten. Or was it eleven? Yael slept late, but Bram and I woke early to go down to the docks to buy the day's catches from the just-returning fisherman, who all smelled of salt and vodka. But following Yael's lead, I excise those bits of nostalgia from my missives.

"Hoi Ma." The cursor blinks like a reprimand and I can't get past it, can't think of what to say. I toggle back to my in-box, scrolling backward in time. The last few years and their occasional notes from Broodje, and the notes from people I met on the road—vague promises to meet up in Tangiers, in Belfast, in Barcelona, in Riga—plans that rarely material-ized. Before that, there's the flurry of emails from various professors on the economics faculty, warning me that unless I appealed "special circumstances," I was in danger of not be-ing asked back next year. (I didn't, and I wasn't.) Before that, condolence emails, some of them still unopened, and before that, notes from Bram, mostly silly things he liked to forward to me, a restaurant review of a place he wanted to try out, a photo of a particularly monstrous piece of architecture, an invitation to help on his latest fix-it project. I scroll back now four years and there are the emails from Saba, who, in the two years between discovering email and getting too sick to use it, had delighted in this instant form of communication, where you could write pages and pages and it didn't cost any more to send.

I return to the note to Yael. "Hoi Ma, I'm back in Utrecht now, hanging out with Robert-Jan and the boys. Nothing much to report. It's pissing down rain every day; no sign of the sun for a week now. You're glad not to be here for it. I know how you hate the gray. Talk soon. Willem."

Postcard Language, the smallest of small talk.

Nine

The boys and I are going to a movie, along with W's new girlfriend. Some Jan de Bont thriller at the Louis Hart-looper. I haven't liked a de Bont film since—I can't even remember—but I've been outvoted because W has a girl-friend, and this is a big thing, and if she wants explosions, we will watch explosions.

The theater complex is packed, people spilling out the front doors. We fight our way through the crowds to the box office. And that's when I see her: Lulu.

Not my Lulu. But the Lulu I named her for. Louise Brooks. The theater has lots of old movie posters in the lobby, but I've never seen this one, which isn't on the wall but is propped up on an easel. It's a still shot from *Pandora's Box*, Lulu, pour-ing a drink, her eyebrow raised in amusement and challenge.

"She's pretty." I look up. Behind me is Lien, W's punked-out math major girlfriend. No one can quite get over how he did it, but apparently they fell in love over numbers theory.

"Yeah," I agree.

I look closer at the poster. It is advertising a Louise Brooks film retrospective. *Pandora's Box* is on tonight.

"Who was she?" Lien asks.

"Louise Brooks," Saba had said. "Look at those eyes, so much delight, you know there's sadness to hide." I was thirteen, and Saba, who hated Amsterdam's mercurial wet summers, had just discovered the revival cinemas. That summer was particularly dreary, and Saba had introduced me to all the silent film stars: Charlie Chaplin, Buster Keaton, Rudolph Valentino, Pola Negri, Greta Garbo, and his favorite, Louise Brooks.

"Silent film star," I tell Lien. "There's a festival on. Unfortunately it's tonight."

"We could see that instead," she says. I can't tell if her tone is sarcastic; she's as dry as W is. But when I get to the front of the line to buy the tickets, I find myself asking for five to *Pandora's Box*.

At first, the boys are amused. They think I'm joking, until I point to the poster and explain about the retrospective. Then they are not so amused.

"There's a live piano player," I say.

"Is that supposed to make us feel *better*?" Henk asks.

"No way I'm seeing this," W adds.

"What if *I* wanted to see it?" Lien interjects.

I offer her a silent thank-you and she gives me a perplexed eyebrow raise in return, showing off her piercing. W acquiesces and the rest follow suit.

Upstairs, we take our seats. In the quiet, you can hear the explosions from the adjacent theater and I can see Henk's eyes go wistful.

The lights go down and the piano player starts in with the overture and Lulu's face fills the screen. The movie starts, all scratchy and black and white; you can almost hear it crackle like an old LP. But there is nothing old about Lulu. She's timeless, flirting gaily in the nightclub, being caught with her lover, shooting her husband on their wedding night.

It's strange because I've seen this film before, a few times. I know exactly how it ends, but as it goes on, a tension starts to build, a suspense, churning uncomfortably in my gut. It takes a certain kind of naiveté, or perhaps just stupidity, to know how things will end and still hope otherwise.

Fidgety, I shove my hands into my pockets. Though I try not to, my mind keeps going to the other Lulu on that hot August night. I tossed her the coin, as I'd done to so many other girls. But unlike the other girls who always came back—lingering by our makeshift stage to return my very valuable worthless coin and to see what it might buy—Lulu didn't.

That should've been my first sign that the girl could see through my acts. But all I'd thought was: *Not to be.* It was just as well. I had an early train to catch the next day, and a big, shitty day after that, and I never slept well with strangers.

I hadn't slept well anyhow, and I'd been up early, so I'd caught an earlier train down to London. And there she was, on that train. It was the third time in twenty-four hours that I'd seen her and when I walked into that train's café car, I remember feeling a jolt. As if the universe was saying: *pay attention.*

So I'd paid attention. I'd stopped and we'd chatted, but then we were in London and about to go our separate ways. By that point, the knot of dread that had been building in me since Yael's request that I return to Holland to sign away my home had solidified into a fist. The banter with Lulu on the way down to London had made it unravel, somehow. But I knew that once I got on that next train to Amsterdam, it would grow, it would take over my insides, and I wouldn't be able to eat or do anything except nervously roll a coin along my knuckles and focus on the next *next*—the next train or plane I'd be boarding. The next departure.

But then Lulu started talking about wanting to go to Paris, and I had all this money from the summer's worth of Guerrilla Will, cash I wouldn't be needing much longer. And in that train station in London, I'd thought, okay, maybe *this* was the meant to be: The universe, I knew, loved nothing more than balance, and here was a girl who wanted to go to Paris and here was me who wanted to go anywhere but back to Amsterdam. As soon as I'd suggested we go to Paris together, balance was restored. The dread in my gut disappeared. On the train to Paris, I was as hungry as ever.

On screen, Lulu is crying. I imagine my Lulu waking up the next day, finding me gone, reading a note that promised a quick return that never materialized. I wonder, as I have so many times, how long it took her to think the worst of me when she already *had* thought the worst of me. On the train from London to Paris, she'd started laughing uncontrollably, because she'd thought I'd left her there. I'd made a joke of it; and of course, it wasn't true. I wasn't planning that. But it had got to me because it was my first warning that somehow, this girl saw me in a way I hadn't intended to be seen.

As the movie goes on, desire and longing and regret and second-guessing of everything about that day start building in me. It's all pointless, but somehow knowing that only makes it worse, and it builds and builds and has nowhere to go. I shove my hands deeper into my pockets and punch a hole right through.

"Damn!" I say, louder than I mean to.

Lien looks at me, but I pretend to be absorbed in the movie. The piano player is building to a crescendo as Lulu flirts with Jack the Ripper and, lonely and defeated, invites him up to her room. She thinks she has found someone to love, and he thinks that he has found someone to love, and then he sees the knife, and you know what will happen. He'll just revert to his old ways. I'm sure that's what she thinks of me, and maybe she's right to think it. The film ends with a frenzied flourish of the piano. And then there's silence.

The boys sit there for a minute and then all start talking at once. "That's it? So he killed her?" Broodje asks.

"It's Jack the Ripper and he had a knife," Lien responds. "He wasn't carving her a Christmas turkey."

"What a way to go. I'll give you one thing, it wasn't boring," Henk says. "Willem? Hey, Willem, are you there?"

I startle up. "Yeah. What?"

The four of them all look at me for what feels like a while. "Are you okay?" Lien asks at last.

"I'm fine. I'm great!" I smile. It feels unnatural I can almost feel the scar on my face tug like a rubber band. "Let's go get a drink."

We all make our way to the crowded café downstairs. I order a round of beers and then a round of *jenever* for good measure. The boys give me a look, though if it's for the booze or for paying for it all, I don't know. They know about my inheritance now, but they still expect the same frugality from me as always.

I drain my shot and then my beer.

"Whoa," W says, passing me his shot. "No *kopstoot* for me."

I knock his shot back, too.

They're quiet as they look at me. "Are you sure you're okay?" Broodje asks, strangely hesitant.

"Why wouldn't I be?" The *jenever* is doing its job, heating me up and burning away the memories that came alive in the dark.

"Your father died. Your mother left for India," W says bluntly. "Also, your grandfather died."

There's a moment of awkward silence. "Thanks," I say. "I'd forgotten all about that." I mean it to come out as a joke, but it just comes out as bitter as the booze that's burning its way back up my throat.

"Oh, don't mind him," Lien says, tweaking his ear affectionately. "He's working on human emotions like sympathy."

"I don't need anyone's sympathy," I say. "I'm fine."

"Okay, it's just you haven't really seemed yourself since . . ." Broodje trails off.

"You spend a lot of time alone," Henk blurts.

"Alone? I'm with you."

"Exactly," Broodje says.

There's another moment of silence. I'm not quite sure what I'm being accused of. Then Lien illuminates.

"From what I understand, you always had a girl around, and now the guys are worried because you're always alone," Lien says. She looks at the boys. "Do I have that right?"

Kind of sort of yeah, they all mumble.

"So you've been discussing this?" This should be funny, except it's not.

"We think you're depressed because you're not having sex," W says. Lien smacks him. "What?" he asks. "It's a viable physiological issue. Sexual activity releases serotonin, which increases feelings of well-being. It's simple science."

"No wonder you like me so much," Lien teases. "All that simple science."

"Oh, so I'm depressed now?" I try to sound amused but it's hard to keep that tinge of something else out of my voice. No one will look at me except for Lien. "Is that what you think?" I ask, trying to make a joke of it. "I'm suffering from a clinical case of blue balls?"

"It's not your balls I think are blue," she says coolly. "It's your heart."

There's a beat of silence, and then the boys erupt into raucous laughter. "Sorry, *schatje*," W says. "But that would be anomalous behavior. You just don't know him yet. It's much more likely a serotonin issue."

"I know what I know," Lien says.

They all argue over this and I find myself wishing for the anonymity of the road, where you had no past and no future either, just that one moment in time. And if that moment happened to get sticky or uncomfortable, there was always a train departing to the next moment.

"Well, if he does have a broken heart or blue balls, the cure is the same," Broodje says.

"And what's that?" Lien asks.

"Getting laid," Broodje and Henk crow together.

It's too much. "I've gotta piss," I say, standing up.

In the bathroom, I splash water on my face. I stare in the mirror. The scar is still red and angry, aggravated, as though I've been picking at it.

Outside, the corridor is crowded, another film having just let out, not the de Bont but one of those treacly British romantic comedies, the kind that promise an everlasting love in two hours.

"Willem de Ruiter, as I live and breathe."

I turn around, and coming out of the cinema, her eyes misty with fabricated emotion, is Ana Lucia Aurelanio.

I stop, letting her catch up. We kiss hello. She gestures for her friends, people I recognize from University College, to go on ahead. "You never called me," she says, adjusting her face into a little girl pout that somehow looks charming on her, though almost anything would.

"I didn't have your number." I say. I have no reason to be sheepish, but it's like a reflex.

"But I gave it to you. In Paris."

Paris. Lulu. The feelings from the movie start to come back, but I push back against them. Paris was make-believe. No different from the romantic movie Ana Lucia just saw.

Ana Lucia leans in. She smells good, like cinnamon and smoke and perfume.

"Why don't you give me your number again," I say, pulling out my phone. "So I *can* call you later."

"Why bother?" she says.

I shrug. I'd heard rumors she wasn't too happy when things ended last time. I put my phone away.

But then she grabs my hand in hers. Mine is cold. Hers is hot. "I mean why bother calling me *later* when I'm right here, right *now*?"

And she is. Here now. And so am I.

The cure is the same, I hear Broodje say.

Maybe it is.

Ten

*A*na Lucia's dorm is like a cocoon, thick feather quilts, radiators hissing full blast, endless cups of custard-like hot chocolate. For the first few days, I am content just to be here, with her.

"Did you ever think we'd get back together?" she coos, snuggling up to me like a warm little kitten.

"Hmm," I say, because there's no right way to answer that. I never thought we'd get back together because I never considered us together in the first place. Ana Lucia and I had a three, maybe four-week fling in that hazy spring after Bram died, when I was spectacularly floundering in school but also spectacularly succeeding with women. Though succeeding isn't the right word, exactly. It implies a kind of effort, when really, it was the one thing in my life that was effortless.

"*I* did," she says, nibbling my ear. "I thought about you so much these past few years. And then we bumped into each other in Paris, and it felt like it meant something, like fate."

"Hmmm," I repeat. I remember bumping into her in Paris and also feeling like it meant something, but not fate. More like the encroachment, a day too soon, of a world I'd left behind.

"But then you didn't call me," she says.

"Oh, you know. Something came up."

"I'm sure *something* did." Her hand drifts between my legs. "I saw you with that girl. In Paris. She was pretty."

She says it offhandedly, dismissively even, but something skitters to life in my gut. A kind of warning. Ana Lucia's hand is still between my legs and it's having the intended effect, but now Lulu's somewhere in the room, too. Just like that day in Paris, when I ran into Ana Lucia and her cousins while I was in the Latin Quarter with Lulu, I want nothing but distance between these two girls.

"She was pretty, but *you're* beautiful." I say it, trying to steer the conversation away. My words are true, but meaningless. Though Ana Lucia is probably technically prettier than Lulu, such contests are rarely won on technicalities.

Her grip tightens. "What was her name?" she asks.

I don't want to say her name. But Ana Lucia has me firmly in hand and if I don't say it, I'll arouse suspicion. "Lulu," I say into the pillow. It's not even her real name, but it feels like a betrayal.

"Lulu," Ana Lucia says. She lets go of me and sits up in the bed. "A French girl. Was she your girlfriend?"

Morning light is filtering through the window, pale and gray and tinting everything in here slightly greenish. Somehow, the gray dawn light had made Lulu glow in that white room.

"Of course not."

"Just another one of your flings then?" Ana Lucia's laughter answers her own question; the knowingness irks me.

That night in the art squat, after everything, Lulu had smudged her finger against her wrist, and I'd done the same. A kind of code for *stain*, for something that lasts, even if you might not want it to. It had meant something, in that moment at least. "You know me," I say lightly.

Ana Lucia laughs again, the sound of it throaty and full, rich and indulgent. She climbs on top of me, straddling my hips. "I *do* know you," she says, her eyes flashing. She runs a finger down my center line. "I know what you've been through now. I didn't understand before. But I've grown up. You've grown up. I think we're both different people, with different needs."

"My needs haven't changed," I tell her. "They're the same as they ever were. Very basic." I yank her toward me. I'm still angry at her, but her invoking of Lulu's name has riled me up. I finger the lace along the trim of her camisole. I dip a finger under the straps.

Her eyes flutter closed for a minute and I close mine, too. I feel the give of the bed and the trail of her waxy kisses on my neck. "*Dime que me quieres*," she whispers. "*Dime que me necesitas.*" *Tell me you want me. Tell me you need me.*

I don't tell her because she's speaking Spanish, which she

doesn't realize I now understand. I keep my eyes closed, but even in darkness I hear a voice telling me she'll be my mountain girl.

"I'll take care of you," Ana Lucia says, and I jump in the bed at hearing Lulu's words come out of Ana Lucia's mouth.

But as Ana Lucia's head dips under the covers, I realize it's a different kind of taking care she's talking about. It's not the kind I really need. But I don't refuse it.

Eleven

After two weeks ensconced in Ana Lucia's dorm, I make my way back to Bloemstraat. It's quiet, a welcome change from the constant hubbub in and around the University College campus, everyone in everyone's business.

In the kitchen, I open the cupboards. Ana Lucia has been bringing me back cafeteria food or ordering takeout, charging it away on her father's credit cards. I crave something real.

There's not much here, a couple of bags of pasta and some onions and garlic. There's a can of tomatoes in the pantry. Enough for a sauce. I start to chop the onions and my eyes immediately tear. They always do this. Yael's too. She never cooked much, but occasionally she'd get homesick for Israel, and she'd play bad Hebrew pop music and make *shakshouka*. I might be all the way upstairs in my room and I'd feel the burn. I'd gravitate down to the kitchen. Bram would find us sometimes, together and red-eyed, and he'd laugh and ruffle my hair and kiss Yael and joke that chopping onions was the only time you'd ever catch Yael Shiloh crying.

Around four, I hear the key click in the lock. I call out a hello.

"Willy, you're back. And you're cook—" Broodje says as he turns the corner into the kitchen. Then he stops midsentence. "What's wrong?"

"Huh?" And then I realize he means my tears. "Just the onions," I explain.

"Oh," Broodje says. "Onions." He picks up the wooden spoon and swirls it in the sauce, blows, then tastes. Then he reaches into the pantry for several dried herbs and rubs them between his fingers before sprinkling them in. He gives a few shakes of salt and several turns of the pepper mill. Then he turns the flame down low and puts on the lid. "Because if it's not the onions . . ." he says.

"What else would it be?"

He shuffles his foot against the floor. "I've been worried about you since that night," he says. "What happened after the movie."

"What about it?" I say.

He starts to say something. Then stops. "Nothing," he says. "So, Ana Lucia? Again."

"Yeah. Ana Lucia. Again." I can think of nothing else to add so I revert to small talk. "She sends her greetings."

"I'm sure she does," Broodje says, not buying it for a minute.

"You want to eat?"

"I do," he says. "But the sauce isn't ready."

Broodje goes up to his room. I'm perplexed. It's unlike him to turn down food, no matter how cooked it is. I've seen him eat raw hamburger meat. I let the sauce simmer. The aroma fills up the house and he still doesn't come down. So I go up and tap on his door. "Hungry yet?" I ask.

"I'm always hungry."

"Do you want to come down? I can make some pasta."

He shakes his head.

"Are you on a hunger strike?" I joke. "Like Sarsak."

He shrugs. "Maybe I will go on a hunger strike."

"What will you strike for?" I ask. "It would have to be very important for you to go without food."

"*You* are very important."

"*Me?*"

Broodje swivels in his desk chair. "Didn't we used to tell each other things, Willy?"

"Of course."

"Haven't we always been good friends? Even when I moved away we stayed close. Even when you were gone and you didn't ever contact me, I thought we were good friends, and now you're back, what if we're not really friends at all?"

"What are you talking about?"

"Where have you been, Willy?"

"Where have I been? With Ana Lucia. Jesus, you were the one who said I needed to get laid to get over it."

His eyes flash. "Get over *what*, Willy?"

I sit down on the bed. Get over what? That's the question, right there.

"Is it your pa?" Broodje asks. "It's okay if it still is. It's only been three years. It took me that long to get over Varken, and he was a dog."

Bram's death gutted me. It did. But that was then and I've been okay so I'm not sure why it feels so raw again *now*. Maybe because I'm back in Holland. Maybe it was a mistake to stay.

"I don't know what it is," I tell Broodje. It's a relief to admit this much.

"But it is *something*," he says.

I can't really explain it, because it makes no sense. One girl. One day.

"It is something," I tell Broodje.

He doesn't say anything, but the silence is like an invitation, and I'm not sure why I'm keeping this a secret. So I tell him: About meeting Lulu in Stratford-upon-Avon. About seeing her again on the train. About our flirtation on the train about *hagelslag* of all things. About calling her Lulu, a name that seemed to fit her so well that I forgot she wasn't actually called that.

I tell him some of the highlights of a day that seems so perfect in retrospect, I sometimes think I invented it: Lulu marching up and down the Bassin de la Villette with a hundred-dollar bill, bribing Jacques to take us down the canal. The two of us almost getting arrested by that gendarme for illegally riding two people on a single Vélib' bike, but then when the gendarme asked me why I'd done something so stupid, I'd quoted that Shakespeare line about beauty being a witch, and he recognized it, and let us off with a warning. Lulu blindly picking a Métro stop to go to and us winding up in Barbès Rochechouart, and Lulu, who claimed to be uncomfortable with traveling, seeming to love the randomness of it all. I tell him about the skinheads, too. About how I didn't really think about it when I intervened and tried to stop them from hassling those two Arab girls about their headscarves. I didn't really think about what they might do to *me*, and just as it was starting to dawn on me that I might have really screwed myself, there was Lulu, hurling a book at one of them.

Even as I explain it, I realize I'm not doing it justice. Not the day. Not Lulu. I'm not telling the whole story, either, because there are things I just don't know how to explain. Like how when Lulu bribed Jacques to give us that ride on the canal, it wasn't her generosity that got to me. I never told her I'd grown up on a boat, or that I was one day away from signing it all away. But she seemed to know. How did she know? How do I explain that?

When I'm done with my story, I'm unsure if I've made any sense. But I feel better somehow. "So," I say to Broodje. "Now what?"

Broodje sniffs the air. The smell of the sauce has infiltrated the entire house. "Sauce is ready. Now we eat."

Twelve

———

"I've been thinking," Ana Lucia says. It's sleeting outside but it's toasty in her dorm, with our little feast of Thai food on her bed.

"Always dangerous words," I joke.

She throws a sachet of duck sauce at me. "I've been thinking about Christmas. I know you don't really celebrate it, but maybe you should come with me to Switzerland next month. So you're among family."

"I didn't realize I had relatives in Switzerland," I tease, popping a spring roll in my mouth.

"I meant my family." She looks at me, her eyes uncomfortably intense. "They want to meet you."

Ana Lucia belongs to a sprawling Spanish clan, the heirs to a shipping company that was sold to the Chinese before the recession crippled their economy. She has endless relatives, siblings and cousins, living all over Europe and the U.S., Mexico, and Argentina, and she speaks to them in a kind of round-robin on the phone each night. "You never know what might happen. One day, you might think of them as your family, too."

I want to say I already have a family, but it hardly seems true anymore. Who's left? Yael and me. And Uncle Daniel, but he barely counted in the first place. The roll sticks in my throat. I wash it down with a gulp of beer.

"It's beautiful there," she adds.

Bram took Yael and me skiing once in Italy. We both stayed huddled in the lodge, freezing. He learned his lesson. The next year we went to Tenerife. "Switzerland's too cold," I say.

"And it's so nice here?" she asks.

Ana Lucia and I have been together for three weeks. Christmas is in six weeks. You don't need to be W to figure out the math on that one.

When I don't answer, Ana Lucia says, "Or maybe you want me to go, so you can have someone else keep you warm?" Just like that, her tone changes, and the suspicion that I now realize has been lurking outside all along comes rushing in.

The next afternoon, when I head back to Bloemstraat, I find the boys at the table, papers sprawled out all over the place. Broodje looks up wearing the expression of a guilty dog who stole the dinner.

"I'm sorry," he says straightaway.

"About what?" I ask.

"I may have told them a little bit about our conversation," he stammers. "About what you said."

"It wasn't much of a surprise," W says. "It was obvious *something* has been wrong since you came back. And I *knew* that scar wasn't from a bicycle accident. It doesn't look like something you'd get from a fall."

"My story was I got hit by a tree branch."

"But you got beaten up by skinheads," Henk tells me. "The same ones the girl threw the book at the day before."

"I think he knows what happened to him," Broodje says.

"Crazy that you saw the same guys," Henk says.

"More like bad luck," Broodje says.

I don't say anything

"We think you have that post-traumatic thing," Henk says. "That's why you've been so depressed."

"So you've scrapped the celibacy theory?"

"Well, yeah," Henk says. "Because you're getting laid now and you're still depressed."

"You think it's because of this," I say, tapping the scar. "Not because of the girl?" I look at W. "You don't think maybe Lien was right?"

The three of them try not to laugh. "What's so funny?" I ask, feeling irritated and defensive all of a sudden.

"This girl didn't break your heart," W says. "She just broke your streak."

"What's that supposed to mean?" I ask.

"Willy, come on," Broodje says, waving his arms to calm us all down. "I know you. I know how you are with girls. You fall in love and then it disappears like snow in the sun.

If you'd had another few weeks with this girl you'd get tired of her, just like you do all the others. But you didn't. It was almost like she dumped you. So you're pining."

You're comparing love to a stain? Lulu had asked. She'd been skeptical at first.

Something that never comes off, no matter how much you might want it to. Yes, stain had seemed about right.

"Okay," W says, clicking his pen. "Let's start at the beginning, with as much detail as you can muster."

"The beginning of what?"

"Your story."

"Why?"

W starts explain about the Principle of Connectivity and how police use that to track down criminals, via who they associate with. He is always talking about theories like this. He believes that all of life boils down to mathematics, that there's a numeric principal or algorithm to describe every event, even the random ones (chaos theory!). It takes me a while to understand that he means to use the Principle of Connectivity to solve the mystery of Lulu.

"Again, why? The mystery's solved," I snap. "I'm pining over the girl who got away, because she got away." I'm not sure if I'm irritated because I think this is true or because I think it's not.

W rolls his eyes, as if this is beside the point. "But you want to find her, don't you?"

By that night, W has spreadsheets and graphs and on the mantel, below the fading Picasso poster, an empty poster board. "Principle of Connectivity. Basically, we track down the people we can find and see what connections they have back to your mystery girl," W says. "Our best bet is to start with Céline. Lulu may have gone back for the suitcase." He writes Céline's name and draws a circle around it.

The thought has crossed my mind a number of times, and each time, I've been tempted to contact Céline. But then I think back to that night, the raw, wounded look on her face. In any case, it doesn't matter. Either the suitcase is at the club, and Lulu hasn't gone back for it, or it's not there and she did somehow retrieve it and she found my notes inside and chose not to respond. Knowing does nothing to change the situation.

"Céline is off the table," I say.

"But she's the strongest connection," W protests.

I don't tell them about Céline and what happened at her flat that night, or what I promised her. "She's out."

W makes a rather dramatic X through Céline's name. Then he draws a circle. Inside he writes, "barge."

"What about it?" I ask.

"Did she fill out any paperwork?" W says. "Pay with a card?"

I shake my head. "She paid with a hundred dollar bill. She basically bribed Jacques."

He writes "Jacques." Circles it.

I shake my head again. "I spent more time with him than she did."

"What do you know about him?"

"He's a typical sailor. Lives on the water all year round. Sails in warm weather, kept the barge anchored in a marina, in Deauville he said, I think."

W writes "Deauville" and puts a circle around it. "What about other passengers?"

"They were older. Danish. One married couple, one divorced couple that seemed married. They were all drunk off their heads."

W writes "Drunk Danes" in a circle way off on the side of the poster board.

"We'll consider them last resorts," W says, moving to the next line. "I think the strongest lead is probably the most time-consuming." Small grin there. Then on the bottom of the poster he writes "TOUR COMPANY" in large block letters.

"Only problem is I don't know which one it was."

"Odds are, it's one of these seven," W says, reaching for a computer printout.

"You found the tour company? Why didn't you say so to begin with?"

"I didn't find it. But I did narrow down the seven companies that do tours for American students that had a tour operating in Stratford-upon-Avon on the nights in question."

"Nights in question," Henk jokes. "This is starting to sound like a detective program."

I stare at the printout. "How did you do that? In one night?"

I expect some complicated mathematical theorem, but he just shrugs and says: "The Internet." He pauses. "There may be more than seven tours, but these are seven that I've confirmed as possibilities."

"More?" Broodje says. "Seven already seems like lot."

"There was a music festival that week," I explain. It was why Guerrilla Will had gone to Stratford-upon-Avon in the first place. Tor generally avoided it; she had a poisonous grudge against the Royal Shakespeare Company, related to her even more toxic grudge against the Royal Academy of Dramatic Art, which had denied her admission twice. It was after that that she'd gone all anarchist and started Guerrilla Will.

W writes and circles the names of the tours on the poster: "Wide Horizons," "Europe Unlimited," "It's a Small World," "Adventure Edge," "Go Away," "Teen Tours!" and "Cool Europa." "My guess is that your mystery girl was on one of these."

"Okay, but there's seven tours," Henk says. "Now what?"

"I call them?" I guess.

"Exactly," W says.

"Looking for . . . damn." Once again, it comes back to me: I don't even know her name.

"What identifying details *do* you know?" W asks.

I know the timbre of her laugh. I know the heat of her breath. I know the cast of moonlight against her skin.

"She was traveling with her friend," I say, "who was blonde, and Lulu had black hair, cut short, in a bob, like Louise Brooks." The boys all exchange a look. "She had a birthmark right here." I touch my wrist. Since she first showed it to me on the train, I'd wondered what it would taste like. "She mostly kept it covered with a watch. Oh, right, she had an expensive gold watch. Or did have. I have it now."

"That's hers?" Broodje asks.

I nod.

W scribbles this down. "This is good," W says. "The watch, especially. It identifies her."

"Also, it gives you a cover," Broodje says. "A reason to be tracking her down other than wanting to bone her a few more times to get her out of your system. You can say you want to return the watch."

A half hour ago the poster board was empty, but now it's half filled, all these circles, these tenuous connections, linking me to her. W turns toward it, too.

"Principle of Connectivity," he says.

Over the next week, one by one, the circles on W's connectivity board become Xs, as connections that I understand never actually existed are severed. It's a Small World is for teens and their parents, so that one's out. Go Away doesn't have any record of anyone with a black bob and a watch on that tour. Adventure Edge refuses to divulge information about their clients and Cool Europa appears to have gone out of business. Teen Tours! doesn't pick up the phone, though I've left several messages and emails.

It's a dispiriting process, this. And complicated, too because I have to dodge time zones and callbacks and the ever-more-suspicious Ana Lucia. She's not pleased with my more frequent absences, which I've attributed to the soccer league I've supposedly joined.

One night the phone rings past eleven. "Your girlfriend?" Ana Lucia says, her voice flat. *Girlfriend* is what she calls Broodje these days, because she thinks I spend more time with him than her. It's a joke, but it gives my stomach a guilty twist every time.

I pick up the phone and cross to the other side of her room.

"Hi. I'm looking for a Willem de Ruiter?" The voice, in English, butchers the pronunciation of my name.

"Yes, hello," I respond, trying to stay businesslike because Ana Lucia is right there.

"Hi Willem! This is Erica from Teen Tours! I'm responding to your email about trying to return a missing watch."

"Oh, good," I say, keeping it breezy, though Ana Lucia is now looking at me with narrowed suspicious eyes and I realize it's because I'm speaking in English, and though I speak English with her, on the phone, with the boys, I always speak Dutch.

"We provide loss and theft insurance for all our travelers so if she'd lost something of value, there'd be a claim."

"Oh," I say.

"But I've checked all the claims for that time period, and all I've found is a claim for a stolen iPad from Rome and a bracelet that was recovered. But if you have a name, I can double check."

I look at Ana Lucia, who's decidedly not looking at me now, so I know she's listening. "I can't give you that now."

"Oh. Okay. Well, maybe you can call me back with that later?"

"I can't really do that either."

"Oh. You sure it was a Teen Tours! tour?"

I now see how the missing-watch story is as cracked as

the watch itself. Even if this was the right tour, there's no way the tour operators would know Lulu lost the watch because she lost it after the tour. It's a fiction. This is *all* a fiction. The truth is, I'm looking for a girl whose name I don't know, who bears a passing resemblance to Louise Brooks. None of which I can say out loud. Nor do I want to. This is absurd.

Erica goes on, "You know, one of our veterans led that tour. She'd know if anything went amiss. Do you want her number?"

I turn to the bed. Ana Lucia is up, throwing off the covers.

"Her name is Patricia Foley," Erica continues. "Would you like her number?"

Ana Lucia walks across the room and stands in front of me, totally naked, like she knows she's offering a choice. But it's not really a choice, when the other option doesn't actually exist.

"That won't be necessary," I say to Erika.

I wake up the next morning to knocking. I squint at the sliding glass door. There's Broodje, holding a bag, and putting a finger to his lips.

I crack open the door. Broodje pops in his head in and hands me the bag.

From the bed, Ana Lucia rubs her eyes, looking grumpy.

"Sorry to wake you," he calls to Ana Lucia. "I need to steal him. We have a soccer match. Lapland forfeited so now we're playing Wiesbaden."

Lapland and Wiesbaden? Ana Lucia is ignorant about

all things soccer, but this is pushing it. But her face registers no suspicion about the pairing, only sourness about Broodje's untimely arrival.

In the bag is someone's old soccer kit, jersey, shorts, cleats, and a thin tracksuit to wear on top. I look at Broodje. He gives me a look. "Better go change now," he says.

"When will you be back?" she asks me when I return. The tracksuit is several centimeters too short for me. I can't tell if she notices.

"Late," Broodje answers. "It's an away game. In France." He turns to me. "In Deauville."

Deauville? No. The search is over. But Broodje is halfway out the door and Ana Lucia already has her hands crossed over her chest. I'm already paying the price, so I may as well do the crime.

I go to give her a kiss good-bye. "Wish me luck," I say, forgetting for a second that there is no game, no soccer game at least, and that she's the last person who should be wishing me luck.

Anyway, she doesn't. "I hope you lose," she says.

Thirteen

Deauville

It's off season in Deauville, and the seaside resort is buttoned up tight, a cold wind whipping in off the Channel. From a distance, I can see the marina, rows of sailboats in drydock, on their stands, their masts unstepped. As we get closer, the whole marina appears shut down, hibernating for the winter. Which seems about the right idea.

On the drive down in Lien's car, which had smelled of lavender when we left and now smells of wet, dirty laundry somehow, the boys had been ebullient. W had located a barge called *Viola* late last night and had then decided we should take a road trip to France. "Wouldn't it be easier to call?" I'd asked after the plan had been explained to me. But no. They seemed to think we should just go. Of course, they were properly dressed for it, and I was in nothing but a thin track-suit. And they had nothing to lose, except a day's worth of studies. Me, I had even less, but it felt like more somehow.

We drive around the labyrinthine marina, finally reaching the main office only to find it closed. Of course. It's now four o'clock on a dark November day; anyone in their right mind is holed up somewhere warm.

"Well, we'll just have to find it ourselves," W says.

I look around. As far as I can see in every directions are masts. "I don't see how."

"Are marinas organized by type of vessel?" W asks.

I sigh. "Sometimes."

"So there might be a section for barges?" he prompts.

I sigh again. "Possibly."

"And you said this Jacques lives on his boat year-round so it wouldn't be drydocked?"

"Probably not." We had to pull our houseboat out of the water every four years for service overhauls. Drydocking for a vessel that size is a massive undertaking. "Probably anchored."

"To what?" Henk asks.

"Probably to a pier."

"There. We walk around until we find the barges," W says, as if it's all that easy.

But it's not easy at all. It's raining hard now, wet below us and above us. And it seems deserted around here, no sound except the steady pounding of rain, the waves against the sides of the hulls, and the clang of the halyards.

A cat streaks out across one of the piers, and behind it, a barking dog, and behind the dog, a man in a yellow slicker, one dot of color in all the gloom. I watch them go and wonder if I'm like that dog, chasing a cat because it's what a dog does.

The boys take shelter under an awning. I'm shivering now, ready to pack it in. I turn around to suggest a warm bistro, a nice meal, and some drinks before the long drive home. But the boys are all pointing behind me. I turn back around.

The *Viola*'s blue steel shutters are closed, making her look lonely out here strapped alongside the cement slips and the massive wooden posts. She looks cold, too, like she also wishes she were back in the hot Paris summer.

I step on the pier, and for a second, I can almost feel the rays of sunlight on my skin, can hear Lulu introducing me to double happiness. It was right there we'd sat, by the railing. Right there we'd disagreed about what double happiness meant. *Luck*, she'd said. *Love*, I'd countered.

"What the hell are you doing here?"

Striding toward us is the man in the yellow slicker, the runaway mutt now leashed and shivering.

"Many a thief has underestimated Napoleon and has paid for it in a pound of flesh, haven't they?" the man says to his dog. He pulls at the leash and Napoleon barks pitifully.

"I'm not a thief," I say in French.

The man wrinkles his nose. "Worse! You are a foreigner. I knew you were too tall. German?"

"Dutch."

"No matter. Get out of there before I call the gendarme or let Napoleon loose on you."

I hold up on my hands. "I'm not here to steal anything. I'm looking for Jacques."

I'm not sure if it's the dropping of Jacques's name or the fact that Napoleon has started licking his balls, but the man backs down. "You know Jacques?"

"A little."

"If you know Jacques even a little, you know where to find him when he's not on the *Viola*."

"Maybe less than a little. I met him last summer."

"You meet lots of people. You don't board a man's vessel without an invitation. That is the ultimate violation of his kingdom."

"I know. I just want to find him, and this is the only place I can think of."

He squints. "Does he owe you money?"

"No."

"You're sure? This isn't about the races? He always backs the wrong horses."

"Nothing to do with that."

"Did he sleep with your wife?"

"No! Last summer he took four passengers through Paris."

"The Danes? Bastards! He lost almost his whole charter fee right back to them. He's a terrible poker player. Did he lose money to you?"

"No! He got money off us. A hundred dollars. Me and this American girl."

"Terrible, those Americans. They never speak French."

"She spoke Chinese."

"What good does *that* do you?"

I sigh. "Look, this girl . . ." I start to explain. But he waves me away.

"If you want Jacques, go to Bar de la Marine. When he's not on the water, he's in the drink."

I find Jacques at the long wooden bar, slung over a near-empty glass. As soon as we walk in, he waves at me, though whether it's because he recognizes me or because this is just his standard greeting, I'm not sure. He is carrying on an in-depth conversation about new slip fees with the bartender. I buy the boys a round of beers, settle them into a corner table, and sit down next to Jacques.

"Two of what he's having," I tell the bartender, and he pours us each a glass of teeth-achingly sweet brandy on the rocks.

"Good to see you again," Jacques tells me.

"So you remember me?"

"Of course I remember you." He squints, placing me. "Paris." He belches and then pounds his chest with his fist. "Don't look so surprised. It was only a few weeks ago."

"It was three months ago."

"Weeks, months. Time is so fluid."

"Yes, I remember you saying that."

"You want to charter the *Viola*? She's dry for the season but we get wet again in May."

"I don't need a charter."

"So what can I do for you?" He downs the rest of his drink and crunches hard on the ice. Then he starts in on the fresh one.

I don't really have an answer for him. What *can* he do for me?

"I was with that American girl and I'm trying to get in touch with her. She didn't by any chance get in touch with you?"

"The American girl. Oh yes, she did."

"Really?"

"Yeah. She said to tell that tall bastard I'm done with him 'cause I've found myself a new man." He points to himself. Then he laughs.

"So she didn't get in touch with you?"

"No. Sorry, boy. She leave you high and dry?"

"Something like that."

"You could ask those bastard Danes. One of them keeps texting me. Let me see if I can find it." He pulls out a smartphone and starts fumbling with it. "My sister got me this, said it would help with navigation, bookings . . . but I can't figure it out." He hands it to me. "You try."

I check his text queue and find a note from Agnethe. I open the text and there are several more before it, including pictures from last summer when they were cruising on the *Viola*. Most are of Jacques, in front of fields of yellow safflower, or cows, or sunsets, but there's one shot I recognize: a clarinet player on a bridge over Canal Saint Martin. I'm about to hand the phone back when I see it: in the corner, a sliver of Lulu. It's not her face, it's the back of her—shoulders, neck, hair—but it's her. A reminder that she's not some fiction of my own making.

I've often wondered how many photos I've been accidentally captured in. There was another photo that day, not accidental at all. An intentional shot of Lulu and me that she'd asked Agnethe to take with her phone. Lulu had offered to send it to me. And I'd said no.

"Can I forward this to myself?" I ask Jacques.

"As you wish," he says, with a wave of the hand.

I forward the shot to Broodje's phone because it was true that mine won't accept photo texts, though that wasn't the reason I didn't want the shot of Lulu and me when she offered it. It was automatic, that denial, a reflex almost. I had almost no pictures from the last year of my traveling. Though I'm sure I am in many people's photos, I'm in none of my own.

In my rucksack, the one that got stolen on that train to Warsaw, had been an old digital camera. And on that camera were photographs of me and Yael and Bram from my eighteenth birthday. They were some of the last photos I had of the three of us together, and I hadn't even discovered them until I was on the road, bored one night and going through all the shots on my memory stick. And there we were.

I should've had those pictures emailed somewhere. Or printed. Done something permanent. I planned to, I did. But I put it off and then my rucksack got nicked and it was too late.

The devastation caught me off guard. There's a difference between losing something you knew you had and losing something you discovered you had. One is a disappointment. The other is truly a loss.

I didn't realize that before. I realize it now.

Fourteen

On the ride back to Utrecht, I call Agnethe the Dane to
see if Lulu sent her any photographs, if there had been any
correspondence. But she hardly remembers who I am. It's de-
pressing. This day, so seared in my memory, is just another
day to everyone else. And in any case, it was just one day, and
it's over now.

It's over now with Ana Lucia, too. I can feel it, even if she
can't. When I come back, defeated, telling her soccer season
is over, she is sympathetic, or maybe victorious. She's full of
kisses and *cariños*.

I accept them. But I know now it's just a matter of time.
In three weeks, she leaves for Switzerland. By the time she
gets back, four weeks later, I will be gone. I make a mental
note to get on that passport renewal.

It's as if Ana Lucia senses all this. Because she starts
pushing harder for me to join her in Switzerland. Every day,

a new appeal. "Look how nice the weather is," she says one morning as she gets ready for class. She opens her computer and reads me the weather report from Gstaad. "Sunny skies every day. Not even so cold."

I don't answer. Just force a smile.

"And here," she says, clicking over to a travel site she likes and tilting the laptop toward me to show me pictures of snowy alps and painted nutcrackers. "Here it shows you all the things you can do besides skiing. You don't have to sit at the lodge. We're close to Lausanne or Bern. Geneva's not even so far. We can go shopping there. It's famous for watches. I know! I'll buy you a watch."

My whole body stiffens. "I already have a watch."

"You do? I never see you wear it."

It's back at Bloemstraat, in my rucksack. Still ticking. I can almost hear it from here. And suddenly, three weeks feels too long.

"We should talk." The words trip out before I know what to follow them with. Breaking up is not something I've done in a while. So much easier to kiss good-bye and catch a train.

"Not now," she says, rising to apply lipstick in the mirror. "I'm already late."

Okay. Not now. Later. Good. It will give me time to find the right words. There are always right words.

After she leaves, I get dressed, make a coffee, and sit down at her computer to check my email before I leave. The travel page she was on is still open, and I'm about to close the window when I see one of the banner ads. MEXICO!!! it screams. Outside, it's cold and gray, but the pictures promise only warmth and sunshine.

I click on the link, and it takes me to a page listing several package holiday specials, not the kind of thing I'd ever do, but I feel warmer just looking at the beaches. And then I see some ads for trips to Cancún.

Cancún.

Where Lulu goes every year.

Where she has gone with her family to the same place every year. Her mother's predictability, so exasperating to her, is now my best hope.

I pull up the details. Like everything from that day, they're as fresh as wet paint. A resort fashioned like a Mayan temple. Like America behind walls with Christmas carols mariachi-style. Christmas. They went for the holidays. Christmas. Or was it New Year's? I can just go for both!

Channeling W, I start searching for resorts in Cancún. One crystalline-water beach after the other flashes across the screen. There is no end to them, these megaresorts like Mayan fortresses and temples. She said it had some kind of river. I'd remembered wondering about that, a resort with a river. There aren't any natural rivers running through Cancún. There are golf courses and swimming pools and diving cliffs, and waterslides. But rivers? I'm looking at the listing for Palacio Maya when I stumble across it. A *lazy* river, a kind of fake stream you ride on in an inflatable tube.

I narrow my search. There don't seem to be *that* many resorts that look like Mayan temples and have lazy rivers.

Four, that I can see. Four that Lulu might be staying at some time between Christmas and New Year's.

Outside it's pouring, but the sites brag that the weather in Mexico is hot, endless blue skies and sunshine. All this time, I've been stuck, trying to figure out where to go next. Why not here? To find her? I click over to an airline consolidator and look up the prices for two tickets to Cancún. Expensive, but then again, I can afford it.

I snap the computer shut, a list forming in my head. It seems so simple.

Get my passport.

Invite Broodje.

Buy the tickets.

Find Lulu.

Fifteen

_B_y six o'clock that night, I've bought Broodje's and my plane tickets and reserved us a room at a cheap hotel in Playa del Carmen. I feel flush with satisfaction, having accomplished more in this single day than I have in the last two months. There's only one thing left to do.

"We need to talk," I text Ana Lucia. She texts me right back, "I know what you want to talk about. Come by at 8." I am limber with relief. Ana Lucia is smart. She knows, like I know, that whatever this is, it's not a stain.

I buy a bottle of wine on my way over. No reason this can't be civilized.

She greets me at the door, wearing a red bikini and redder lips. Taking the wine from my hand, she pulls me inside. There are lit votive candles everywhere, like a cathedral on a saint's day. I get a bad feeling.

"Cariño, I understand it now. All that talk about how much you hate the cold. I should've guessed."

"You should've guessed?"

"Of course you want to go somewhere warm. And you know my aunt and uncle are in Mexico City but what I can't figure out is how you know about the villa on Isla Mujeres?"

"Isla Mujeres?"

"It's beautiful. Right on the beach, with a pool and servants. They have invited us to stay there if we want, or we can stay on the mainland, though not at one of those cheap places," She wrinkles her nose. "I insist to pay for the hotel, no arguments. Because it's only fair you bought the tickets."

"Bought the tickets." All I can do is repeat.

"Oh cariño," she coos. "You'll meet my family, after all. They are going to throw us a party. My parents were upset about me canceling Switzerland but they understand the things you do for love."

"For love," I repeat although with a sickening feeling I'm starting to piece together what has happened. Her Internet browser. My entire search history. Tickets for two. The hotel. My smile is pulled taut, full of false sweetness. How can I find the words for this? A misunderstanding, I will tell her; the tickets are for a boys' holiday, for me and Broodje, which *is* true.

"I know you wanted it to be a surprise," she continues. "Now I know why you have been sneaking off on the telephone, but *amor*, we leave in three weeks, when did you plan to tell me?"

"Ana Lucia," I begin. "There's been a misunderstanding."

"What do you mean?" she says. And the hope is still there, as if the misunderstanding is about a minor detail, like the hotel.

"Those tickets. They're not for you. They're for—"

She cuts me off. "It's that other girl isn't it? The one from Paris?"

Maybe I'm not so good an actor as I think. Because the way her expression has tectonically shifted from adoration to suspicion shows me that she's probably always known. And I must be a terrible actor now, because even as my mouth starts to form a plausible explanation, my face must be giving it all away. I can tell it is by what's happening to Ana Lucia's face—her pretty features puckering into disbelief, and then into belief.

"*Hijo de la gran puta!* It's the French girl? You've been with her all this time, haven't you?" Ana Lucia screams. "*That's* why you went to France?"

"It's not what you think," I say holding up my hands.

She flings open the sliding-glass door leading onto the quad. "It's exactly what I think," she says, shoving me out the door. I just stand there. She reaches for a candle and hurls it at me. It flies past me and lands on one of the throw pillow she keeps on the cement stoop. "You've been sneaking around all this time with that French whore!" Another candle whizzes by, landing in the shrubbery.

"You're going to start a fire."

"Good! I'll burn the memory of you, *culero*!" She flings another candle at me.

The rain has stopped, and though it's a chilly night, it

seems as if half the college has now gathered around us. I try to bring her back inside, to calm her down. I am unsuccessful at both.

"I canceled my trip to Switzerland for you! My relatives arranged a party for you. And all along, you were sneaking off to see your French whore. In my land. Where my family lives." She pounds on her bare chest, as if she's claiming ownership not just of Spain but of all of Latin America.

She hurls another candle. I catch this one, and it explodes, spilling glass and hot wax down my hand. My skin bubbles to a blister. I wonder, vaguely, if it'll scar. I suspect it won't.

Sixteen

*T*he height of the Mayan civilization was more than a thousand years ago, but it's hard to imagine the holiest of temples back then were as well guarded as the Maya del Sol is now.

"Room number?" The guards ask Broodje and me as we approach the gate in the imposing carved wall that seems to stretch a kilometer in each direction.

"Four-oh-seven," Broodje says before I have a chance to speak.

"Key card," the guard says. There are sweat patches all down the side of his sweater vest.

"Um, I left it in the room," Broodje replies.

The guard opens a binder and looks through a sheaf of papers. "Mr. and Mrs. *Yoshimoto*?" he asks.

"Uh-huh," Broodje replies, linking arms with me.

The guard looks annoyed. "Guests only." He snaps the binder shut and goes to close the little window.

"We're not guests," I say, smiling conspiratorially. "But we're trying to *find* a guest."

"Name?" He picks up the binder again.

"I don't know, exactly."

A black Mercedes with tinted windows glides up and barely stops before the guards lift the gate and wave it through. The guard turns back to us, weary, and for a second I think we've won. But then he says, "Go now, before I have to call the police."

"The police?" Broodje exclaims. "Whoa, whoa, whoa. Let's just all cool down a minute. Take off our sweater vests. Maybe have a drink. We can go to the bar; the hotel must have some nice bars. We'll bring you back a beer."

"This is not a hotel. It's a vacation club."

"What does that mean, exactly?" Broodje asks.

"It means you can't come in."

"Have a heart. We came from Holland. He's looking for a girl," Broodje says.

"Aren't we all?" the guard behind him asks, and they both laugh. But they still don't let us in.

I give the moped a good frustrated kick, which at least means it sputters to life. Nothing so far is going quite how I'd expected it to, not even the weather. I'd thought Mexico would be warm, but it's like being in an oven all day long. Or maybe it only feels that way because instead of spending our first day on a breeze-cooled beach as Broodje had the good sense to do, I spent yesterday at the Tulum ruins. Lulu had mentioned her family went to the same ruins every year and Tulum is the closest one, so I'd thought I might just catch her there. For four hours I watched thousands of people as they belched out of tour buses and minivans and rental cars. Twice, I thought I saw her and ran after a girl. Right hair, wrong girl. And I realized she might not even have that haircut anymore.

I'd come back to our little hotel with a sunburn and a headache, the optimism I'd had about this trip souring into a sinking feeling. Broodje cheerfully suggested we try the hotels, a more contained environment. And if that didn't work out, he'd pointed toward the beach. "There are so many girls here," he'd said in a hushed, almost reverent tone, gesturing out to the sand, which was covered, every square yard of it, with bikinis.

So many girls, I'd thought. *Why am I trying to find just one?*

Palacio Maya, another of the faux-Mayan resorts on my hit list, is a few kilometers north of here. We putter up the highway, breathing in the fumes of the passing tour buses and trucks. This time, we stash the moped in some flowering shrubs along the winding manicured road that leads to the front gates. Palacio Maya looks a lot like the Maya del Sol, only instead of a monolithic wall, it is fronted by a giant pyramid, with a guard gate in the middle. This time, I'm ready. In Spanish, I tell the guard I'm trying to find a friend of mine who's staying here but I want to surprise her. Then I slip him a twenty-dollar bill. He doesn't say a word—he just opens the gates.

"Twenty dollars," Broodje says, nodding his head. "Much classier than a couple of beers."

"It's probably what a couple of beers go for in a place like this."

We walk along the paved roadway, expecting to find a hotel, or some evidence of one, but what we find is another guard gate. The guards smile at us and call *buenos días*, as if they're expecting us, and by the way they're appraising us, like they're cats and we're mice, I see the other guards have called ahead. Without saying a word, I reach into my wallet and hand over another ten.

"Oh *gracias, señor*," the guard says. "*Que generoso!*" But then he looks around. "Only there are two of us."

I reach back into my wallet. The well's dry. I show my empty wallet. The guard shakes his head. I realize I overplayed it back at the first gate. I should've offered up the ten first.

"Come on," I say. "It's all I have left."

"Do you know how much rooms here are?" he asks. "Twelve hundred dollars a night. If you want me to let you in, and your friend, to enjoy the pools, the beaches, the tennis, the buffets, you have to pay."

"*Buffets?*" Broodje interrupts.

"Shh!" I whisper. To the guard I say, "We don't care about any of that. We're just trying to find a guest here."

The guard raises his eyebrow. "If you know guests, why you sneak in like a thief? You think just because you have white skin, and a ten-dollar bill, we think you are rich?" He laughs. "It's an old trick, amigo."

"I'm not trying to sneak anything. I'm trying to find a girl. An American girl. She might be staying here."

This makes the guard laugh even harder. "An American girl? I'd like one of those, too. They cost more than ten dollars."

We glare at each other. "Give me my money back," I say.

"What money?" the guard asks.

I'm furious when we get back to the bike. Broodje, too, is muttering about getting ripped off that thirty dollars. But I don't care about the money, and it's not the guards I'm mad at.

I keep replaying a conversation with Lulu in my head. Then one when she'd told me about Mexico. About how frustrating it was to go to the same resort with her family every year. I'd told her maybe she should go off the grid next time she went to Cancún. "Tempt fate," I'd said. "See what happens." Then I'd joked that maybe I'd go to Mexico one day, too, bump into her, and we'd escape into the wilds, having no idea at the time that this silly aside would become a mission of sorts. "You think that would happen?" she'd asked. "We'd just randomly bump into each other?" I'd told her it would have to be another big accident and she'd teased back: "So you're saying *I'm* an accident?"

After I told her that she was, she'd said something strange. She'd said that me calling her an accident might be the most flattering thing anyone has ever said about her. She wasn't simply fishing for compliments. She was revealing something with that honesty of hers, so completely disarming it was like she was stripping not just herself bare but me, too. When she said that, it had made me feel as if I'd been entrusted with something very important. And it also made me sad, because I sensed it was true. And if it was, it was wrong.

I've flattered lots of girls, many who deserved it, many who didn't. Lulu deserved it, she deserved so much more flattery than being called an accident. So I opened my mouth to say something nice. What came out, I think, surprised us both. I told her that she was the sort of person who found money and returned it, who cried in movies you weren't meant to cry in, who did things that scared her. I wasn't even sure where these things were coming from, only that as I said them, I was certain that they were true. Because improbable as it was, I *knew* her.

Only now it strikes me how wrong I was. I didn't know her at all. And I didn't ask the simplest of questions, like where she stayed in Mexico or when she visited or what her last name was, or what her first name was. And as a result, here I am, at the mercy of security guards.

We ride back to our hostel in the dusty part of Playa del Carmen, full of stray dogs and rundown shops. The cantina next door serves cheap beer and fish tacos. We order several of each. A couple of travelers from our hostel roll in. Broodje waves them over, and he starts telling them about our day, embellishing it so that it almost sounds fun. It's how all good travel stories are born. Nightmares spun into punch lines. But my frustration is too fresh to make anything seem funny.

Marjorie, a pretty Canadian girl, clucks sympathetically.

A British girl named Cassandra, with short spiky brown hair, laments the state of poverty in Mexico and the failures of NAFTA, while T.J., a sunburnt guy from Texas, just laughs. "I seen that place Maya del Sol. It's like Disneyland on the Riviera."

At the table behind us, I hear someone snicker. "*Más como Disneyland del infierno.*"

I turn around. "You know the place?" I ask in Spanish.

"We work there," the taller one answers in Spanish.

I put out my hand. "Willem," I say.

"Esteban," he answers.

"José," says the shorter. They're a bit of a spaghetti-and-meatball pair, too.

"Any chance you can sneak me in?"

Esteban shakes his head. "Not without risking my job. But there's an easy way to get in. They'll pay you to visit."

"Really?"

Esteban asks me if I have a credit card.

I pull out my wallet and show him my brand new Visa, a gift from the bank after my large deposit.

"Okay, good," Esteban says. Then he looks at my outfit, a t-shirt and a beat-up pair of kakis. "You'll also need better clothes. Not these surfer things."

"No problem. Then what?"

Esteban explains how Cancún is full of sales reps trying to get people into those resorts to buy a timeshare. They hang out at car-rental places, in the airports, even at some of the ruins. "If they think you *have* money, they'll invite you to take a tour. They'll even pay *you* for your trouble, money, free tours, massages."

I explain this all to Broodje.

"Sounds too good to be true," he says.

"It's no too good, and it is true," José answers in English. "So many people buy, make such a big decision after just one day." He shakes his head, in wonderment, or disgust, or both.

"Fools and their money," T.J. says, laughing. "So y'all gotta look like you're loaded."

"But he *is* loaded!" Broodje says. "What does it matter what he looks like?"

José says, "No matter what you is; only matter what you seem."

I buy Broodje and myself some linen pants and button-up shirts for next to nothing and spend a ridiculous amount on a couple of pairs of Armani sunglasses from one of the stalls in the touristy section of town.

Broodje is aghast at the cost of the glasses. But I tell him they're necessary. "It's the little details that tell the big story." That was what Tor always said, to explain why we had such minimal costumes in Guerilla Will.

"What's the big story?" he asks.

"We're slacker playboys with trust funds, renting a house on Isla Mujeres."

"So, aside from the house, you're pretending to be you?"

The next day is Christmas so we wait until the day after to set off. At the first car rental agency, we've practically rented a car by the time we realize that there's no one there offering us a tour. At the second car rental agency, we're met by a smiling, big-toothed American blonde who asks us how long we're in town for and where we're staying.

"Oh, I love the Isla," she purrs after we tell her about our villa. "Have you eaten at Mango yet?"

Broodje looks mildly panicked but I just give a little smile. "Not yet."

"Oh," she says. "Does your villa come with a cook?"

I just continue to smile, a little bashfully this time, as if the largesse embarrasses me.

"Wait. Are you renting the white adobe place with the infinity pool?"

Again, I smile. Little nod.

"So Rosa is the cook there?"

I don't answer, I don't need to. An embarrassed shrug will do.

"Oh, I *love* that place. And Rosa's mole is divine. Just thinking about it makes me hungry."

"I'm always hungry," Broodje says, leering. She looks at him quizzically. I give him a discreet kick.

"That place is very expensive," she says. "Have you ever considered buying something down here?"

I chuckle. "Too much responsibility," says Willem, Millionaire Playboy.

She nods, as if she too understands the burdens of juggling multiple properties. "Yes. But there is another way. You can own, and have someone else take care it for you, even rent it out for you." She pulls out glossy brochures of several different hotels—including the Maya del Sol.

I glance at the brochures, scratching my chin. "You know, I heard about such an investment for tax-sheltering purposes," I say, channeling Marjolein now.

"Oh, fantastic moneymaker and money saver. You really should see one of these properties."

I pretend to casually glance at the brochures. "This one looks nice," I say, flicking a finger at the Maya del Sol brochure.

"It's sinfully decadent." She starts telling me all the things I know about the place, about the beach and the pools and the restaurants and the movie theater and the golf. I feign disinterest.

"I don't know," I say.

"Oh, at least take a tour!" She's practically pleading now. "You could even do one today."

I heave a big sigh and allow my eyes to flicker toward her for a brief minute. "We'd planned to see the ruins. That's why we're renting a car."

"I can arrange a free tour of the ruins for you." She reaches for another brochure. "This one goes to Coba, and you swim in a cenote and go on a zip line. I can throw that in for you two. Gratis."

I pause, as if considering it.

"Look, you can go, spend the day." She beckons me closer. "Don't tell them I told you but you could even spend the night. Once you get past the gates, you're in."

I look at Broodje, as if seeking his permission to do the girl this favor and take her tour. He gamely plays along, giving me a put-upon look that says, *well, if you must.*

I crack a smile at the girl and she positively beams in return. "Oh, fantastic!" She starts to write us up the paperwork, all the while chatting about the tour we'll go on. "And when you get back on the Isla, you must go to Mango. The brunches are to die for." She looks up from her paperwork. "Maybe I can take you."

"Maybe," I allow.

"Will you still be here for New Year's?"

I nod.

"What are you doing?"

I shrug, open my hands, as if to suggest so many, many options.

"There's this great party on the beach at Puerto Morelos. Las Olas de Molas, this wild reggae band are playing. It's usually the best thing going in all of the Playa. A lot of us dance all night, and sometimes catch a ferry to the Isla for hangover brunch."

"Maybe I'll see you there."

She grins. "I'll cross my fingers. Here's everything you need for your tours," she says, handing me some paperwork, as well as a card with her personal cell phone number on it. "I'm Kayla. Call me if you need anything. *Anything* at all."

The same sweating, sweater-vested security guards are manning the gate to Maya del Sol, but they don't recognize us. Or they don't care. In the backseat of a taxi, with official paperwork in triplicate in hand, I am transformed.

We are deposited in the front lobby, an enormous atrium

full of bamboo, flowers, and tropical birds tied to perches. We sit down on a wicker loveseat while a burnished Mexican woman takes our IDs and makes copies of my credit card. Then we are delivered to an older Mexican man with a flip of golden hair held back by a pair of tortoiseshell Ray-Bans.

"Welcome!" he says. "My name is Johnny Maximo, and I'm here to tell you that at Maya del Sol, fantasy becomes reality."

"That's just what he's hoping for," Broodje says.

Johnny grins. He glances at the piece of paper in hand. "So, William, Robert. Is it Robert or Bob?"

"Robert-Jan, actually," Broodje says.

"Robert then. Have you ever owned a vacation property?"

"I can't say that I have."

"What about you, William?"

"I'm more of a see-the-world kind of guy."

Johnny laughs. "Me, too. See all the ladies of the world. So I take it you two bachelors have never to been to a vacation club before."

"Can't say that I have, Johnny," Broodje says.

"I am telling you: this is the life. Why rent your vacation when you can own it? Why live half a life when you can live a whole one?"

"Or two lives, even," Broodje says.

"Here is one of our pools. We have six of them," Johnny brags. It's surrounded by chaise longues and flowering shrubs. Beyond, the Caribbean glitters as if its sole purpose is to be a backdrop. "The view is nice, no?" Johnny laughs, pointing to a row of sunbathing women.

"Very," I say, scanning them, one by one.

"So, what do you do, William?"

"Real estate," I say.

"Ahh, so you already know how lucrative it is. You know . . ." He motions me closer. "I used to be a big movie star in Mexico," he says in an exaggerated whisper. "But now—"

"You were an actor?" I interrupt.

This catches him off guard. "Before. But I make more money as an owner here than I ever did in the film business."

"What films were you in?" I ask.

"Oh, nothing you'd ever hear of."

"We get lots of foreign films in Holland. Try me."

"Really, I don't think you'd hear of them. I was in a film with Armand Assante. Mostly I was in the telenovelas."

"Soap operas? Like *Good Times, Bad Times*," Broodje says, scoffing a little.

"Here, they are taken very seriously," Johnny says with a sniff.

"That's cool," I say. "That you made your living like that."

For a second, Johnny's face flattens out. Even his tan seems to fade. And then he snaps to. "That was then. I make so much more money now." He claps his hands together and turns toward me. "So, William, what would you like to see?" He gestures out toward the grounds, and I have this first inkling, tiny but real, that she might be here. It's a small thing, but somehow it's the happiest I've felt in months.

"Every single centimeter of the resort," I say.

"Well, we are more than one square kilometer so that might take a while, but I am glad to see you are so motivated."

"Oh, you have no idea how motivated I am." Which is a funny thing to say because I wasn't that motivated yesterday. But now it's like I've switched into character.

"Why don't we start with one of our world-class restaurants. We have eight. Mexican, Italian, burger bar, sushi . . ."

"Yes," Broodje says.

"Why don't you show us the one that is the most popular for guests having lunch at this time," I suggest. "I'd like to see the makeup of the crowds."

"Oh, that would be Olé, Olé, our open-air cantina. It has a lunch buffet."

Broodje grins. Lunch buffet. Magic words.

Lulu is not at the lunch buffet, or any of the seven other restaurants we visit during our five-hour tour. She's not at any of the six pools or the two beaches or the twelve tennis courts or the two nightclubs or the three lobbies or the Zen day spa or the endless gardens. She's not at the petting zoo, either.

As the day lags on, I realize there are just too many variables. Maybe this is the wrong place. Or maybe this is the right place, but it's the wrong time. Or maybe it's the right place and the right time but she was watching TV in her room when I was at the pool. Maybe right now she is sitting by one of the pools while I'm looking at one of the model rooms.

Or maybe I walked right past her and I didn't even know it.

The good feeling from earlier begins to collapse in on itself. She could be anywhere. She could be nowhere. And worst of all, she could be right here and I didn't even recognize her.

A couple of girls in bikinis sashay past me, laughing. Broodje nudges me but I barely look at them. I'm beginning to think that I've talked myself into a lie of my own telling. Because the truth is I don't know her. All I know is that she's a girl who bears a passing resemblance to Louise Brooks. But what is that? The contours of a person, but really no more real that a fantasy projected onto a screen.

Seventeen

"Cheer up, hombre, it's almost a new year."

Esteban hands me a bottle. He, José, Broodje, Cassandra, and I are crammed into a taxi, crawling through holiday traffic as we head north to that party in Puerto Morelos, the one Kayla told me about. José and Esteban know about it, too, so apparently it really is the place to be.

"Yeah, come on. It's New Year's," Cassandra says.

"And you won't go home empty-handed if you don't want to," Broodje says. "Unlike some of us," he adds, full of exaggerated self-pity.

"Poor Broodje," Cassandra says. "Am I saying it right?"

"Bro-djuh," Broodje corrects, adding, "it means sandwich."

Cassandra smiles. "Don't worry, Sandwich Boy. We'll make sure somebody takes a bite out of you tonight."

"I think she wants a bite of my sandwich," Broodje says in Dutch, grinning at the prospect. I attempt a smile back. But really, I'm done. I've been done since Maya del Sol, though I have dutifully checked out a few other resorts, thanks to José and Esteban, who told me how to get into Palacio Maya and got me wristbands for Maya Vieja. But it's felt like going through the motions. I don't even know who I'm looking for, so how am I going to find her?

The taxi skids onto a strip of undeveloped beach. We pay the driver and emerge onto a scene. Music throbs from huge speakers, and hundreds of people are scattered up and down the beach. Everyone seems to be barefoot, judging by the enormous piles of shoes right at the entrance to the party.

"Maybe you can find by her shoe," Cassandra says. "Like Cinderella. What would a glass slipper for the modern girl look like? How about this?" She holds up a pair of shiny orange flip-flops. She tries them on. "Too big," she says, flinging them back onto the piles.

"Would beautiful lady like to dance?" José asks Cassandra.

"Sure," she says, grinning. They walk away, José already with a hand on her hip.

Broodje's face falls. "I guess his taco was more appetizing than my sandwich."

"As you keep reminding me, there are lots of girls. I'm sure one of them will want a bite of your sandwich."

And there are so many girls. Hundreds of them, in all shapes and colors, perfumed and primed for partying. On any other New Year's, it would be a promising start.

The line for the bar snakes all the way around the palm trees and hammocks. We're inching our way forward when a girl wearing a sarong, a smile, and not much else stumbles into me.

"Steady there," I say, righting her by the elbow. She holds up a half-empty bottle of tequila, curtseys, and takes a long slug.

"You might want to pace yourself," I say.

"Why don't *you* pace me?"

"Okay." I take the bottle from her and swig. I hand it to Broodje who does the same. He gives the bottle back to her.

She holds it up, swishes it around so the larva inside somersaults. "You can have the worm, if you want to," she says in a slurry voice. "Worm, worm, can the hottie eat you?" She holds the bottle up to her ear. "The worm says yes." She leans in closer, and in a hot whisper adds, "So do I."

"It's not really a worm," Broodje says. "It's an agave larva." Jose is a bartender and he explained this all to us.

Her eyes roll unfocussed in her head. "What's the diff? Worm, larva. You know what they say? The early bird gets the worm." She hands Broodje the bottle, then puts both arms on my shoulder and kisses me, fast, wet, and boozy, on the mouth. She reels back, grabbing her tequila bottle. "Gets the kiss, too," she says, laughing. "Happy New Year."

Broodje and I watch her stumble through the sand. Then he turns to me. "I forgot what it's like, being out with you. What you're like."

Six months ago, I'd have kissed the girl back, and the night would be set. Broodje may know what I'm like, but I don't.

When we get our drinks, Broodje makes his way toward the dance area. I tell him I'll meet up with him later. Up the beach, away from the stage and dance area, I spot a small bonfire with a group of people sitting around it, strumming on guitars. I start off in that direction, but then I see someone walking toward me. Kayla of the car rental agency, waving tentatively, as if she's not sure it's really me.

I pretend to not be me, and pivot toward the shoreline. As crowded and chaotic as the party is, the water is surprisingly quiet. There are a few people splashing about. Farther out, it's empty, just moonlight reflecting on the water. Even at night, the water is bluer than I imagined it; it's the only part of this trip that is coming close to meeting expectations.

I strip down to my boxers and dive in, swimming far out, until I reach a floating raft. I grip the splintering wood. The sounds of the guitars strumming "Stairway to Heaven" and the heavy bass of a reggae band reverberate through the water. It's a good party, on a beautiful beach, on a soft, warm night. All the things that used to be enough.

I swim out a little farther and duck back under. Tiny silvery fish zip by. I reach out to touch them, but they whip out of reach so fast it's like they're leaving contrails behind. When I can't hold my breath any longer, I come up for air to hear the reggae singer announce: "Half hour until the New Year. Until it all starts again. *Año nuevo*. It's a tabula rasa."

I take a breath and go back under. I scoop up a handful of

sand and let it go, watching the grains disperse in the water. I come back up.

"Come the stroke of midnight, before you kiss your *amor*, save *un beso para tí*."

A kiss for you.

Moments before I'd kissed her for the first time, Lulu had said another one of her strange things: *I escaped danger*. She was emphatic about it, her eyes had a fire to them, just as they had when she'd come between me and the skinheads. It had seemed a peculiar thing to say. Until I'd kissed her. And then I felt it, as visceral and all-encompassing as the water around me now. Escaping danger. I'm not sure what danger she'd been referring to. All I knew was that kissing Lulu made me feel relief, like I'd landed somewhere after a long journey.

I turn onto my back, looking at the canvas of a star-spangled sky.

"Tabula rasa . . . time to *hacer borrón y cuenta nueva*, wipe the board clean," the singer chants.

Wipe the board clean? I feel like my board is too clean, perpetually wiped bare. What I want is the opposite: a messy scrawl, constellations of indelible things that can't ever be washed away.

She *must* be here. Maybe not at this party, or on this beach, or at the resorts I visited, but *somewhere* here. Swimming in *this* water, the same water I'm in now.

But it's a big ocean. It's an even bigger world. And maybe we've gotten as close as we're supposed to get.

Eighteen

The bus is shaped like a monkey, it's full of old people, and I don't want to be on it. But Broodje does, and after dragging him to half the resorts on the Mayan Riviera, I'm not one to argue.

"First stop, Coba, then we go to a Mayan village. Then a zip line—not sure about these folks and a zip line," Broodje says, nodding to our mostly gray-haired tour mates. "Then swimming in a cenote—it's a kind of underground cave lake—then Tulum." He flips the brochure around. "This tour costs a hundred and fifty dollars per person and we got it for free."

"Hmm," I say.

"I don't get it. You're Dutch on one side, Israeli on the other. By all rights, this should make you the cheapest bastard alive."

"Uhh-huh."

"Are you listening?"

"Sorry. I'm tired."

"Hungover more like. When we stop for lunch, we'll get some tequila. Hair of the dog is what T.J. calls it."

I bunch my rucksack into a makeshift pillow and lean my head against the window. Broodje pulls out a copy of *Voetbal International*. The bus chugs off. I fall asleep, waking when we arrive at Coba. We plod off the bus, standing in a little clump as the guide tells us about the ancient Mayan ruins, a series of isolated temples and pyramids half overtaken by the trees and vines of the jungle. "It's very unique," she says. "This is one of the few ruins you can still climb. And you'll also be interested in the lagoon, La Iglesia, or church, and of course, the ball courts."

Behind us, a girl, the only other person our age, asks, "Ball courts? What kind of ball did they play?"

"A sort of basketball," the guide answers.

"Oh." She sounds disappointed.

"You don't like basketball?" Broodje asks her. "I thought Americans loved basketball."

"She's a soccer player," an older woman says. "She was all-state in high school."

"Nana!"

"Really? What position?" Broodje asks.

"Striker."

"Midfield." He taps his chest.

They look at each other. "Wanna go check out the ball courts?" she asks.

"Sure."

"Be back in a half hour, Candace," the older lady says.

"Okay."

Broodje looks at me to come, but I nod for him to go alone. When the rest of the tour sets off toward the lagoon, I turn straight for the Nohoch Mul pyramid, climbing the 120 near-vertical steps to the top. It's midday and hot so there's hardly anyone up here, just a family taking pictures. It's still enough for the quiet to be loud: the rustle of the breeze in the trees, the squawk of tropical birds, the metallic chirp of crickets. A gust of hot wind picks up a dry leaf and carries it over the jungle canopy.

The stillness is interrupted by a couple of kids, who have started shouting each other's names in bird chirps. *"Josh!"* the girl squawks, as her brother laughs.

"Allie!" the boy, Josh, presumably, chirps back.

"Joshua, Allison, *shh*," their mother chides, gesturing to me. "You're not the only ones up here."

The kids look at me, cocking their heads, as if inviting me to call out a name, too. I hold up my hands and shrug because I don't actually know the name I want to yell. I'm not even sure I want to yell it anymore.

Back at the Monkey Bus, I find Broodje and Candace sharing a Coke, one bottle, two straws. When we lumber back on board, I slip into a seat next to an older man traveling solo, allowing Broodje and Candace to sit together in our row. When I hear them arguing about whether Van Persie or Messi is the best striker, I smile, and my gentleman seatmate smiles back.

After lunch, we stop at a traditional Mayan village and are given the option of a ten-dollar spiritual cleansing by a Mayan priest. I stay off to the side as the others take turns standing under a smoking canopy. Then we're herded back on the bus. The doors wheeze open. Broodje climbs on, Candace climbs on, my seatmate with the sandals and the socks climbs on, the guide climbs on. Everyone climbs on, except me.

"Willy, you coming?" Broodje calls.

He sees me hesitating by the door and comes back down the aisle to talk to me. "Willy, all is good? Are you mad that I'm sitting with Candace?"

"Of course not. I think it's great."

"Come on."

I do the calculations in my mind. Candace said she was in town until the eighth, longer than we are. Broodje will have company.

"I'm getting off here." As soon as I say it, I feel that familiar relief. When you're on the road, there is always the promise of the next stop being better than the last.

His face goes serious. "Are you staying away because of what I said before, about you getting all the girls? Don't worry. I think one actually likes me."

"I'm sure of it. So you should make the most of it. I'll see you back at the airport for the flight home."

"*What?* That's in four days. And you don't have your things."

"I have what I need. Just bring the rest to the airport."

The bus driver guns the engine. The guide taps her watch. Broodje looks panicked.

"It's okay," I reassure him, tightening the straps on my rucksack.

"You won't get lost?" he asks.

I paste on a reassuring smile. But of course, the truth is, that is exactly what I intend to do.

Nineteen

*T*wo hitched truck rides later, I find myself on the outskirts of Valladolid, a small colonial town. I wander around the central square, full of low-rise, pastel colonial buildings reflecting in a large fountain. Soon I stumble upon a cheap hotel.

It feels a world away from the Mayan Riviera here. Not just the lack of megaresorts or partying tourists, but how I got here. Not looking, just finding.

I have no schedule. I sleep when I'm tired, eat when I'm hungry, grabbing something hot and spicy from one of the food carts. I linger late into the night. I don't look for anyone. I don't talk to anyone. After the last few months on Bloemstraat, the boys always around, or if not them, Ana Lucia, I'm not used to being alone.

I sit at the edge of the fountain and watch people and, for a minute, indulge myself imagining Lulu being one of them, imagining that we really had escaped into the wilds of Mexico. Is this where we'd go? Would we sit at a café, our ankles intertwined, our heads close, like that couple over there under the umbrella? Would we walk all night, ducking into the alleyways to steal a kiss? Would we wake up the next morning, untangle our bodies, pull out a map, close our eyes and decide where to next? Or would we just never get out of bed?

No! Stop it! This is pointless. A road nowhere. I get up, brush off my pants and return to the hotel. Lying in bed, I spin a twenty-peso coin around my knuckles and ponder what to do next. When the coin falls to the floor, I reach for it. And then I stop. Heads, I'll stay in Valladolid another day. Tails, I'll move on. Tails.

It's not pointing at the map. But it'll do.

The next morning I go downstairs in search of coffee. The worn dining room is practically empty—one Spanish-speaking family at one table, and in the corner by the window, a pretty woman about my age with hair the color of rust.

"I was wondering about you," she calls in English. She sounds American.

I pour some coffee from the samovar. "I often wonder about me, too," I reply.

"I saw you last night at the food carts. I've been trying to brave up to eat at them, but I wasn't sure what they were serving or if it would kill a gringo like me."

"I think it was pork. I don't ask too many questions."

"Well, it didn't kill you." She laughs. "And whatever doesn't kill you makes you stronger."

We stand there for a second. I gesture to join her at the same time she gestures for me to take a seat. I sit down across from her. A waiter in a tired tuxedo drops off a plate of Mexican sweet bread.

"Careful there," she says, flicking at her own stale bread with a turquoise-painted nail. "I almost chipped a tooth."

I knock at it. It sounds like a hollow log. "I've had worse."

"What are you, some kind of a professional adventure eater?"

"Something like that."

"Where are you from?" She holds up a hand. "No, wait, let me guess. Say something else."

"Something else?"

She taps a finger to her temple, then snaps her fingers. "You're Dutch."

"Good ear."

"Not much of an accent, though."

"Very good ear. I grew up speaking English."

"Did you live in England?"

"No, it was just my mother didn't like speaking Dutch, thought it sounded too much like German. So at home, it was English."

She glances at the phone on the table. "Well, I suspect there is a fascinating story behind that, but I'm afraid it'll have to remain a mystery." She pauses. "I'm a day late already."

"Late for what?"

"For Mérida. I was supposed to be there yesterday, but my car broke down, and, well, it's been a cascading comedy of errors. What about you? Where are you headed?"

I pause. "Mérida—if you'll give me a ride."

"I wonder what would piss off David more—driving alone or giving a ride to strangers."

"Willem." I hold out my hand. "Now I'm not a stranger."

She narrows her eyes at my outstretched hand. "You'll need to do better than that."

"Sorry. I'm Willem de Ruiter." I reach into my backpack for my stiff new passport and hand it over. "Here's some identification."

She flips through it. "Nice picture, Willem. I'm Kate. Kate Roebling. And I'm not showing you my passport because the picture is very unfortunate. You'll just have to trust me on that."

She smiles and slides my passport back across the table. "Okay, then, Willem de Ruiter, traveling adventure-eater. The garage just opened so I'm grabbing the car. Assuming it's actually ready, I'll be hitting the road in about a half hour. Does that give you time to get packed and ready to go?"

I point to my rucksack on the floor next to me. "I'm always packed and ready to go."

Kate picks me up in a sputtering Volkswagen jeep, the seats torn, the foam stuffing coming out. "*This* is fixed?" I ask, climbing in.

"That's just cosmetic. You should've seen it before. The

muffler was falling out, literally dragging behind the car, sparking. The whole rainforest could've gone up in flames because of this baby. No offense. Who's a pretty girl?" She pats the dashboard and turns to me, whispering. "You have to be nice to her. Or she won't go."

I tip an imaginary hat to the car. "My apologies."

"This is actually a great car. Appearances can be quite deceiving, you know." She guns the engine.

"Yes, I've noticed."

"Thank God, or I'd be out of a job."

"Bank robber?"

"Ha! I'm an actor."

"*Really?*"

She turns to me. "Why? Are you of the tribe?"

"Not really."

She raises an eyebrow. "'Not really'? That's like being 'a little' pregnant. You either are or you're not."

"How about I was, not seriously, and now I'm not."

"Oh, did you need to get a 'real job'?" she asks sympathetically.

"No. I don't have one of those, either."

"So you just travel and eat dangerously?"

"More or less."

"Nice life."

"More or less." The car hits a pothole and my stomach seems to smack against the roof and then just as abruptly, plummet back to the floor. "What kind of acting do you do?" I ask when I've regained my equilibrium.

"I'm a cofounder and artistic director of a small theater

company in New York called Ruckus. We do productions, but also training and teaching programs."

"That's not impressive at all."

"I know, right? I never meant to be quite so ambitious, but when my friends and I moved to New York, we couldn't get the kind of roles we wanted, so we started our own company. And it's just kind of grown. We produce our own plays and we teach, and now we've started this overseas initiative. That's why we're in Mexico. We're running a workshop on Shakespeare in Mérida in conjunction with Universidad Autónoma de Yucatán."

"You're teaching Shakespeare in Spanish?"

"Well, *I'm* not, because I don't speak a lick of Spanish. I'll work with the English speakers. David, my fiancé, he speaks Spanish. Though the funny thing is, even when we do the Shakespeare in translation, I somehow know where we are in the plays. Maybe because I know them so well. Or because Shakespeare transcends language."

I nod. "The first time I did Shakespeare, I did it in French."

She turns to me. Her eyes are green, bright as autumn apples, and there's a smattering of freckles across the bridge of her nose. "You did Shakespeare then? And in French?"

"Mostly in English, of course."

"Oh, *of course.*" She pauses. "That's pretty good for a not-serious actor."

"I never said I was any good."

She laughs. "Oh, I can tell you were good."

"Really?"

"Yep. I have a Spidey-sense for these things." She pulls

out a package of gum, takes a stick, and offers me a piece. It tastes like talcum powder and coconuts and makes my still-churning stomach rebel a little bit more. I spit it out.

"Vile, right? Yet strangely addictive." She pops a second piece. "So how in the world did a Dutchman wind up doing Shakespeare in French?"

"I was traveling. I was broke. I was in Lyon. I met this Shakespeare troupe called Guerrilla Will. They mostly performed in English but the director is a little . . . eccentric and she thought the way to one-up the other street performers was to do Shakespeare in the native language. She'd cobbled together a cast of French speakers to do *Much Ado About Nothing* in France, in French. But the guy who'd been playing Claudio ran off to be with some Norwegian guy he'd met; everyone was already doubling up parts so they just needed someone who could get by in French. And I could."

"You'd never done Shakespeare before?"

"I'd never acted before. I'd been traveling with an acrobatic troupe. So when I tell you it was all by accident, I'm not kidding."

"But you did other plays?"

"Yeah, *Much Ado* was a disaster but we ran it for four nights before Tor realized it. Then Guerrilla Will switched back to English and I stayed on. It was decent money."

"Oh, you're one of *those*. Doing Shakespeare just for the money," she jokes. "You whore."

I laugh.

"So what other plays did you do?"

"*Romeo and Juliet*, of course. *A Midsummer's Night Dream. All's Well That Ends Well. Twelfth Night.* All the crowd-pleasers."

"I love *Twelfth Night*; we're talking about doing that next year when we have time. We just closed a two-year off-Broadway run of *Cymbeline* and we've been touring it. Do you know it?"

"I've heard of it, but I've never seen it."

"It's a lovely, funny, romantic play and there's lots of music in it. At least the way we do it."

"Us, too. We had a drum circle in our *Twelfth Night*."

She glimpses at me sidelong as she keeps her eyes on the road. "*Our Twelfth Night?*"

"Theirs. Guerrilla Will's."

"Sounds like the whore fell in love with the john."

"No. No falling in love," I say.

"But you miss it?"

I shake my head. "I've moved on."

"I see." We're quiet for a while. Then she says, "Do you do that a lot? Move on?"

"Maybe. But only because I travel a lot."

She taps out a beat on the steering wheel, audible only to herself. "Or maybe you travel a lot because it lets you move on."

"Perhaps."

She's quiet again. Then: "So are you moving on now? Is that what brought you to the grand metropolis of Valladolid?"

"No. The wind just blew me there."

"What? Like a plastic bag?"

"I prefer to think of myself as a ship. Like a sailboat."

"But sailboats aren't steered by the wind; they're powered by it. There's a difference."

I look out the window. The jungle is everywhere. I look back at her. "Can you move on from something when you're not sure what it is you're moving on from?"

"You can move on from absolutely anything," she replies. "But that does sound a little complicated."

"It is," I say. "Complicated."

Kate doesn't answer, and the silence stretches out, shimmery, like the road ahead of us.

"And a long story," I add.

"It's a long drive," she replies.

There's something about Kate that reminds me of Lulu. Maybe it's just that they're both American or how we met: during journeys, talking food.

Or maybe it's because in a few hours, I'll never see her again. There's nothing to lose. So as we drive, I tell Kate the story of that day, but it's a different version from the one I told Broodje and the boys. You play to your audience, Tor always said. Which is maybe why I can tell Kate the parts of the story that I didn't—couldn't—tell Broodje and the boys. "It was like she knew me," I tell her. "Straightaway, she knew me."

"How?"

I tell Kate about Lulu thinking I'd deserted her on the train when I'd spent too long in the café. Hysterically laughing, and then out of the blue—my glimmer of her strange honesty—telling me she'd thought I'd got off the train.

"Were you going to?" Kate asks, her eyes wide.

"No, of course not," I answer. And I wasn't, but the memory of it still shames me because of what I was going to do later.

"So how did she *see* you, exactly?"

"She said she couldn't understand why I invited her without an ulterior motive."

Kate laughs. "I hardly think you wanting to sleep with a pretty girl qualifies as an ulterior motive."

I wanted to sleep with her, of course. "But that wasn't the ulterior motive. I invited her to Paris because I didn't want to go back to Holland that day."

"Why not?"

My stomach lurches again. Bram, gone. Yael, all but gone. The houseboat, a signature away from gone. I force a smile. "That is a much longer story and I'm not done with this one."

I tell Kate the double happiness story Lulu told me. About the Chinese boy traveling to take some important exam, and along the way, falling sick. About the mountain doctor taking care of him. About the doctor's daughter telling him this strange line of verse. About the emperor who, after the boy does well on the exam, recites a mysterious line to him. About the boy immediately recognizing the line as the other half of what the girl told him, and repeating the line the girl had told him, pleasing the emperor, getting the job, going back, and marrying the girl. About double happiness.

"*Green trees against the sky in the spring rain while the sky set off the spring trees in the obscuration. Red flowers dot the land in the breeze's chase while the land colored up in red after the kiss.*" That had been the couplet. As soon as Lulu told it to me, there had been something instantly familiar about it, even though I'd never heard it before, never heard the story before. Unknown and familiar. Which, by that point, was how Lulu was seeming.

I tell Kate about Lulu asking who took care of me—as if she knew the answer—and then doing it herself. Stepping between me and the skinheads. Throwing that book. Distracting them so we could get away before we got hurt. Only she got hurt. Even now, the memory of the blood on her neck from when one of the skinheads threw the bottle at her, after all these months, it makes me sick. And ashamed. I don't tell Kate that.

"That was very brave of her," Kate says when I tell her what Lulu did.

Saba used to say there was a difference between bravery and courage. Bravery was doing something dangerous without thinking. Courage was walking into danger, knowing full well the risks.

"No," I tell Kate. "It was courageous."

"You both were courageous."

But I wasn't. Because I tried to send Lulu back. Cowardly. And then I didn't manage to. Cowardly. I don't tell Kate this part either.

"So you're here in Mexico to do what?" she asks.

I think of the boys. They think I'm here to inoculate myself. To find Lulu, sleep with her a few more times, and get on with things.

"I don't know . . . find her. At the very least, set the record straight."

"What record? You left a note."

"Yes, but . . ." I almost say it. Then I stop myself.

"But what?" Kate asks.

"But . . . I didn't come back," I finish.

Kate looks at me for a long moment. The car starts to drift off the road before she returns her attention to driving.

"Willem, in case you haven't noticed, Cancún is back that way?" She points in the reverse direction. I nod. "The chances of you finding this girl seem unfavorable enough without you going to an entirely different city."

"It wasn't going to happen. I could tell."

"How could you tell?"

"Because you don't ever find things when you're looking for them. You find them when you're not."

"If that were true, nobody would ever find their keys."

"Not keys. The bigger things."

She sighs. "I don't get it. On one hand, you put all this faith into these accidents of yours, and on the other hand, you write off the chance of one even happening."

"I didn't write it off. I came all the way to Cancún."

"And promptly went to Mérida."

"I wasn't going to find her. By looking." I shake my head. It's hard to explain this part. "It wasn't meant to be."

"Meant to be," Kate scoffs. "Excuse me but I'm having a hard time buying all this woo-woo stuff." She waves her arms in the air and I have to reach out for the steering wheel until she takes it again. "Nothing happens without intention,

Willem. Nothing. This theory of yours—life is ruled by accidents—isn't that just one huge excuse for passivity?"

I start to disagree, but then the image of Ana Lucia flits through my head. Right place at the right time. It had seemed like a fortuitous accident back then. Now, it feels more like surrender.

"How do you explain us?" I point back and forth to me and her. "Right now, right here, having this conversation, if not for accidents? If not because your car muffler broke and put you in Valladolid, where I wasn't even meant to be?" I don't mention the flipped coin being a deciding factor, even though it would seem to support my case.

"Oh, no, don't go falling in love with me." She laughs and taps the ring on her finger. "Look, I don't discount a magical hand of fate. I am an actor, after all, and a Shakespearian, no less. But it can't be the ruling force of your life. You have to be the driver. And by the way, yes, we are having this conversation because my car—lovely, sweet car that you are," she baby talks, stroking the dashboard, "had some mechanical issues. But *you* were the one who asked *me* for a ride, persuaded me to give you a ride, so you discredit your own theory right there. That was pure will, Willem. Sometimes fate or life or whatever you want to call it, leaves a door a little open and you walk through it. But sometimes it locks the door and you have to find the key, or pick the lock, or knock the damn thing down. And sometimes, it doesn't even show you the door, and you have to build it yourself. But if you keep waiting for the doors to be opened for you. . . ." she trails off.

"What?"

"I think you'll have a hard time finding single happiness, let alone that double portion."

"I'm beginning to doubt that double happiness even exists," I say, thinking of my parents.

"That's because you're looking for it. Doubt is part of searching. Same as faith."

"Aren't those opposites?"

"Maybe they're just two parts of the couplet."

It reminds me of something Saba used to say: *A truth and its opposite are flip sides of the same coin.* It never quite made sense to me before.

"Willem, I suspect deep down you know *exactly* why you're here, *exactly* what you want, but you're unwilling to commit to it, unwilling to commit to the wanting, let alone the having. Because both of those propositions are terrifying."

She turns to me and gives me a long, searing look. It goes on a while, and the car starts to drift. Again, I take the wheel to right us. She lets go of the wheel entirely and I grasp it with both hands.

"Look there, Willem. You grabbed the wheel."

"Only to keep us from crashing."

"Or, you might say, to keep us from having an accident."

Twenty

Mérida, Mexico

---

*M*érida is a bigger version of Valladolid, a colonial pastel-painted city. Kate drops me off in front of a historic peach-colored building that she has heard is a decent hostel. I book myself a room with a balcony overlooking the square and I sit out and watch people taking shelter from the afternoon sun. Shops are closing up for siesta and though I'd planned to scout out the area and find some lunch, I'm not actually hungry. I'm a little wrung out from the morning's drive and my stomach still feels as if it's on the bumpy highway. I decide to take a siesta, too.

I wake up covered in sweat. It's dark outside, the air in my room still and stale. I sit up to open my window or the balcony door, but when I do, my stomach heaves. I flop back down on the bed and close my eyes, willing myself back to sleep. Sometimes I can trick my body into righting itself before it realizes something's wrong. Sometimes that works.

But not tonight. I think of the pork in the brown sauce I ate for dinner last night and the memory of it makes my stomach wave and flutter, like there's a small feral animal trapped inside.

Food poisoning. It must be. I sigh. Okay. A few hours discomfort, and then sleep. Then it will be over. It's all about getting to the sleep.

I'm not sure of the time so I don't know how long it takes for the sun to come up, but when it does, I haven't even touched sleep. I've puked so many times the plastic wastebin is almost full. I tried, a few times, to crawl to the shared bathroom down the hall, but I couldn't make it past my door. Now that the sun is up, the room is heating up. I can almost see the toxic fumes from the wastebin spreading out, poisoning me all over again.

I keep throwing up. There's no respite or relief in between bouts. I puke until there's nothing left: no food, no bile, none of me left, it seems.

That's when the thirst hits. I've long since drunk the rest of the water in my bottle, and thrown that up too. I start to fantasize about mountain streams, waterfalls, rain showers, even the Dutch canal; I'd drink from those if I could. They sell bottled water downstairs. And there's a tap in the bathroom. But I can't sit up, let alone stand up, let alone make it to water.

Is anyone there? I call. In Dutch. In English. I try to remember the Spanish but the words get jumbled. I think I'm talking but I can't tell and it's noisy in the square and my weak voice stands no chance.

I listen for a knock at the door, praying for an offering of water, clean sheets, a cool compress, a soft hand on my forehead. But none comes. This is a hostel, bare bones, no housekeeping, and I prepaid two nights.

I retch again. Nothing comes out except my tears. I am twenty-one years old and I still cry when I puke.

Finally, sleep comes to rescue me. And then I wake up, and I see her, so close. And all I can think is: *It was worth it if it brought you.*

Who takes care of you now? she whispers. Her breath feels like a cooling breeze.

You, I whisper back. *You take care of me.*

I'll be your mountain girl.

I try to reach for her, but now she's gone and the room is full of the others: Céline and Ana Lucia and Kayla and Sara and the girl with the worm, and there's more yet—a Franke in Riga, a Gianna in Prague, a Jossra in Tunis. They all start talking at me.

We'll take care of you.

Go away, I want Lulu back. Tell her to come back.

Green turtles, red blood, blue sky, double happiness, la-lala, they singsong.

No! That's not how it goes. That's not how double happiness goes.

But I can't remember how it goes either.

She left you like this.
I'll take care of you.
French whore.
Call me if you need anything.
Wanna share with me?
Stop it! I yell.

Take the wheel! Now it's Kate yelling. Only I can't see any wheel and I have the awful feeling, like in the dreams, that I'm going to crash.

No! Stop. Go away! All of you! You're not real. None of you! Not even Lulu. I screw my eyes shut and cover my ears with the sweat-soaked pillow and curl up into a fetal ball. And finally, finally, like this, I fall asleep.

I wake up. My skin is cool. The sky is purple. I'm not sure if it's twilight or dawn, how long I've been out. I'm coherent enough to know that I'm supposed to be back in Cancún soon to meet Broodje and fly back to Holland, and I need to get word to him somehow, that he might have to leave without me. I swing my legs over the side of the bed. The room teeters before my eyes, but it doesn't totter over. I plant my feet. I pull to a stand. Like a toddler or a very old man, I take the steps, one at a time, to the lobby.

In the corner is an Internet café where you can make long-distance phone calls. I feel like I've been in the dark for months, the lights from all those monitors hurt my eyes so. I hand over some money and ask for a phone and am guided to a bank of computers with a telephone handset. I open my address book. Kate's card, RUCKUS THEATER

COMPANY splashed across the top in red lettering, falls out.

I start to dial. The digits swim on the page and I'm not sure if I have the country code right or if I dialed correctly.

But there's a tinny ring. And then a voice: faraway, tunnel-like, but unmistakably hers. As soon as I hear it, my throat closes.

"Hello. Hello? Who is this?"

"Ma?" I manage to croak out.

Silence. And when she says my name I want to cry.

"Ma," I say again.

"Willem, where are you?" Her voice is crisp, officious, businesslike as always.

"I'm lost."

"You're *lost*?"

I've been lost before, in new cities with no familiar land-marks to set me straight, waking up in strange beds, unsure of where I was or who was next to me. But I realize now, *that* wasn't lost. It was something else. This . . . I may know exactly where I am—in a hostel, in the central square, in Mérida, Mexico—but I have never been so utterly unmoored.

There's a long silence on the line and I'm afraid the call has dropped. But then Yael says: "Come to me. I'll send you a ticket. Come to me."

It's not what I really want to hear. What I want—what I ache—to hear is *come home.*

But she can't tell me to come to a place that no longer exists, any more than I can go to that place. For now, this is the best either of us can do.

Twenty-one

FEBRUARY
Mumbai, India

Emirates 148
13 Feb: Departure 14:40 Amsterdam—00:10 Dubai
Emirates 504
14 Feb: Departure 03:55 Dubai—08:20 Mumbai
Have a safe trip.

This email, containing my itinerary, comprises the bulk of the communication between Yael and me since I returned from Mexico last month. When I got back from Cancún, a friendly travel agent named Mukesh called to request a copy of my passport. A week later, I got the itinerary from Yael. I've heard little else since.

I try not to read too much into it. This is Yael. And this is me. The most charitable explanation is that she's hoarding the small talk so we will have something to say to each other for the next . . . two weeks, month, six weeks? I'm not sure. We haven't discussed it. Mukesh told me that the ticket was valid for three months and that if I wanted help booking flights within India, or out of India, I should contact him. I try not to read too much into that, either.

In the immigration line, I'm jangly with nerves. The bar of duty-free Toblerone (meant for Yael) that I wound up eating as the plane descended into Mumbai probably didn't help matters. As the line lurches forward, an impatient Indian woman pushes into me with her prodigious sari-wrapped belly, as if that will make us go faster. I almost switch places with her. To stop the pushing. And to make us go slower.

When I exit into the airport arrivals hall, the scene is both space age and biblical. The airport is modern and new, but the hall is thronged with people who seem to be carrying their entire lives on metal trolleys. The minute I get out of customs, I know that Yael is not here. It's not that I don't see her, though I don't. It's that I realize, belatedly, she never specifically said she'd meet me. I just assumed. And with my mother, you never assume.

But it's been almost three years. And she invited me here. I go back and forth through the hall. All around me, people swarm and push and shove, as if racing for some invisible finish line. But there's no Yael.

Ever optimistic, I go outside to see if she's waiting there. The bright morning light hurts my eyes. I wait ten minutes. Fifteen. There's no sign of my mother.

There's a gladiator match of taxi drivers and porters vying for passengers. *Psst,* they hiss at me. I stare at the itinerary now gone limp in my hand, as if it will somehow impart critical new information.

"Are you being met?"

In front of me is a man. Or a boy. Somewhere in between. He seems about my age, except for his eyes, which are ancient.

I give the area one more sweep. "It appears I'm not."

"Do you need a driver?"

"It appears I do."

"Where are you going?"

I recall the address from the immigration forms I just filled out in triplicate. "The Bombay Royale. In Colaba. Do you know it?"

He gives his head a half nod, half shake that isn't exactly reassuring. "I take you there."

"Are you a driver?"

He wags his head again. "Where is your suitcase?"

I point to the small rucksack on my back.

He laughs. "Like Kurma."

"The food?"

"No. That is korma. Kurma is one of Vishnu's incarnations, a tortoise, carries his home on his back. But if you like korma, I can show you a good place."

The boy introduces himself as Prateek and then confidently threads us through the crowd past the airport garage and to a dusty lot. On one side are the runways, the other, high-rise buildings and even higher cranes, swinging in the wind. Prateek locates the car—something that back home might be called vintage, but when I compliment it, he makes a face and tells me it belongs to his uncle and one day, he will buy his own car, a good one made abroad, a Renault, or a Ford, not a Maruti or a Tata. He pays the skinny dusty boy who was guarding the car a few coins and opens the backseat. I toss my rucksack there and try to open the front door. Prateek tells me to wait, and with a complicated sequence of rattles and twists, opens it from the inside, sweeping a pile of magazines from the passenger seat.

The car shudders to life and the little brass statue cemented to the dash—a tiny elephant with a sort of smile of the perpetually amused—starts to dance.

"Ganesha," Prateek says. "Remover of obstacles."

"Where were you last month?" I ask the statue.

"He was right here," Prateek answers solemnly.

We drive out of the airport complex, past a bunch of ramshackle houses, before climbing onto an elevated expressway. I tilt my head out the window. It's pleasantly hot, but not as hot as it will be, Prateek warns. It's still winter; it will get warmer until the monsoons come in June.

As we drive, Prateek points out landmarks. A famous temple. A spidery suspension bridge crossing Mahim Bay. "Many Bollywood stars live in this area. Closer to the studios, which are near the airport." He thumbs behind us. "Though some live in Juhu Beach, and some in Malabar Hill. Some even in Colaba where you are staying. Taj Mahal Hotel is there. Angelina Jolie, Brad Pitt, Roger Moore, Double-Oh Seven. Also American presidents all stayed there."

Traffic starts to back up. We slow down and Ganesha stops his dance. "What is your favorite movie?" Prateek asks me.

"Hard to pick just one."

"What is the last movie you saw?"

I flipped through a half dozen of them on the flights over, but was too antsy to focus on any one. I suppose the last movie I watched in full was *Pandora's Box*. That was the movie that started it all, that led to the disastrous trip to Mexico, which funnily enough, has now landed me here. Lulu. If she was far away before, she's farther now. Not one but two oceans between us now.

"Never heard of that movie," Prateek says, wagging his head. "My favorite movie of the last year is a tie. *Gangs of Wasseypur*. Thriller. And *London, Paris, New York*. Do you know how many films Hollywood studios produce a year?"

"No idea."

"Take a guess."

"A thousand."

He frowns. "I speak of the studios, not an amateur with a camera. One thousand, that would be impossible."

"A hundred?"

His smile flips on like a switch. "Wrong! Four hundred. Now do you know how many films Bollywood produces a year? I won't make you guess because you will be wrong." He pauses for dramatic effect. "Eight hundred!"

"Eight hundred," I repeat because it's clear he thinks the number warrants repeating.

"Yes!" He's smiling broadly now. "Twice the number of Hollywood. Do you know how many people in India go to the movies every single day?"

"I have a feeling you're going to tell me."

"Fourteen million. Do fourteen million people go to the movies every day in Germany?"

"I wouldn't know. I'm from Holland. But given that the entire population isn't much more than sixteen million, I doubt it."

He beams with pride now.

We exit the expressway onto the streets of what must be colonial Mumbai and turn into an area with an arbor of trees and a line of idling double-decker buses belching out black exhaust.

"There is the Gateway of India," Prateek says, pointing out a carved arch monument on the edge of the Arabian Sea. "The Taj Mahal Hotel I told you about," he says, pulling past a massive confection of a hotel, all domes and cornices. A group of Arab men in billowing white robes are piling into a series of window-tinted SUVs. "Inside is a Starbucks." He lowers his voice to a whisper. "Have you ever had a Starbucks coffee?"

"I have."

"My cousin said that in America they drink it with every meal." He pulls up in front of another graying building, Victorian, and it seems, almost sweating in the heat. The sign, in fading elaborate cursive, reads BO BAY RO AL. "Here you are. Bombay Royale."

I follow Prateek into a darkened, cool lobby, quiet except for the whoosh and squeak of ceiling fans and the faint chirping of crickets nesting somewhere in the walls. Behind a long mahogany desk, a man so old he seems original to the building is napping. Prateek loudly rings the bell and he startles awake.

Immediately, the two start arguing, mostly in Hindi but with a few English words thrown in here and there. "Regulations," the old man keeps saying.

Eventually, Prateek turns to me. "He says you can't stay here."

I shake my head. *Why did she bring me here? Why did I come?*

"It's a private residence club, not a hotel," Prateek explains.

"Yes. I've heard of those."

Prateek frowns. "There are other hotels in Colaba."

"But this must be the place." This is the address I've had for her for the last few years. "Look under my mother's name. Yael Shiloh."

At the mention of her name, the old man's head whips up. "Willem saab?" he asks.

"Willem. Yes, that's me."

He squints his eyes and grasps my hands. "You are nothing like the memsahib," he says.

I don't have to know what that means to know who he's talking about. It's what everyone says.

"But where is she?" he asks.

There's a kernel of comfort. I'm not the only one in the dark. "Oh, you know her," I say.

"Yes, yes, yes," he says, doing the same head nod/shake as Prateek.

"So can I go to her flat?" I ask the old man.

He considers it, scratching the gray stubble on his chin. "Regulations say only members can stay here. When memsahib makes you a member, you will be a member."

"But she's not here," Prateek points out helpfully.

"Regulations," the old man says.

"But you knew I was coming," I say.

"But you are not with her. What if you are not really you? Do you have proof?"

Proof? Like what. A surname? Mine is different. Photos? "Here," I say, pulling out the email, now damp and creased.

He squints at it with dark eyes that have gone filmy with age. He must decide it's enough. Because he gives two quick nods of his head and says, "Welcome, Willem saab."

"At last," Prateek says

"I am Chaudhary," the old man says, ignoring Prateek and handing me a sheaf of papers to fill out. When I finish, he heaves at the opening to the front desk and creaks out from behind. He shuffles down the scuffed wooden hallway. I follow him. Prateek trails behind me. When we reach the elevators, Chaudhary makes a tick-tock gesture to Prateek with his fingers. "Members only in the elevator," he tells him. "You may take the stairs."

"But he's with me," I say.

"Regulations, Willem saab."

Prateek shakes his head. "I should probably get the car back to my uncle," he says.

"Okay, let me pay you." I pull out a wad of filthy rupees.

"Three hundred rupees for no AC. Four hundred with," Chaudhary says. "That's the law."

I hand Prateek five hundred rupees, about the price of a sandwich back home. He backs up to leave. "Hey, what about that korma?" I ask him.

His smile is goofy, a little like Broodje's. "I will be in touch," he promises.

The elevator lurches to the fifth floor. Chaudhary opens the gate onto a light-filled corridor, smelling of floor wax and incense. He leads me past a series of slatted wood doors, stopping at the farthest one, and pulls out a master key.

At first, I think the old man got the wrong room. Yael has lived here for two years, but this is an empty suite of rooms. Anonymous bulky wood furniture, generic paintings on the wall of desert forts and Bengal tigers. A small round table against a pair of French doors.

And then I smell it. Beneath the competing scents of onion and incense and ammonia and wax, is the undeniable smell of citrus and wet earth. The scent, I realize with the clarity of something you've always known, but never needed to recognize before, of my mother.

I take a tentative step into the hallway and another blast hits me. And just like that, I'm not in India. I'm back in Amsterdam, at home, a long summer twilight. It had finally stopped raining, so Yael and Bram were outside, celebrating the minor miracle of sunshine. Still cold from the rain, I stayed huddled inside under a scratchy wool blanket and watched them through the big picture window. Some students who lived in one of the flats across the canal were blasting music. A song came on, something old and New Wave from when Yael and Bram were younger, and he grabbed her and they danced, head to head, even though it wasn't a slow song. I watched them through the glass, fixed on the sight of them, pretending not to be. I must've been eleven or twelve, an age when such displays should've embarrassed me, but didn't. Yael saw me watching, and—this is what surprised me then, still surprises me now as I remember it—she came inside. She didn't exactly drag me out or invite me to dance with them, as Bram might've. She just folded up the blanket and pulled me up by the elbow. I was enveloped by her smell, oranges and leaves, that ever-present loamy tang of her tinctures, and the canals and all their murky secrets. I tried to make it like I was acquiescing, allowing myself to be led, giving no trace of how happy I was. But I must not have been able to fully contain it because she smiled back at me and said, "We have to snatch the sun when we have it, don't we?"

She could be warm like that. But it came and went with as much regularity as the Dutch sun. Except with Bram. But maybe it was reflected warmth—he was her sun, after all.

After Chaudhary leaves, I lie down on the sofa. My head rests uncomfortably against the heavy wood arm but I don't move, because I'm in the sunlight and the heat feels necessary, like a transfusion of sorts. *I should probably get in touch with Yael*, I think, but drowsiness and jetlag and a certain kind of relief are pulling me under, and before I can do so much as remove my shoes, I am asleep.

I'm flying again. Back on a plane, which feels wrong because I just got off a plane. But it's so vivid and real it takes a beat longer than usual to recognize it as the dream; and then it warps and becomes lurid and surreal, heavy and slow, the way dreams do when your mind is rebelling against a betrayed body clock. Maybe that's why in this dream, there is no landing. No illumination of the seatbelt sign, no inaudible announcement from the captain. Just the buzz of the engines, the feeling of being aloft. Just flying.

But there is someone next to me. I turn and try to ask, *Where are we?* But everything is heavy, lugubrious, I can't get my mouth to work right because what comes out is, *Who are you?*

"Willem," a voice in the distance calls.

The person in the dream turns. Still faceless. Already familiar.

"Willem." The voice again. I don't answer it. I don't want out of the dream quite yet, not this time. Again, I turn toward my seatmate.

"Willem!" The voice is sharp this time and it pulls me out of the honey stickiness of sleep.

I open my eyes. I sit up and for a second, we just look at each other, blinking.

"What are you doing here?" she asks.

I've been wondering that myself for the past month, after my initial optimism about this trip faded to ambivalence and then curdled into pessimism and now has withered into regret. *What* am *I doing here?*

"You sent me a ticket." I try to make it seem like a joke, but my head is cloudy with the dream, and Yael only frowns.

"I mean what are you doing *here*? We've been looking everywhere for you at the airport."

We? "I didn't see you."

"I was needed at the clinic. I sent a driver and he was running a bit late. He said he sent you several texts."

I take out my phone and turn it on. Nothing happens. "I don't think it works here."

She looks, disgusted, at my phone, and I feel a sudden and fierce loyalty to it. Then she sighs. "The important thing is you made it," she says, which seems both obvious and optimistic.

I stand up. My neck has a crick and when I circle it, it gives off a loud pop that makes Yael frown again. I stand up, stretch, and look around the room.

"Nice place," I say, continuing the small talk that has sustained us for the past three years. "I like what you've done with it."

It's like a reflex, trying to make her smile. It never worked for me before and it doesn't work now. She walks away, opening the French doors leading to the balcony, overlooking the Gateway, the water beyond. "I should probably get something closer to Andheri, but I seem to have grown too accustomed to living on the water."

"Andheri?"

"Where the *clinic* is," she says, as if I should know this. But how, exactly? Talk of her work has been strictly off limits in our casual chit-chat emails. The weather. The food. The myriad Indian festivals. Postcards, without the pretty pictures.

I know that Yael came to India to study Ayurvedic medicine. It was what she and Bram had intended to do once I left for university. Travel more. For Yael to study traditional healing methods. India was to be the first stop. The tickets were booked before Bram died.

After he died, I expected Yael to fall apart. Only this time, I would be there. I would put aside my own grief and I would help her. Finally, instead of me being an interloper into her great love affair, I would be the product of it. I would be a comfort to her. What she wasn't as a mother, I would be as a son.

For two weeks, she locked herself in the top-floor room, the one Bram had built for her, shutters closed, door locked, ignoring most of the visitors who'd stopped by. In life, Bram had been all hers, and in death, that hadn't changed.

Then, six weeks later, she'd left for India as scheduled, as if nothing had happened. Marjolein said Yael was just licking her wounds. She'd be back soon.

Two months later, though, Yael sent word that she wasn't coming back. Long ago, before she studied naturopathic medicine, she'd had a nursing degree, and now she was going back to that, working in a clinic in Mumbai. She said she was closing down the boat; she'd already boxed up the important things and everything else was being sold. I should take what I wanted. I packed up a few boxes and stored them in my uncle Daniel's attic. Everything else, I left. Not long after that, I got kicked off of my program. Then I packed up my own rucksack and took off.

"You're just like your mother," Marjolein had said, somewhat mournfully, when I told her I was leaving.

But we both knew that wasn't true. I am nothing like my mother.

The same emergency that kept Yael from the airport is apparently pulling her back to the clinic after all of an hour in my company. She invites me to come with her, but the invitation is halfhearted and rote, a lot like this invitation to come to India, I suspect. I politely decline, with excuses of jetlag.

"You should be out in the sunshine; it's the best cure." She looks at me. "Though make sure you cover this." She touches the mirror image on her face where my scar is. "It looks fresh."

I touch the scar. It's six months old now. And, for a minute, I imagine telling Yael about it. It would infuriate her if she knew what I said to the skinheads to take their attention off the girls and onto me. *A one four six oh three*—the identification number the Nazis tattooed on Saba's wrist—but at least I would get a reaction.

But I don't tell Yael. This goes way beyond small talk. It goes to painful things we never mention: Saba. The war. Yael's mother. Yael's entire childhood. I touch the scar. It feels hot, as if merely thinking about that day has inflamed it. "It's not that fresh," I tell her. "It's just not healing right."

"I can mix you up something for that." Yael brushes the scar. Her fingers are rough and callused. Workers' hands, Bram used to say, though he was the one who should've had the rougher hands. I realize then we haven't embraced or kissed or done any of the things one might expect for a re-union.

Still, when she takes her hand away, I wish she hadn't. And when she starts packing up with promises of things we will do when she has a day off, I'm wishing I had told her about the skinheads, about Paris, about Lulu. Except even if I'd tried, I wouldn't have known how. My mother and I, we both speak Dutch and English. But we never could speak the same language.

Twenty-two

I am awoken by the ringing of a phone. I reach for my mobile, remember it doesn't work here. The phone keeps ringing. It's the house line. It doesn't stop. Finally, I pick it up.

"Willem saab. Chaudhary here." He clears his throat. "On the line for you, Prateek Sanu," he continues formally. "Would you like me to ask the nature of his business?"

"No, that's okay. You can put him through."

"One moment." There is a series of clicks. Then Prateek's voice echoing hellos, interrupted by Chaudhary, declaring. "Prateek Sanu calling for Willem Shiloh."

It's funny to be called by Yael and Saba's surname. I don't correct him. After a moment of silence, Chaudhary clicks off.

"Willem!" Prateek booms, as if it's been months, not hours, since we last spoke. "How are you?"

"I'm good."

"And what do you think of the Maximum City?"

"I haven't seen much of it," I admit. "I've been asleep."

"You are awake now. What are your plans?"

"Haven't worked that out yet."

"Let me make a proposal: Pay a visit to me at Crawford Market."

"Sounds good."

Prateek gives me instructions. After a cold shower, I head outside, Chaudhary trailing behind me with dire warnings of "pickpockets, thieves, prostitutes, and roving gangs." He ticks off the threats on his thick fingers. "They will accost you."

I assure him I can take it, and in any case the only people to accost me are begging mothers, who congregate in the grassy medians in the center of the shady streets, asking for money to buy formula for the sleeping babies in their arms.

This part of Mumbai reminds me a bit of London with its decaying colonial buildings, except it's supersaturated with color: the women's saris, the marigold-festooned temples, the crazily painted buses. It's like everything absorbs and reflects the bright sun.

From the outside, Crawford Market seems like another building plucked out of old England, but inside it is all India: bustling commerce and yet more surreally bright colors. I walk around the fruit stalls, the clothing stalls, making my way toward the electronics stalls where Prateek told me to find him. I feel a tap on my shoulder.

"Lost?" Prateek asks, a grin splitting his face.

"Not in a bad way."

He frowns at that, confounded. "I was worried," he says. "I wanted to call you but I don't have your mobile."

"My mobile doesn't work here."

The smile returns. "As it happens, we have many mobile phones at my uncle's electronics stall."

"So that's why you lured me here?" I tease.

Prateek looks insulted. "Of course not. How did I know you lacked a phone?" He gestures to the stalls around us. "You can buy from another stall."

"I'm joking, Prateek."

"Oh." He takes me to his uncle's stall, crammed to the ceiling with cellphones, radios, computers, knockoff iPads, televisions, and more. He introduces me to his uncle and buys us all cups of tea from the chai-wallah, the traveling tea salesman. Then he takes me to the back of the stall and we sit down on a couple of rickety stools.

"You work here?"

"On Mondays, Tuesdays, and Fridays."

"What do you do the other days?"

He does the head nod/wag thing. "I'm studying accounting. I also work for my mother some days. And I help my cousin sometimes to find *goreh* for movies."

"*Goreh.*"

"White people, like you. It's why I was at the airport today. I had to drive my cousin."

"Why didn't you ask *me*?" I joke.

"Oh, I am not a casting director, or even an assistant to an assistant. I just drove Rahul to the airport to look for backpackers needing money. Do you need money, Willem?"

"No."

"I did not think so. You are staying at the Bombay Royale. Very high class. And visiting your mother. Where is your father?" he asks.

It's been a while since anyone asked me that. "He's dead."

"Oh, mine, too," Prateek says almost cheerfully. "But I have many uncles. And cousins. You?"

I almost say yes. I have an uncle. But how do you explain Daniel? Not so much a black sheep as an invisible one, eclipsed by Bram. And Yael. Daniel, the footnote to Yael and Bram's story, the small print that nobody bothers to read. Daniel, the younger, scragglier, messier, less directed—and not to forget, shorter—brother. Daniel, the one relegated to the backseat of the Fiat, and consequently, it seemed, the backseat of life.

"Not much family," is all I say in the end, bookending my vagueness with a shrug, my own version of the head wag.

Prateek presents me a choice of phones. I choose one and buy a SIM card. He immediately programs his number and, for good measure, his uncle's into it. We finish our tea and then he announces, "Now I think you must go to the movies."

"I just got here."

"Exactly. What is more Indian than that? Fourteen million people—"

"A day go to the movies here," I interrupt. "Yes, I've been told."

He pulls a heap of magazines out of his bag, the same ones I'd seen in the car. *Magna. Stardust.* He opens one and shows me pages of attractive people, all with extremely white teeth. He rattles off a bunch of names, dismayed that I know none of them.

"We will go now," he declares.

"Don't you have to work?"

"In India, work is the master, but the guest is god," Prateek says. "Besides, between the phone and taxi . . ." He smiles. "My uncle will not object." He opens a newspaper. "*Dil Mera Golmaal* is on. So is *Gangs of Wasseypur.* Or *Dhal Gaya Din.* What do you think, Baba?"

Prateek and his uncle carry on a spirited conversation in a mix of Hindi and English, debating the merits and deficits of all three films. Finally they settle on *Dil Mera Golmaal.*

The theater is an art deco building with peeling white paint, not unlike the revival houses Saba used to take me to when he visited. I buy our tickets and our popcorn. Prateek promises to translate in return.

The film—a sort of convoluted take on *Romeo and Juliet*, involving warring families, gangsters, a terrorist plot to steal nuclear weapons, plus countless explosions and dance numbers—doesn't require much translation. It is both nonsensical and oddly self-explanatory.

Still, Prateek gives it a shot. "That man is that one's brother but he doesn't know it," he whispers. "One is evil, the other is good, and the girl is engaged to the bad one, but she loves the good one. Her family hates his family and his family hates her family but they don't really because the feud has to do with the other one's father, who engineered the feud when he stole the baby at birth, you see. He is also a terrorist."

"Right."

Then there's a dance number and a fight scene and then suddenly we are in the desert. "Dubai," Prateek whispers.

"Why, exactly?" I ask.

Prateek explains that the oil consortium is there. As are the terrorists.

There are several scenes in the desert, including a duel between two monster trucks that Henk would appreciate.

Then the film switches abruptly to Paris. One moment, there's a generic shot of the Seine. And then, a second later, a shot down the banks of the river. Then we see the heroine and the good twin brother, who, Prateek explains, have gotten married and fled together. They break out into song. But they're no longer on the Seine; now they are on one of the arched bridges that span the canals in Villette. I recognize it. Lulu and I cruised under it, sitting side by side, our legs knocking against the hull. Occasionally, we'd accidentally knock ankles and there had been something electric about it, a turn-on, just in that.

I feel it now in this musty theater. Almost like a reflex, my thumb goes to the inside of my wrist, but the gesture is meaningless, here in the dark.

Soon the song is over and we're back in India for the grand finale when the families reunite and reconcile and there's another wedding ceremony and a big dance number. Unlike Romeo and Juliet, these lovers get a happy ending.

After the movie, we walk through the crowded streets. It's dark now, and the heat's gone wavy. We meander our way to a wide crescent of sand. "Chowpatty Beach," Prateek tells me, pointing out the luxury highrises on Marine Drive. They sparkle like diamonds against the slender curving wrist of the bay.

It's a carnival atmosphere with all the food vendors and clowns and balloon shapers and the furtive lovers taking advantage of the darkness to steal kisses behind a palm tree. I try not to watch them. I try not to remember stealing kisses. I try not to remember that first kiss. Not her lips, but that birthmark on her wrist. I'd been wanting to kiss it all day. Somehow, I knew exactly what it would taste like.

The water laps against the shore. The Arabian Sea. The Atlantic Ocean. Two oceans between us. And still not enough.

Twenty-three

After four days, Yael finally has a day off. Instead of waking up from my fold-up bed to find her rushing out the door, I see her in her pajamas. "I've ordered up breakfast," she says in that crisp voice of hers, the gutturalness of her Israeli accent ironed out from all the years of speaking English.

There's a knock at the door. Chaudhary, who seems to always work and to do every single job here, shuffles in, pushing a trolley. "Breakfast, Memsahib," he announces.

"Thank you, Chaudhary," Yael says.

He studies the two of us. Then shakes his head. "He is nothing like you, Memsahib," he says.

"He looks like his baba," Yael replies.

I know it's true, but it's strange to hear her say it. Though not as strange, I'd imagine, as seeing the face of her dead husband staring back at her. Sometimes when I'm feeling charitable, I'll justify this as the reason she's put such distance between us these last three years. Then the less charitable side of me will ask, *What about the eighteen years before that?*

With a dramatic flourish, Chaudhary sets out toast, coffee, tea, and juice. Then he backs out of the door.

"Does he ever leave?" I ask.

"No, not really. His children are all overseas and his wife passed. So he works."

"Sounds miserable."

She gives me one of her inscrutable looks. "At least he has a purpose."

She flips open the newspaper. Even that is colorful, a salmony shade of pink. "What have you been doing the last few days?" she asks me as she eyes the headlines.

I went back to Chowpatty Beach, the markets around Colaba, the Gateway. I went to another movie with Prateek. I've wandered mostly. Without purpose. "This and that," I say.

"So today we do that and this," she replies.

Downstairs, we are besieged by the usual congregation of beggars. "Ten rupees," a woman carrying a sleeping baby says. "For formula for my baby. You come with me to buy it."

I start to pull out money, but Yael snaps at me to stop and then snaps at the woman in Hindi.

I don't say a word. But my expression must give me away, because Yael gives an exasperated explanation. "It's a scam, Willem. The babies are props. The women are part of begging rings, run by organized crime syndicates."

I look at the woman, now standing across from the Taj Hotel, and shrug. "So? She still needs the money."

Yael nods and frowns. "Yes, *she* does. And the *baby* needs food, no doubt, but neither of them will get what they need. If you bought milk for that woman, you'd pay an inflated price, and you'd get an inflated sense of goodwill. You helped a mother feed her baby. What could be better?"

I don't say anything, because I've been giving them money every day and now I feel foolish for it.

"As soon as you walk away, the milk's returned to the shop. And your money? The shopkeeper gets a cut; the crime bosses get a cut. The women, the women are indentured, and they get nothing. As for what happens to babies . . ." She trails off ominously.

"What happens to the babies?" The question pops out before I realize I might not want to know the answer.

"They die. Sometimes of malnutrition. Or sometimes of pneumonia. When life is so tenuous, something small might do it."

"I know," I say. *Sometimes even when life isn't that tenuous*, I think and I wonder if she's thinking the same thing.

"In fact, the day you arrived, I was late because of an emergency with one of those very children." She doesn't elaborate, leaving it for me to put the pieces together.

Yael's non-admission manages to make me feel retroactively guilty for faulting her—there was something more important—and bitter—there always is something more important. But mostly it makes me tired. Couldn't she have just told me and saved me the trouble of my guilt and bitterness?

Then again, sometimes I think that guilt and bitterness may be Yael's and my true common language.

Our first stop is the Shree Siddhivinayak Temple, an ornate wedding cake of a temple that is being attacked by a tourist horde of ants. Yael and I take our place among the masses and push into a stuffy gold hall, wending our way to a flower-covered statue of the elephant god. He's beet-red, as if embarrassed, or maybe he's just hot, too.

"Ganesha," Yael tells me.

"The remover of obstacles."

She nods.

All around us, people are laying garlands around the shrine or singing or praying.

"Do you have to make an offering?" I ask. "To get your obstacles removed?"

"You can," she replies. "Or just chant a mantra."

"What mantra?"

"There are several." Yael doesn't say anything else for a while. And then, in a low and clear voice, she chants: "*Om gam ganapatayae namaha.*" She gives me a look, like that's enough of that.

"What does it mean?"

She cocks her head. "Roughly I've heard it translated as: 'Wake up.'"

"Wake up?"

She looks at me for a second, and though we have the same eyes, I really have no idea what she sees through hers.

"It's not the translation that matters with a mantra. It's the intention," she says. "And this is what you say when you want a new beginning."

———————————

After the temple, we hail a rickshaw. "Where to now?" I ask.

"We are meeting Mukesh for lunch."

Mukesh? The travel agent who booked my flights?

We spend the next half hour in silence as we weave through more traffic and dodge more cows, finally arriving at a sort of dusty shopping center. As we're paying the driver, a tall, broad, smiling man in a voluminous white shirt comes barreling out of a place called Outbound Travels.

"Willem!" he says, greeting me warmly, grasping both my hands. "Welcome."

"Thank you," I say, looking back and forth between him and Yael, who's decidedly not looking at him, and I wonder what exactly is going on. Are they together? It would be just her way, introduce the idea of a boyfriend by not introducing him as her boyfriend and leaving me to figure it out.

Mukesh tells our driver to wait and then goes back into the travel agency to pick up a plastic bag, and then we climb back in and drive through fifteen more minutes of traffic to the restaurant.

"It's middle eastern," Mukesh says proudly. "Like Mummy."

Mukesh pushes the menu aside and calls over the waiter, ordering platters of hummus and grape leaves, baba ghanoush and tabouli.

When the first platter of hummus arrives, Mukesh asks me how I'm liking Indian food so far.

I explain about the dosas and the pakoras I've been eating off the stands. "I still haven't had a proper curry."

"We will have to arrange that for you," he says. "Which is why I'm here." He reaches into the plastic bag and pulls out a number of glossy brochures. "You don't have so much time here, so I suggest you pick one region—Rajasthan, Kerala, Uttar Pradesh—and explore that. I have taken the liberty of coming up with a few sample itineraries." He slides me over a computer printout. One is for Rajasthan. It has everything. Return flights to Jaipur, transfers to Jodhpur, Udaipur and Jaisalmer. There's even a camel trip. There's a similar packed itinerary for Kerala, flights, transfers, river cruises.

I'm confused. "Are we taking a trip?" I ask Yael.

"Oh, no, no," Mukesh answers for her. "Mummy has to work. This is a special trip for you, to make sure your time in India is tip-top."

And then I understand the guilty look. Mukesh isn't the boyfriend. He's the travel agent. The one enlisted to bring me here. The one enlisted to send me away.

At least I know why I'm here. Not for new beginnings. A hasty invitation that was foolish to issue, foolish to accept—and most foolish of all to solicit.

"Which trip do you prefer?" Mukesh asks. He seems unaware of the thorny dynamic he's stumbled into.

My anger feels hot and bilious but I keep it bottled until it doubles back and I'm mad at myself. What's the definition of insanity? Doing the same thing over and over and expecting different results.

"This one," I say, flicking the brochure on top of the pile. I don't even look where it goes to. It hardly seems the point.

Twenty-four

Jaisalmer, India

It's ten o'clock in Jaisalmer and the desert sun is beating down on the sand-colored stones of the fortress city. The narrow alleys and staircases are thick with heat and smoke from the early morning dung fires, and that, along with the ever-present camels and cows, gives the city a particular aroma.

I skirt past a group of women, their eyes kohl-dipped, downturned, shy it seems, though they manage to flirt in other ways, with the swoosh of their electric-colored saris, the tinkle of their ankle bracelets.

At the bottom of the hill, I pass several stalls hawking local textiles. I stop at one of them, peering at a purple-mirrored wall-hanging.

"You like what you see?" the young man behind the counter asks casually, no sign that he knows me except for the twinkle in his eye.

"Perhaps," I say noncommittally.

"Is there something particular you like?"

"I have my eye on something."

Nawal nods solemnly, no hint of a smile, no hint that we have had almost this exact same conversation for the past four days. It's like a game. Or a play we started acting in when I first found the tapestry I want. Or rather, Prateek wants.

Two days into my tour of Rajasthan, when I was still full of bitterness and bile and of half a mind to just fly back to Amsterdam early, Prateek sent me a text about his "grand proposal!!!!!!!!!!!" Turned out to be not so grand. He wanted me to shop for Rajasthani handicrafts that he'd sell back in Mumbai for a markup. He'd reimburse me for what I spent and we'd split the profit. At first I told him no, especially after he texted the shopping list. But then one day in Jaipur I wound up in the Bapu Bazaar with nothing much to do, so I started looking for the kind of leather sandals he wanted. And from there, I kept going. Combing the markets for spices and bangles and a very particular kind of slipper has given the trip a sort of shape, allowing me to forget that it's actually an exile. And because of that, I've extended the exile, having Mukesh lengthen it by a week. I've now been gone three weeks, and I'll get back to Mumbai with only a handful days before my return flight to Amsterdam.

In Jaisalmer, Prateek has instructed me to buy a particular kind of tapestry that the area is known for. It must be silk, and I will know it is silk because I must burn a thread, and it will give off the odor of burnt hair. It should be embroidered, sewn, not glued, and I will know it's sewn because I must turn it over and yank the thread, which also must be silk and must be tested with a match. And it's to cost no more than two thousand rupees, and I must bargain, hard. Prateek had grave doubts about my bargaining ability, because he claims I overpaid him for the taxi, but I assured him that I'd seen my grandfather barter down a wheel of cheese by half in the Albert Cuyp market, so it was in me.

"Some tea, perhaps, while you look?" Nawal asks. I look under the counter and see that, like yesterday, the tea is already prepared.

"Why not?"

At which point, the script ends and conversation takes over. Hours of it. I sit down in the canvas chair next to Nawal's, and as we have done for the past four days, we talk. When it gets too hot, or when Nawal gets a serious customer, I leave. Before I do, he will drop the price of the tapestry by five hundred rupees, insuring that I'll come back and do the whole thing again the next day.

Nawal pours the spicy tea from the ornate metal pot. His radio is playing the same crazy Hindi pop that Prateek loves. "Cricket game on later. If you want to listen," he informs me.

I take a sip of the tea. "Cricket? Really? The only thing duller than watching cricket is listening to it."

"You only say that because you don't understand the particulars of the game."

Nawal enjoys schooling me about all the things that I don't understand. I don't understand cricket, or soccer for that matter, and I don't understand the politics between India and Pakistan, and I don't understand the truth about global warming, and I certainly don't understand why love marriages are inferior to arranged marriages. Yesterday, I made the mistake of asking what was so wrong with love marriages, and I got quite a lecture.

"The divorce rate in India is the lowest in the world. In the West, it's fifty percent. And that's if they even get married," Nawal had said, disgusted. "Here, I tell you a story: All my grandparents, my aunties, my uncles, my parents, my brothers, all had arranged marriages. Happy. Long lives. My cousin, he chose a love marriage, and after two years, no children, the wife leaves him in disgrace."

"What happened?" I'd asked.

"What happened is they were not compatible," he'd said. "They were driving without a map. You cannot do that. You must have it arranged properly. Tomorrow I will show you."

So today, Nawal has brought a copy of the astrological chart that was drawn up to decide if he and his fiancé, Geeta, are compatible. Nawal insists it shows his and Geeta's happy future, ordained by the gods. "With matters such as these, you have to rely on forces larger than the human heart," he says.

The chart looks not unlike one of W's mathematical equations, with the paper divided into sections and different symbols in each one. I know W believes that all of life's questions can be solved through mathematical principle, but I think even he would find this a stretch.

"You don't believe in it?" Nawal challenges. "Name me one good love marriage that lasts."

Lulu had asked me a similar question. Sitting at that café, arguing about love, she'd demanded to know one couple who'd stayed in love, who'd stayed stained. And so I'd said *Yael and Bram*. Their names had just popped out. And it was so strange because in two years on the road, I had never told anyone about them, not even people I'd traveled with for a long time. As soon as I said that, I'd wanted to tell her *everything* about them, the story of how they met, how they seemed like interlocking puzzle pieces and how sometimes I didn't seem to fit into the equation. But it had been so long since I'd spoken of them, I hadn't known know how to do it. Though in some strange way, it seemed like another unsaid thing she already knew. Still, I wish I'd told her everything. Add it to my list of regrets.

I'm about to tell Nawal about them. My parents, who had a pretty spectacular love marriage, but then again, maybe it was there, in the charts all along, how it would end. I have wondered: If you could know going in that twenty-five years of love would break you in the end, would you risk it? Because isn't it inevitable? When you make such a large withdrawal of happiness, somewhere you'll have to make an equally large deposit. It all goes back to the universal law of equilibrium.

"I think this whole falling in love business is a mistake," Nawal continues. "I mean look at *you*." He says it like an indictment.

"What about *me*?"

"You are twenty-one and you are all alone."

"I'm not all alone. I'm here with you."

Nawal eyes me pitifully, reminding me that, pleasant as these days have been, he is here to sell something and I am here to buy something.

"You have no wife. And I'll wager you have been in love. I'll wager you have been in love many times like they always seem to be in Western films."

"Actually, I have never been in love." Nawal looks surprised at that, and I'm about to explain that while I haven't been in love, I've fallen in love many times. That they're separate entities entirely.

But then I stop. Because once again, I'm transported from the deserts of Rajasthan to that Paris café. I can almost hear the skepticism in Lulu's voice when I'd told her: *There's a world of difference between* falling *in love and* being *in love.* Then I'd dabbed the Nutella on her wrist, supposedly to demonstrate my point, but really because it had given me an excuse to see what she tasted like.

She'd laughed at me. She'd said the distinction between falling in love and being in love was false. *It sounds like you just like to screw around. At least own that about yourself.*

I smile at the memory of it, although Lulu, who had been right about me so much that day, was wrong about this. Yael had trained as a paratrooper in the Israel Defense Forces, and she once described how it felt to jump out of a plane: hurtling through the air, the wind everywhere, the exhilaration, the speed, your stomach in your throat, the hard landing. It always seemed the exact right way to describe how things felt with girls—that wind and the exhilaration, the hurtling, the wanting, the freefall. The abrupt end.

Oddly enough, though, that day with Lulu it didn't feel anything like falling. It felt like arriving.

Nawal and I drink our tea and listen to music, talk about upcoming elections in India and upcoming soccer tournaments. The sun blazes through the canopy roof and we go quiet in the heat. No customers come this time of day.

The ringing of my phone disturbs the idyll. It'll be Mukesh. He is the only one who calls me here. Prateek texts. Yael does neither.

"Willem, is everything tip-top?" he asks

"A-okay," I say. In Mukesh's hierarchy, A-okay is one step above tip-top.

"Excellent. Not to worry you but I call with a change in plans. Camel tour is canceled."

"Canceled? Why?"

"Camels got sick."

"Sick?"

"Yes, yes, vomiting, diarrhea, terrible, terrible."

"Can't we book another one?" The three-night desert camel tour was the one part of his planned itinerary I was actually looking forward to. When I extended my trip a week, I'd asked Mukesh to reschedule the camel trip for me.

"I tried. But unfortunately, next tour I could get you on was not for another week, and if you take that, you miss your flight to Dubai next Monday."

"Is there a problem?" Nawal asks.

"My camel tour was canceled. The camels are sick."

"My cousin runs a tour." Nawal is already picking up his mobile. "I can arrange it for you."

"Mukesh, I think my friend here can book me on a different tour."

"Oh, no! Willem. That will be most unacceptable." His ever-friendly tone goes brusque. Then, in a milder voice he continues: "I already booked your train back to Jaipur tonight, and a flight back to Mumbai tomorrow."

"Tonight? What's the rush? I don't leave for a week." When I asked Mukesh to extend my Rajasthan trip by a week, I also asked him to book my return flight to Amsterdam for a few days after I am due to get back to Mumbai. I had it all timed out perfectly so I'd only have to see Yael for a couple of days at the tail end. "Maybe I could stay here another few days?"

Mukesh clucks his tongue, which, in his particular argot, is the exact opposite of A-okay. He starts rattling on about flight schedules and change fees and warnings of me being stuck in India unless I come back to Mumbai now, and finally there is nothing to do but give in. "Good, good. I'll email you the itinerary," he says.

"My email's not working right. I got locked out of it and had to reset the password and then a whole bunch of recent messages disappeared," I say. "Apparently there's a virus going around.

"Yes, that would be the Jagdish virus." He tsks again. "You must set up a new account. In the meantime, I will text you your train and flight itinerary."

I get off the phone with Mukesh and reach into my backpack for my wallet. I count out three thousand rupees, the last price Nawal had dropped to. His face falls.

"I have to leave," I explain. "This evening."

Nawal reaches behind the counter for a thick square

wrapped up in brown paper. "I set it aside on day one so no one else would get it." He peels back the paper, showing me the tapestry. "I put a little something extra in it for you."

We say good-bye. I wish him luck with his marriage. "I don't need luck; it's in the stars. You, I think, are the one who needs luck."

It makes me think of something Kate said when she dropped me off in Mérida. "I'd wish you luck, Willem, but I think you need to stop relying on that."

I'm not sure which one of them is right.

I pack up my things and then walk to the train station through the late afternoon heat. The city looks golden up the hills, the sand dunes rippling behind it, and it all makes me feel wistful, nostalgic already.

The train gets me into Jaipur at six the next morning. My flight to Mumbai is at ten. I haven't had a chance to set up a new email, and Mukesh has texted nothing about a ride from the airport. I text Prateek. He hasn't replied to any of my texts in the last two days. So I try ringing him.

He answers, distracted.

"Prateek, hey it's Willem."

"Willem, where are you?"

"On a train. I've got your tapestry here." I rattle the package.

"Oh, good." For all his manic enthusiasm about this latest venture, he seems oddly blasé.

"Everything okay?"

"Better than okay. Very good. My cousin Rahul, he is sick with influenza."

"That's terrible. Is he okay?"

"Fine. Fine. But bed rest for him," Prateek says cheerfully. "I am helping him out." He lowers his voice to a whisper. "With the movies."

"The movies?"

"Yes! I find the *goreh* to act in the movies. If I can get ten, they will put my name in the credits. Assistant to assistant director of casting."

"Congratulations."

"Thank you," he says formally. "But only if I find four more. Tomorrow, I return to Salvation Army and maybe to the airport."

"Actually, if you're coming to the airport, that's perfect. I need a ride."

"You return on Saturday, I thought."

"Change of plans. I'm coming back tomorrow now."

There's a silence, during which Prateek and I have the same idea. "Do you want to be in?" he asks at the same time I offer, "Would you want me to be in . . . ?"

The line echoes with our laughter. I give him my flight information and hang up. Outside, the sun is setting; a bright flame behind the train, and darkness in front of us. A short while later, it's all dark.

Mukesh has booked me a sleeper seat in an air-conditioned car, which India Rail chills like a meat locker. The bed has nothing but a sheet. I shiver, and then think of the tapestry, thick and warm. I unwrap the paper; out tumbles something small and hard.

It's a small statue of Ganesha, holding his ax and his lotus, smiling his smile, like he knows something the rest of us haven't figured out yet.

Twenty-five

Mumbai

*T*he movie is called *Heera Ki Tamanna*, which translates, roughly, as *Wishing for a Diamond*. It is a romance starring Billy Devali—big star—and Amisha Rai—big, big star— and is directed by Faruk Khan, who apparently is so big, he needs no further description. Prateek tells me all this in a breathless monologue; he has hardly stopped talking since he swooped me out of the arrivals hall and rushed me to the car, barely glancing at the various Rajasthani goods I painstakingly shopped and bargained for over the past three weeks.

"Oh, Willem, that was the last plan," he says, shaking his head, dismayed that he must explain such things. "I am working in Bollywood now." Then he tells me that yesterday, Amisha Rai swept by him so close that the edge of her sari brushed his arm. "Can I tell you what it felt like?" he asks, not waiting for me to answer. "It felt like a caress from the gods. Can I tell you what she smelled like?" He closes his eyes and inhales. Apparently, her odor defies words.

"What exactly do I do?"

"Do you remember in *Dil Mera Golmaal*, the scene after the shootout?"

I nod. It was like *Reservoir Dogs*, but on a ship. With dancing.

"Where do you think all those white people came from?"

"From the same magical place as the go-go dancers?"

"From casting directors like me." He pounds his chest.

"Casting director? So it's official. You're up to ten?"

"You make eight. But I will get there. You are so tall and handsome and . . . white."

"Maybe I can count for two?" I joke.

Prateek looks at me like I'm an idiot. "No, you count for one. You are only one man."

We arrive in Film City, the suburb that houses many of the studios, and then we pull into the complex and then into what looks like a large airplane hangar.

"Oh, by the way, the payment," Prateek says nonchalantly. "I must tell you, it's ten dollars a day."

I don't answer. I hadn't planned on being paid anything.

He mistakes my silence. "I know for Westerners it is not much," he explains. "But you get meals, and also lodging so you do not need to commute back to Colaba each night. Please, please tell me you'll agree to it."

"Of course. I'm not in it for the money." Which is exactly what Tor used to say about Guerrilla Will. *We're not in it for the money*. But half the time she would say this as she was carefully counting the night's take or checking weather reports in the *International Herald Tribune* to determine the sunniest—and most lucrative—places to hit next.

Back then, I was very much in it for the money. Even the little I earned from Guerrilla Will kept me from having to return to an unwelcoming home.

Funny that, how little things have changed.

On the set, Prateek introduces me to Arun, the assistant casting director, who takes a brief pause from his mobile phone conversation to appraise me. He says something to Prateek in Hindi and then nods at me and barks, "Costume."

Prateek squeezes my arm, as he leads me to the costume room, which is a series of rolling racks full of suits and dresses, tended to by a harried woman with glasses. "Find something that fits," she orders.

Everything is at least a head too short for me. Which is about the amount by which I tower over most Indians. Prateek looks worried. "Do you have a suit?" he asks.

The last time I wore a suit was to Bram's funeral. No, I don't have a suit.

"What seems to be the problem?" Neema, the wardrobe lady snaps.

Prateek grovels, apologizing for my height, as if it were a personality defect.

She sighs impatiently. "Wait here."

Prateek looks at me in alarm. "I hope they do not send you back. Arun just told me that one of the ashram people left this morning and now I am back down to seven."

I slouch, make myself shorter. "Does that help?"

"The suit still will not fit," he says, shaking his head as if I'm an imbecile.

Neema returns with a garment bag. Inside is a suit, freshly pressed, shiny blue, sharkskin. "This is from the actors' wardrobe, so don't mess it," she warns, shoving me into a curtained area to try it on.

The suit fits. When Prateek sees me, he grins. "You look so first-class," he says, amazed. "Come, walk by Arun. Casual, casual. Oh, yes, he sees. Very good. I think I am almost assured a spot in the credits. To think, one day, I might be like Arun."

"Dare to dream."

I'm teasing, but I keep forgetting that Prateek takes everything literally. "Oh, yes. To dream is the ultimate dare, is it not?"

The film set is a faux cocktail lounge, with a grand piano right in the middle. The Indian stars circle the area around the bar, and then deeper into the set mill the fifty or so extras. The majority of them are Indians, but there are about fifteen or twenty Westerners. I go stand next to an Indian in a tux, but he narrows his eyes at me and scoots away.

"They're such snobs!" a skinny, tan girl in a sparkly blue dress says, laughing. "They won't talk to us."

"It's like reverse colonialism or something," says a guy with dreadlocks tied back into a band. "Nash," he says, sticking out a hand.

"Tasha," says the girl.

"Willem."

"Willem," they repeat, dreamily. "You at the ashram?"

"No."

"Oh. We didn't think so. We'd have recognized *you*," Tasha says. "You're so tall. Like Jules."

Nash nods his head. I do too. We all nod at this Jules's height.

"What brings you to India?" I ask, slipping easily back into Postcard Language.

"We are refugees," Tasha says. "From the fame-and-celebrity-obsessed materialistic world in the States. We are here to cleanse ourselves."

"Here?" I gesture to the set.

Nash laughs. "Enlightenment ain't free. It's kind of expensive, actually. So we're here trying to buy some more time. What about you, dude? Why brings you to Bollywoodland?"

"The fame, of course."

They both laugh. Then Nash asks, "Wanna go get baked? They aren't doing anything except making us wait." He pulls out a fat joint. "I wait just as well stoned."

I shrug. "Why not?"

We sneak off outside where half of the extras seem to be smoking cigarettes in the shade of the overhang. Nash lights up and takes a hit, passes it to Tasha, who takes a long, deep drag and passes it to me. The hash is strong and it's been a while, so it hits me immediately. We pass the joint around a few more times.

"You're really . . . tall, Willem," Tasha says.

"Yes, I think you mentioned that."

"We really have to introduce him to Jules," Tasha drawls. "She's tall. And Canadian."

"Totally," Nash says. "Righteous idea."

The world's gone a bit washed out, overbright and spinny. "Who's Jules?" I ask.

"She's a girl," Nash answers. "Cute. Ginger hair. She's at the ashram but she might come out in a day or two. She's tall. Oh, Tasha already said that. Shit, here comes the assistant director dude. Hide the joint."

Tasha pinches the joint between her fingers just as a bird-like man comes and looks at us. Even though Tasha is holding the joint, it's me he focuses on. He takes out his phone and snaps a picture, and then disappears without saying a word.

"Oh. Shit," Tasha says, giggling. "We got caught."

"*He* got caught," Nash says. "They only took his picture." He sounds a bit insulted.

"If there's hash, you always blame the Dutchman," I say.

"Oh, right," Nash says, nodding.

"I'm paranoid now," Tasha says.

"Let's get back. Save the rest of that for later," Nash says.

With the hash buzzing around my head, the waiting on set goes slower, not faster. I spend a few minutes twirling a rupee coin across my hand but I keep dropping it. I turn on my phone to play some solitaire, but then, on a strange stoned whim, use my phone for its intended purpose. I make a call.

"Hello . . . this is Willem," I say when she picks up.

"I know who this is." I can hear fury in her voice. Even calling her gets me in trouble? "Where are you?" she asks.

"I'm on a film set. I'm acting in a Bollywood movie for the next few days."

Silence. Yael never had much patience for "low" culture, outside of the cheesy Israeli pop music she couldn't resist. She didn't like movies or TV shows. She surely thinks all this is a waste of time.

"And when did you decide to do this?" she says at last. Her voice is flinty enough to spark a fire.

"Yesterday. This morning officially."

"And when did you think to tell me?"

Maybe it's the hash, but I actually laugh out loud. Because it's just funny—in the way that absurd things are.

Yael doesn't think so. "What's so amusing?"

"What's so amusing?" I ask. "You wanting to know my itinerary, that's pretty amusing. When you haven't given a thought to my whereabouts, my well-being for the last three years. When you brought me over to India and then a week later shipped me right back off again and didn't bother to call once. You couldn't even be bothered to come to the airport to pick me up. Oh, I know there was an emergency, something more important, but there always is, isn't there? So why would you need to know that I was acting in a Bollywood movie?"

I stop. And it's like the effects of the hash have worn off, taking my anger—or my bravery—with them.

"The reason I would need to know," she says, her voice

measured, infuriatingly so, "is so I would know not to come to the airport this time to pick you up."

After she hangs up, I turn my phone over. I see the half dozen missed calls, the *Where are you?* texts.

Another missed connection. Story of my life these days.

Twenty-six

*T*hat night, we finish up at eight and pile into a rickety bus for an hour-long ride to a squat cement hotel where we're put four to a room. I wind up with Nash and Tasha and Argin, another acolyte from their ashram. The three of them pass a joint around and tell repeating stories about reaching enlightenment. They offer the joint to me, but after the afternoon's hash-fueled debacle with Yael, I don't trust myself. Eventually, I fall asleep, but I'm woken up in the middle of the night to the enthusiastic squeaking of the bedframe. Nash and Tasha. Or maybe all three of them. It is extremely unpleasant—and it's pathetic because I can't think of anywhere else I'd rather be.

The next day, on set, it's more of the same. After I put on my suit, I see Prateek for half a second before he dashes off. "Must find more people," he calls to me. "Three left yesterday. I need four today!" Neema evil-eyes me. The assistant director snaps another picture. They really are serious about the suit.

Late that afternoon Prateek returns with new recruits, including a leggy woman with reddish hair streaked through with pink.

"Jules!" Nash and Tasha scream when she arrives. They all hug and dance in a small circle and then Tasha waves me over.

"Jules," she says. "This is Willem. We've decided he's perfect for you."

"Oh have you?" Jules rolls her eyes a bit. She is tall, not quite as tall as me, but nearly. "I'm Jules, but apparently you already know that," she says.

"I'm Willem."

"I like your suit, Willem."

"You should. It's a very special suit. So special they keep snapping my picture to make sure I don't mess it up."

"Clearly you're a man who knows his way around a closet. I'm supposed to get into wardrobe. Show me where to go?"

"Glad to."

She links an arm around mine as we walk to the racks. "So you met Nash and Tash, I see?"

"I had the pleasure of spending the night with them."

She makes a face. "They had sex, didn't they?"

I nod.

She shakes her head. "My condolences."

I laugh at that.

"Well, I'm staying in the room with you tonight. I'll try to even things out." She gives me a look. "Not like that, if that's what you're thinking."

"All I'm thinking about is getting you into a dress," I say.

"Really?" she asks. "Getting me *into* a dress?"

I laugh again. Jules has got her arm wrapped around mine, which is a pleasant distraction from the hangover I've had since yesterday's fight with Yael. Girls have always been the best distractions.

Until a girl became the thing I needed distraction from.

Twenty-seven

It's after five when we finally get around to shooting. Our scene is a song, the moment when Billy Devali's character first meets Amisha Rai's and is so besotted he breaks out singing and playing the piano. We are all supposed to watch, mesmerized by this authentic display of love at first sight. At the end, we clap.

We spend the rest of the day shooting. When we break for the day, the assistant director tells us to plan on staying at least two more days. Prateek takes me aside to say it'll probably be more than that and would I mind staying? I don't mind. I'm quite happy to stay until I fly back to Holland.

We're lining up for the bus again, when the assistant director snaps yet another picture of me. "Man, they're building a serious case against you," Nash says.

"I don't understand," I say. "I'm not even wearing the suit right now."

That night in the hotel, there are five of us. Nash, Tasha, Argin, me and Jules. Jules and I share a mattress on the floor. Nothing happens. Not with us, anyhow. Her presence does little to stop Nash and Tasha from their late-night calisthenics, but when it happens, I can see Jules quaking with laughter, and then I am, too.

She rolls over on her side to face me. "Misery loves company," she whispers.

The next day, I'm in the lunch queue for some dal and rice when the assistant director taps me on the back. I even pose this time for the anticipated photo, but there's no camera. Instead he instructs me to come with him.

"Did you stain the suit?" Jules calls after me.

Arun trots up behind us, followed by Prateek, who looks stricken. How much can this suit be worth?

"What's going on?" I ask Prateek as we walk past the set and toward the row of trailers.

"Faruk! Khan!" He sputters the name like a cough.

"What about Faruk Khan?" But before Prateek can answer, I'm pulled up the stairs and pushed into one of the trailers. Inside, Faruk Khan, Amisha Rai, and Billy Devali are sitting in a huddle. They all stare at me for what seems like an eternity, until Billy finally booms, "There! Did I not tell you?"

Amisha lights another cigarette and kicks up her bare feet, which are covered with vinelike henna tattoos. "You are absolutely right," she says in a lilting accent. "He looks like an American movie star."

"Like that one," Billy snaps his fingers. "Heath Ledger."

"Only not dead," Faruk says.

They cluck in agreement.

"I think Heath Ledger was from Australia," I say.

"Never mind that," Faruk says. "Where are you from? America? UK?"

"Holland."

Billy wrinkles his nose. "You don't have an accent."

"You almost sound British," Amisha says. "Close enough to South African."

"This is closer to South African," I say in a clipped Afrikaans accent.

Amisha claps her hands. "He can do accents."

"Afrikaans is close to Dutch," I explain.

"Have you ever acted before?" Faruk asks.

"Not really."

"Not really?" Amisha asks, arching an eyebrow.

"A little Shakespeare."

"You cannot say 'not really' and then say you've done William Shakespeare," Faruk says scornfully. "What is your name? Or should we call you Mr. Not Really?"

"I prefer Willem. Willem de Ruiter."

"Bit of a mouthful," Billy says.

"Not a good stage name," Amisha says.

"He can change it," Billy says. "All the Americans do."

"Like the Indians don't," Amisha says. "*Billy.*"

"I'm not American," I interrupt. "I'm Dutch."

"Oh, yes. Mr. de . . . Willem," Faruk says. "No matter. We have a problem. One of our Western actors, an American named Dirk Digby, he lives in Dubai, perhaps you've heard of him?"

I shake my head.

"Never mind. It appears Mr. Digby had some last-minute problems with the contract and had to make other plans, and this leaves us with a small part open. It's a South African diamond dealer, shady character, who tries to woo our Miss Rai while also trying to steal her family's Shakti diamond. Not a large part, but significant, and we find ourselves in a bit of a bind. We were looking for someone who can look the part and who can manage a few lines of Hindi and a few lines of English. How are you with languages?"

"Pretty good," I say. "I grew up speaking several."

"Okay, try this line," Faruk says, and he reads me something.

"Tell me what it means."

"You see?" Amisha says. "A natural actor would want to know. I don't think Dirk ever knows what he's saying."

Faruk waves her off. He turns to me. "You are trying to keep Amisha's character, Heera, from marrying Billy here, but really, you only want her family's diamonds. It's in English with some Hindi. This is the part where you tell Heera you know who she is, and that her name means diamond. I'll say it, you repeat?"

"Okay."

"*Main jaanta hoon tum kaun ho*, Heera Gopal. Heera, it means diamond, doesn't it?" Faruk says

"*Main jaanta hoon tum kaun ho*, Heera Gopal. Heera, it means diamond, doesn't it?" I repeat.

They all stare at me.

"How did you do that?" Amisha asks.

"Do what?"

"You sounded as if you spoke Hindi fluently," Billy says.

"I don't know. I've always had an ear for languages."

"Incredible, really." Amisha turns to Faruk. "You wouldn't have to cut the dialogue."

Faruk stares at me. "It is three days shooting, starting next week. Here in Mumbai. You will have to learn lines. I can have someone help you with the Hindi pronunciation and translations, but there is a good bit of English." He strokes his beard. "I can pay you thirty thousand rupees."

I pause, trying to do the conversions.

Faruk takes my silence for bargaining. "Okay," he counters. "Forty thousand rupees."

"How long would I have to stay?"

"Shoot starts Monday, should last three days," Faruk says.

Monday is when I'm meant to fly back to Amsterdam. Do I want to stay three more days? But then Faruk continues. "We would put you up in the cast hotel. It's on Juhu Beach."

"Juhu Beach is very nice," Billy says.

"I'm meant to leave on Monday. I have a flight."

"Can't you change your flight?" Faruk asks.

I'm sure Mukesh can. And if they're putting me up in a hotel, it would keep me from having to go back to the Bombay Royale.

"Fifty thousand," Faruk says. "But that's my final offer."

"That's more than a thousand dollars, Mr. de Ruiter," Amisha informs me with a husky laugh and a billowing exhale of cigarette smoke. "Too good to turn down, I think."

Twenty-eight

The production immediately relocates me to a posh hotel in Juhu Beach. The first thing I do is shower. Then I plug in my phone, which has been dead for the past day. I half expect a text or call from Yael, but there isn't one. I consider telling her I'm staying longer, but after our last conversation, after the last three weeks—three years—I feel like she has no right to this information. Instead, I text Mukesh, asking him to bump my departure date by another three days.

Immediately, he calls back. "You've decided to stay with us longer!" he says. He sounds delighted.

"Just a few days." I explain to him about being an extra and now being cast in a small part.

"Oh, that is most exciting," he says. "Mummy must be thrilled."

"*Mummy* doesn't know, actually."

"Doesn't know?"

"I haven't seen her. I've been staying out by the studios, and now I'm in a hotel in Juhu Beach."

"Juhu Beach. Very classy," Mukesh says. "But you haven't seen Mummy since you came back from Rajasthan? I thought she picked you up at the airport."

"Change of plans."

"Oh. I see." There's a pause. "When do you want to leave?"

"I'm supposed to start shooting on Monday, and it's meant to take three days."

"Safer to assume it'll take double," Mukesh says. "I'll see what I can do."

We hang up and I pick up my script. Faruk has written English translations above the Hindi and someone has made me a tape recording of the Hindi. I spend the afternoon repeating the lines.

When I'm done, I pace the room for a bit. It's all modern and posh, with a bathtub and a shower and a wide double bed. I haven't slept somewhere this nice in ages, and it's a little too quiet, a little too pristine. I sit on the bed, watch Hindi TV just to have some company. I order dinner in my room. That night when I go to bed, I find I can't sleep. The bed is too soft, too big, after so many years of sleeping on trains, in cars, on bunkbeds, sofas, futons, Ana Lucia's cramped bed. Now I'm like one of those rescued shipwrecked men who, once rescued and back in civilization, can only sleep on the floor.

Friday I wake up and practice my lines again. The shoot doesn't start for three more days, and they stretch in front of me, endlessly, like the gray blue sea out my window. When my phone rings, I am embarrassed by my relief.

"Willem, Mukesh here. I have news about your flights."

"Great."

"So soonest I can get you out is April." He tells me some dates.

"*What*? Why so long?"

"What can I say? All the flights are booked until then. Easter."

Easter? In a Hindu/Muslim country? I sigh. "You're sure there's nothing sooner? I don't mind paying a bit extra."

"Nothing to be done. I did the best I could." He sounds a bit insulted when he says the last bit.

"What about booking me a new flight?"

"Really, Willem, it is only a matter of weeks, and flights are expensive this time of year, and also full." His voice has gone scolding. "It is just a few extra days."

"Can you keep looking? See if any seats open up?"

"Certainly! Will do."

I hang up and try to fight off the sense of impending doom. I'd thought the film would keep me here a few extra days, all of them in a hotel. Now I'm stuck. I remind myself that I don't need to stay in Mumbai past the shoot. Nash and Tasha and Jules are going to Goa for a few days if they can cobble the cash together. Maybe I'll go with them. Maybe I'll even pay.

I send Jules a text: *Is Goa still a go?*

She texts back: *Only if I don't kill N&T. Last night unbearably loud. You are a traitor for deserting.*

I look around my hotel room where last night it was unbearably quiet. I take a shot of the view from the balcony and send it to Jules. *It's quiet here. And there's room for two if you want to desert*, I write.

I like dessert, she texts back. *Tell me where you are.*

A few hours later, there's a knock at the door. I open it and Jules comes in. She admires the view and hops on the bed. She picks up the script from the coffee table.

"Want to run lines?" I ask. "There's English translations."

She smiles. "Sure."

I show her where to start. She clears her throat and arranges her face. "And who do you think you are?" she asks in a haughty voice, her attempt, I think, to mimic Amisha.

"Sometimes I wonder," I reply. "The name on my birth certificate reads Lars Von Gelder. But I know who *you* are, Heera Gopal. Heera, it means diamond, doesn't it? And you glitter as brightly as your name."

"I don't care to discuss my name with you, Mr. Von Gelder."

"Oh, so you know me after all?"

"I know all I care to."

"Then you know I am the top exporter of diamonds in South Africa, so I know a thing or two about precious gems. I can see more with my naked eye than most jewelers can with a loupe. And looking at you, I can tell that you are a million carats. And flawless."

"Word has it that you're after my family's diamond, Mr. Von Gelder."

"Oh, I am, Miss Gopal. I am." I pause for a beat. "But perhaps not the Shakti Diamond."

At the end of the section, Jules puts down the script. "This is quite cheesy, Mr. Van Gelder."

"It's Von Gelder, actually."

"Oh. Sorry. Mr. *Von* Gelder."

"It's very important, you know? Names," I say.

"Oh, yeah? What's Jules short for?"

"Juliana?" I try. "Like the Dutch queen?"

"Nope." Jules stands up from her chair and walks toward me, smiling as she folds herself into my lap. Then she kisses me.

"Juliet," I try.

She shakes her head, smiling as she unbuttons her shirt. "Not Juliet. But you're welcome to be my Romeo tonight."

Twenty-nine

The next morning, Jules leaves, back to Pune and the ashram with Nash and Tasha. We make vague plans to meet up in Goa the following week. I never do find out what Jules is short for.

I feel hungover even though we didn't drink, and lonely even though I'm used to being on my own. I call Prateek to see what he's doing this weekend, but he's helping his mother at home today and tomorrow he is going to a big family dinner with his uncle. I spend the day wandering Juhu Beach. I watch a bunch of men play soccer on the sand and it all makes me miss the boys in Utrecht. And then all the missing congeals, and it's Lulu I miss, and I know it must be displaced, my loneliness a heat-seeking missile, her the heat. Only I can't seem to find a new source of heat. I don't miss Jules at all.

By Sunday, I'm going stir-crazy. I decide to take a train out of
the city, a day trip somewhere. I've just opened my guidebook
to figure out where to go when my phone rings. I practically
leap on it.

"Willem!" Mukesh's jovial voice echoes through the line.
I don't think I've ever been happier to hear from him. "What
are you doing today?"

"I'm just trying to suss that out. I was thinking of making
a day trip to Khandala."

"Khandala is very nice, but far for one day so you must
leave early. If you like, I can arrange a driver for you another
day. I have a different proposal for you. How about I take
you around?"

"Really?"

"Yes. There are some very lovely temples in Mumbai,
smaller temples tourists so rarely see. My wife and daughters
are away, so I have the day free."

I gratefully accept, and at noon, Mukesh picks me up in a
small battered Ford and proceeds to speed me around Mumbai. We stop at three different temples, watching young men
do yoga-like calisthenics, watching old Sadhus meditating in
prayer. The third stop is a Jain temple, the acolytes all hold
small brooms sweeping in front of them as they walk. "To
brush any living creatures out of their way so not to inadver-
tently take a life," Mukesh explains. "Such care for life," he
says. "Just like Mummy."

"Right. Mummy is practically a Jain," I say. "Or maybe
she's aiming to be the next Mother Teresa?"

Mukesh gives me a sympathetic look that makes me want to break something. "You know how I met Mummy, do you not?" he asks as we walk through a breezeway in the temple.

"I assume it had something to do with the fascinating world of air travel." I'm being unfair to Mukesh, but such is the price for making himself her emissary.

He shakes his head. "That came later. I was with my own mummy who had the cancer." He clucks his tongue. "She was having her treatments, tip-top doctor, but it was in the lungs, so not much to be done. We were coming from the specialist one day, waiting for a taxi, but Amma, that's my mummy, was quite weak and dizzy and she fell on the street. Your mummy happened to be nearby and she rushed up to ask if she could help. I explained to her about Amma's condition—it was terminal," he lowers his voice to a whisper. "But your mummy told me about different things that could help, not to cure her, but to make the dizziness and the weakness better. And she came, every week, to my home, with her needles and her massages and it helped so much. When my amma's time came, her journey to the next life was so much more peaceful. Thanks to your mummy."

I see what he's doing. Mukesh is attempting to interpret my mother to me much in the way Bram used to do when he'd explain why Yael seemed so gruff or distant. He was the one to quietly tell me stories about Saba, who, after the death of Yael's mother, Naomi, came undone by one tragedy too many. He turned overprotective, paranoid, or more overprotective and paranoid, Bram said, not allowing Yael to do the simplest things—swim in a public pool, have a friend over—and forcing her to keep disaster preparation checklists for any kind of emergency. "She promised she would do everything differently," he said. "So it would be different for you. So it wouldn't be oppressive."

As if there's only one kind of oppressive.

After the temples, we have lunch. I'm feeling bad about how I acted toward Mukesh, so when he tells me he has something extra special he wants to show me—something very few tourists ever see—I paste on my smile and act excited. As we bump across Mumbai, the streets becomes more dense: bicycles, rickshaws, cars, donkey-pulled carts, cows, women with bundles on their heads, all converge onto choked streets that don't seem built for such traffic. The buildings themselves suffer from the same syndrome; the mix of high-rises and shacks are all overflowing with rivers of people, sleeping on mats, hanging laundry on lines, cooking on small fires outside.

We turn down a dank narrow alley, shrouded somehow from the bright sunlight. Mukesh points to the row of young girls in tattered saris, standing. "Prostitutes," he says.

At the end of the alley we stop. I look back at the prostitutes. Some are younger than me, and their eyes look blank, and it all makes me feel ashamed somehow. Mukesh points to a squat cement building with a name written on it in both swirly Hindi and block English. "Here we are," he says.

I read the sign. MITALI. It's vaguely familiar.

"What is this?" I ask.

"Why, Mummy's clinic, of course," he says.

"Yael's clinic?" I ask in alarm.

"Yes, I thought we might pay her a visit."

"But, but . . ." I sputter for excuses. "It's Sunday," I finish, as if the day of the week is the problem.

"Sickness does not take a Sabbath." Mukesh points to a small teashop on the corner. "I will wait for you there." And then he's gone.

I stand in front of the clinic for a minute. One of the prostitutes—she looks no older than thirteen—starts to walk toward me and I can't stand the thought that she thinks I'm a client, so I shove open the door to the clinic. The door swings open, right onto an old woman crouched just inside. There are people everywhere, with homemade bandages, and listless babies, napping on pallets on the floor. They're camped all up the cement stairs and all around the waiting room, giving new meaning to the term.

"Are you Willem?" From behind the glass partition a no-nonsense Indian woman in a lab coat is looking at me. Two seconds later, she opens the door to the waiting room. I feel all the eyes turn to me. The woman says something in Hindi or Marathi and there is much silent nodding, giving new meaning to the term *patient*, too.

"I'm Doctor Gupta," she says, her voice brisk, efficient but warm. "I work with your mother. Let me go find her. Would you like some tea?"

"No thank you." I have the sickening feeling that everyone else is in on a joke but me.

"Good, good. Wait here."

She leads me to a small windowless room with a ripped gurney, and a rush of memory overtakes me. The last time I was in a hospital: Paris. The time before that: Amsterdam. Yael had called me at my dorm, very early that morning, telling me to come. Bram was sick.

I couldn't understand the urgency. I'd seen him not a week before. He'd been a little off his game, a sore throat, but Yael was tending to him with her usual teas and tinctures. I had an exam that day. I asked if I could come after.

"Come now," she said.

At the hospital, Yael had stood in the corner while three doctors—the traditional kind, with stethoscopes and guarded expressions—surrounded me in a grim little circle and explained to me that Bram had contracted a rare strain of strep that had sent his body into septic shock. His kidneys had already failed and now his liver was going, too. They were doing everything they could, putting him on dialysis and pumping him full of the most powerful antibiotics, but so far, nothing had been effective. I should brace myself for the worst.

"I don't understand," I said.

Neither did they, really. All they could say was, "It's one of those one-in-a-million cases." Such comforting odds, except when you were the one.

It was like finding out the world was made of gossamer and could be so easily ripped apart. To be so solely at the mercy of fate. Even with all Bram's talk of accidents, it seemed inconceivable.

I looked to Yael, mighty Yael, to intervene, to swoop in, to take care of Bram like she always had. But she just shrank into that corner, not saying a word.

"*Do something, goddammit!*" I screamed at her. "*You have to do something.*"

But she didn't. Couldn't. And two days later, Bram was gone.

"Willem."

I turn around and there's Yael. I always think she's so frightening, but she's actually tiny, barely reaching my shoulder.

"You're crying," she says.

I reach out and touch my face and I find it wet with tears. I'm mortified to be doing this. In front of her. I turn away. I want to run. Out of this clinic. Out of India. Forget the shoot. Forget the flight delay. Buy a new ticket. It doesn't have to be back to Amsterdam. Anywhere that's not here.

I feel her hands on me, turning me back around. "Willem?" she asks. "Tell me why you're lost."

It's shocking to hear her words, my words. That she remembered.

But how can I answer her? How can I answer when I've been nothing but lost these last three years? So much more than I ever anticipated. I keep thinking of another one of the stories Bram used to tell, a horror story really, about when Yael was a girl. She was ten and Saba had taken her camping in the desert. Just the two of them. As the sun started to set, Saba said he'd be right back, and then left her alone with one of those disaster preparation checklists that he was always having her make. Yael, terrified, but capable because of those very disaster preparation checklists, made a fire, made dinner, made camp, fended. When Saba showed up the next day, she screamed at him, *How could you leave me alone?* And Saba had said, *I wasn't leaving you alone. I was watching the whole time. I was preparing you.*

Why didn't she prepare me? Why didn't she teach me about the universal law of equilibrium before I had to find it out for myself? Maybe then I wouldn't miss everything so much.

"I miss . . ." I start to say, but I can't get the words out.

"You miss Bram," she says.

And yes, of course I do. I miss my father. I miss my grandfather. I miss my home. And I miss my mother. But the thing is, for almost three years, I managed not to miss any of them. And then I spent that one day with that one girl. One day. One day of watching the rise and fall of her sleep under the rolling clouds in that park and feeling so peaceful that I fell asleep myself. One day of being under her protection—I can still feel the grasp of her hand as we flew through the streets after she threw the book at the skinheads, her grip so strong that it felt like we were one person, not two. One day of being the beneficiary of her strange generosity—the barge ride, the watch, that honesty, her willingness to show fear, her willingness to show courage. It was like she gave me her whole self, and somehow as a result, I gave her more of myself than I even realized there was to give. But then she was gone. And only after I'd been filled up by her, by that day, did I understand how empty I really was.

Yael watches me a moment longer. "Who else do you miss?" she asks, like she already knows the answer.

"I don't know," I say, and for a minute she looks frustrated, like I'm keeping it from her, but that's not it, and I don't want to keep things from her anymore. So I clarify. "I don't know her name."

Yael looks up, surprised, and not. "Whose name?"

"Lulu."

"Isn't *that* her name?"

So I tell my mother. About finding this girl, this strange and nameless girl, whom I showed nothing but who saw everything. I tell her how since losing her, I have felt bereft. And the relief at telling my mother this is almost as profound as the relief of finding Lulu was.

When I finish telling Yael the story about that day in Paris, I look at her. And I'm shocked all over again because she's doing something I've only seen her do in the kitchen while cutting onions.

My mother is crying.

"Why are *you* crying?" I ask her, now crying again myself.

"Because it sounds just like how I met Bram," she says, laughing on a sob.

Of course it does. I've thought about that every single day since I met Lulu. Wondered if that's not why I'm stuck on her. Because the story is so much like Yael and Bram's.

"Except for one thing," I say.

"What's that?" she asks, swiping at her eyes.

The most important detail. And you'd think I would've known better, having heard Bram's story so many times.

"You give the girl your address."

Thirty

APRIL
Mumbai

As Mukesh expected, the shoot goes over schedule by double, so for six days I have the pleasure of becoming Lars Von Gelder. And it is. A pleasure. A surprising one. On set, in costume, with Amisha and the other actors across from me, Lars Von Gelder's cheesy Hindi lines cease to feel cheesy. They don't even feel like another language. They roll off my tongue and I feel like I am him, the calculating operator who says one thing and wants another.

In between takes, I hang out in Amisha's trailer, playing games of hearts with her and Billy. "We're all impressed with your abilities," Amisha tells me. "Even Faruk, though he'll never say so."

He doesn't. Not exactly. But at the end of each day, he pats me on the back and says, "Not bad, Mr. Not Really." And I feel proud.

But then it's the last day and I know it's over, because

instead of saying "not bad," Faruk says "good work," and thanks me.

And that's it. Next week, Amisha and the principles are packing for Abu Dhabi where they will shoot the final scenes of the film. And me? Yesterday I got a text from Tasha. She and Nash and Jules are in Goa. I'm invited to go with them. But I won't.

I have a couple more weeks here. And I'm spending them with my mother.

My first night back at the Bombay Royale, I get in late. Chaudhary is snoring behind the desk, so I take the stairs up to the fifth floor rather than wake him. Yael has left the door propped open, but she's also asleep when I get in. I'm both relieved and disappointed. We haven't really spoken since that day at the clinic. I don't quite know what to expect between us. Have things changed? Do we speak a common language now?

The next morning she shakes me awake.

"Hey," I say, blinking my eyes.

"Hey," she says back, almost shyly. "I wanted to know, before I leave for work, if you wanted to join me tonight for a Seder. It's the first night of Passover."

I almost think she's joking. When I was growing up, we only celebrated the secular holidays. New Year's. Queen's Day. We never once had a Seder. I didn't even know what they were until Saba started visiting and told me about all the holidays he celebrated, that Yael used to celebrate when she was a child.

"Since when do you go to Seders?" I ask. My question is hesitant, because the mere asking of it touches on the tender spot of her childhood.

"Two years now," she answers. "There's an American family that started a school near the clinic, and they wanted to have one last year and I was the only Jew they knew, so they begged me to come, because they said they'd feel funny having one without a Jew."

"They're not Jewish then?"

"No. They're Christians. Missionaries, even."

"You're kidding?"

She shakes her head, but she's smiling. "I have discovered that no one likes a Jewish holiday quite like a Christian fundamentalist." She laughs, and I can't remember the last time I heard her do that. "There might be a Catholic nun there, too."

"A nun? This is starting to sound like one of Uncle Daniel's jokes. A nun and a missionary walk into a Seder."

"You need three. A nun, a missionary, and an imam walk into a Seder," Yael says.

Imam. I think of the Muslim girls in Paris, and I'm reminded, again, of Lulu. "She was Jewish, too," I say. "My American girl."

Yael's eyebrows go up. "Really?"

I nod.

Yael raises her hands into the air. "Well, maybe she's having her own Seder tonight."

The thought hadn't occurred to me, but as soon as she says it, I get a strange feeling that it's true. And for a second, even with those two oceans and everything else between us, Lulu doesn't feel quite so far away.

Thirty-one

_T_he Donnellys, the family hosting tonight's Seder, live in a large sprawling white stucco house with a makeshift soccer pitch out front. When we arrive, several blond people spill out the front door, including three boys who Yael has told me she can't tell apart. I can see why. Aside from their height, they are identical, all tousled hair and gangly limbs and knobby Adam's apples. "One's Declan, one's Matthew, and the little one, I think, is Lucas," Yael says, not so helpfully.

The tallest one bounces a soccer ball in his hand. "Time for a quick game?" he asks.

"Don't get too muddy, Dec," the blonde woman says. She smiles. "Hi, Willem. I'm Kelsey. This is Sister Karenna," she says, gesturing to a weathered old smiling woman in a full Catholic habit.

"Welcome, welcome," the nun says.

"And I'm Paul," a mustached man in a Hawaiian shirt says, bundling me into a hug. "And you look just like your mama."

Yael and I stare at each other. No one ever says that.

"It's in the eyes," Paul says. He turns to Yael. "You hear about the cholera outbreak in the Dharavi slum?"

They immediately start talking about that, so I go play some soccer with the brothers. They tell me how they've been discussing Passover and the Exodus all week long as part of their studies. They are homeschooled. "We even made matzo over a campfire," the smallest one, Lucas, tells me.

"Well, you know more than me," I say.

They laugh, like I'm joking.

After a while, Kelsey calls us inside. The house reminds me of a flea market, a little of this, a little of that. A dining table on one side, a chalkboard on the other. Chore charts on the wall, alongside pictures of Jesus, Gandhi, and Ganesha. The entire house is fragrant with roasting meat.

"It smells wonderful," Yael says.

Kelsey smiles. "I made roast leg of lamb stuffed with apples and walnuts." She turns to me. "We tried to get a brisket, but it's impossible here."

"Holy cow and all," Paul says.

"This is an Israeli recipe," Kelsey continues. "At least that's what the website said."

Yael is quiet for a minute. "It's what my mother would've made."

Yael's mother, Naomi, who escaped the horrors Saba had lived through only to be struck by a delivery truck on the way back from walking Yael to school. Universal law of equilibrium. Escape one horror, get hit by another.

"What else do you remember?" I ask hesitantly. "About Naomi." She was another unmentionable when I was growing up.

"She sang," Yael says quietly. "All the time. At the Seders too. So there was lots of singing at the Seders—before. And people. When I was a child, we had a full house. Not after. Then it was just us. . . ." She trails off. "It wasn't as joyful."

"So tonight, there will be singing," Paul says. "Someone get my guitar."

"Oh, no. Not the guitar," Matthew jokes.

"I like the guitar," Lucas says.

"Me, too," Kelsey says. "Reminds me of when we met." Her and Paul's eyes meet and tell a quiet story, the way Yael and Bram's used to, and I feel a longing pull at me.

"Shall we sit down?" Kelsey asks, gesturing to the table. We take our seats.

"I know I railroaded you into this again, but Yael, would you mind being the leader?" Paul asks. "I've been studying up since last year and I'll chime in, but I feel you're better qualified. Otherwise we can ask Sister Karenna to do it."

"What? I do it?" Sister Karenna jerks up.

"She's a little deaf," Declan whispers to me.

"You don't have to do anything, Sister, but relax," Kelsey says in a loud voice.

"I'll do it," Yael tells Paul. "If you help."

"We'll tag-team it," Paul says, winking at me.

But Yael hardly seems like she needs the help. She says

an opening prayer over the wine in a clear strong voice, as if she's done this every year. Then she turns to Paul. "Maybe you might explain the point of the Seder."

"Sure." Paul clears his throat and starts a long meandering explanation about how a Seder is meant to commemorate the Jews' exodus from Egypt, their escape from slavery and their return to the Promised Land, the miracles that ensued to make this happen. "Though this happened thousands of years ago, Jews today retell the story every year to rejoice in the triumphant history, to remember it. But here's why I wanted to jump on the bandwagon. Because it's not just a retelling or a celebration of history. It's also a reminder of the price and the privilege of liberation." He turns to Yael. "That sound right?"

She nods. "It's a story we repeat because it's a history we want to see repeated," she says.

The Seder continues. We say blessings over the matzo, we eat the vegetables in salt water, and then the bitter herbs. Kelsey serves soup. "Not matzo ball, mulligatawny," she says. "I hope lentils are okay."

While we're eating our soup, Paul suggests that since the point of the Seder is to retell a story of liberation, we all take a turn and talk about a time in our lives when we escaped some sort of oppression. "Or escaped anything really." He goes first, talking about his life as it used to be, drinking, drugs, aimless and sad before he found God, and then found Kelsey and then found meaning.

Sister Karenna goes next, talking about escaping the brutality of poverty when she was taken in by a church school, and going on to become a nun to serve others.

Then it's my turn. I pause. My first instinct is to tell about Lulu. Because really that was a day I felt like I escaped danger.

But I decide to tell a different story, in part because I don't think this one has been told out loud since he died. The story of one hitchhiking girl and two brothers and the three centimeters that sealed all our fates. It's not really my escape. It's hers. But it is my story. The founding tale of my family. And as Yael said about the Seder, it's a story I repeat because it's a history I want to see repeated.

Thirty-two

The night before I fly back to Amsterdam, Mukesh calls to go over all my flight details. "I got you an exit row seat," he says. "You'll be more comfortable, with all your height. Though maybe if you tell them you are a Bollywood star, you'll get business class."

I laugh. "I'll do my best."

"When does the film come out?"

"I'm not sure. They just finished shooting."

"Funny how it all worked out."

"Right place, right time," I tell him.

"Yes, but you wouldn't have been in the right place in the right time had we not canceled your camel trip."

"You mean it got canceled. Because the camels got sick."

"Oh, no, camels just fine. Mummy asked me to bring you back early." He lowers his voice. "Also, plenty of flights back to Amsterdam before tomorrow, but when you disappeared to the movie, Mummy asked me to keep you here a little bit longer." He chuckles. "Right place, right time."

The next morning, Prateek comes to drive us to the airport. Chaudhary shuffles to the curb to see us off, wagging his fingers and reminding us of the legally mandated taxi fares.

I sit in the backseat this time, because this time Yael is coming to with us. On the ride to the airport, she is quiet. So am I. I don't quite know what to say. Mukesh's confession last night has rattled me, and I want to ask Yael about it, but I don't know if I should. If she'd wanted me to know, she would've told me.

"What will you do when you get back?" she asks me after a while.

"I don't know." I really have no idea. At the same time, I'm ready to go back.

"Where will you stay?"

I shrug. "I can stay on Broodje's couch for a few weeks."

"On the couch? I thought you were living there."

"My room's been rented." Even if it hadn't, everyone is moving out at the end of the summer. W is moving in with Lien in Amsterdam. Henk and Broodje are going to get their own flat together. *It's the end of an era, Willy*, Broodje wrote me in an email.

"Why don't you go back to Amsterdam?" Yael asks.

"Because there's nowhere to go," I say.

I look straight at her and she looks straight at me and it's like we're acknowledging that. But then she raises her eyebrow. "You never know," she says.

"Don't worry. I'll land somewhere." I look out the window. The car is climbing onto the expressway. I can already feel Mumbai falling away.

"Will you keep looking for her? That girl?"

The way she says it, *keep looking*, as if I haven't stopped. And I realize in some way, I haven't. Which is maybe the problem.

"What girl is this?" Prateek asks, surprised. I never told him of any girl.

I look at the dashboard, where Ganesha is dancing away just as he did on that first drive from the airport. "Hey, Ma. What was that mantra? The one from the Ganesha temple?"

"*Om gam ganapatayae namaha*?" Yael asks.

"That's the one."

From the front seat, Prateek chants it. "*Om gam ganapatayae namaha*."

I repeat it. "*Om gam ganapatayae namaha*." I pause as the sound floats through the car. "That's what I'm after. New beginnings."

Yael reaches out to touch the scar on my face. It's faded now, thanks to her ministrations. She smiles at me. And it occurs to me that I might have already gotten what I asked for.

Thirty-three

A week after I get back from India, while I'm still camped out at the couch on Bloemstraat trying to get over my jetlag and figure out what my next move is, I get an unlikely call.

"Hey, little man. You coming to clear your shit out of my attic?" There's no introduction, no preamble. Not that I need one. Even though we have not spoken in years, I know the voice. It's so much like his brother's.

"Uncle Daniel," I say. "Hey. Where are you?"

"Where am I? I'm in my flat. With my attic. That has your shit in it."

This is a surprise. All the years I grew up, I have never actually seen Daniel in the flat he owns. It's the same flat on the Ceintuurbaan that he and Bram used to live in. Back then, it was a squat. It's where they were living when Yael came and knocked on the door and changed everything.

Within six months, Bram had married Yael and moved them into their own flat. Within another year, he'd cobbled together the funds to buy a broken-down old barge on the Nieuwe Prinsengracht. Daniel stayed in the squat, eventually getting a lease for it and then buying it from the city government for a pittance. Unlike Bram, who went on to fix up his boat, floorboard by floorboard, until it was the "Bauhaus on the Gracht," Daniel left the flat in its state of anarchist disrepair and rented it out. He got almost nothing for it. "But nothing is enough to live like a king in Southeast Asia," Bram used to say. So that's where Daniel stayed, riding the ups and down of the Asian economy with a series of business ventures that mostly went nowhere.

"Your ma called," Daniel continues. "Told me you were back. Said you might need a place to stay. I told her you needed to come get your shit out of my attic."

"So I have shit in the attic?" I ask him, stretching out from the too-short sofa and trying to digest my surprise. Yael called Daniel? For me?

"*Everyone* has shit in the attic," Daniel says, laughing a huskier, smokier version of Bram's laugh. "When can you come over?"

We arrange for me to come over the next day. Daniel texts me the address, though that's hardly necessary. I know his flat better than I know him. I know the stuck-in-time furniture—the zebra-striped egg chair, the 1950s lamps that Bram used to find at flea markets and rewire. I even know the smell, patchouli and hash. "It's how this place has smelled for twenty years," Bram would say when he and I would visit the flat together to fix a faucet or deliver keys to a new tenant. When I was younger, the lively multi-ethnic area where Daniel lived, right across from the treasures of the Albert Cuyp street market, seemed like another country from the quiet outer canal where we lived.

Over the years, the neighborhood has changed. The once working-class cafés around the market now serve things with truffles, and in the market, alongside the stalls hawking fish and cheese, there are designer boutiques. The houses have smartened up, too. You can see them through picture windows, the sparkling kitchens, the expensive clean-lined furniture.

Not Daniel's place, though. As his neighbors renovated and upgraded, his flat dug into its time warp. I suspect that's still the case, especially after he warns me that the buzzer doesn't work and instructs me to call upon arrival so he can throw down the keys. So I'm caught a little off guard when he opens the door to the flat and I'm ushered into a lounge, all wide-plank bamboo floors, sage-colored walls, low, modern sofas. I look around the room. It's unrecognizable, except for the egg chair, and even that's been reupholstered.

"Little man," Daniel says, though I am not little at all, a few fingers taller than him. I look at Daniel. His reddish hair is maybe a little shot through with gray, the smile lines cut a little deeper, but otherwise he's the same.

"Little uncle," I joke back, patting him on the head as I hand him back the keys. I walk around. "You've done something to the place," I say, tapping a finger to my chin.

Daniel laughs. "Oh. I'm only halfway there, but that's halfway farther than no way."

"True enough."

"I've got big plans. Actual plans. Where are my plans?" Out the window, there's the roar of a jet rumbling through the clouds. Daniel watches it, then he resumes his search, spinning around peering at the crowded bookshelves. "It's a little slow going because I'm doing the work myself, though I can afford to hire it out, but it just seemed like I should do it this way."

Afford it? Daniel has always been broke; Bram used to help him out. But Bram's not here. Maybe one of his Asian business ventures finally hit. I watch Daniel skitter around the room in search of something, finally locating a set of blueprints shoved halfway under the coffee table.

"I wish he was here to help me; I think he'd be happy that I'm finally making this place mine. But in a way I feel like he is here. Also, he's footing the bill," he says.

It takes me a minute to understand who he's talking about, what he's talking about. "The boat?" I ask.

He nods.

Back in India, Yael barely spoke of Daniel. I figured that they weren't in touch anymore. With Bram gone, why would they be? They never liked each other. At least that's how it seemed to me. Daniel was flakey, messy, a spendthrift—all the things that Yael loved in Bram in less extreme form—and Yael was the person who swept in and upended Daniel's life. If there wasn't much room for me, I can only imagine how it felt for him. It made sense to me why Daniel moved half a world away a few years after Yael showed up.

"There wasn't a will," Daniel says. "She didn't have to do that, but of course she did. That's your ma for you."

Is it? I think about my trip to Rajasthan, an exile that turned out to be what I needed. Then I think about Mukesh, not just canceling the camel tour and delaying my return flight at Yael's behest, but also dropping me off at the clinic that day, when everyone seemed to be expecting me. I'd always assumed my mother was so hands off, taking care of everyone but me. But I'm starting to wonder if perhaps I misunderstood her brand of caretaking.

"I'm beginning to get that," I tell Daniel.

"Good timing, too," he says. He scratches his beard. "I didn't offer you coffee. You want coffee?"

"I wouldn't say no to a coffee."

I follow him into the kitchen, which is the old kitchen, all chipped cupboards, cracked tiles, ancient tiny gas range, cold-water-only sink.

"Kitchen's next. And the bedrooms. Maybe halfway was a bit optimistic. I'd better get on it. You should come live with me. Help me out," he says with a loud clap of his hands. "Your pa always said you were handy."

I'm not sure if I'm handy, but Bram was always drafting me for help with some home-improvement project or another.

He puts the coffee on the stove. "I gotta get into gear. I've got two months now, so tick-tock, tick-tock."

"Two months until what?"

"Oh, shit. I didn't tell you. I only just told your ma." His face breaks out into a smile that looks so much like Bram's it hurts.

"Told her what?"

"Well, Willem, I'm going to be a father."

As we drink coffee, Daniel fills me on the big news. At the age of forty-seven, the perennial bachelor has at last found love. But, because apparently the de Ruiter men can never do things the simple way, the mother of Daniel's child is Brazilian. Her name is Fabiola. They met in Bali. She lives in Bahia. He shows me a picture of a doe-eyed woman with a lit-from-within smile. Then he shows me an accordion folder, several centimeters thick, his correspondence with the various government agencies to prove the legitimacy of their relationship so she can get a visa and they can be married. In July, he is going to Brazil in preparation for the birth in September, and, he hopes, the wedding soon after. All going well, they'll be in Amsterdam in the fall, and return to Brazil for the winter. "Winters there, summers here, and when he is old enough for school, we'll reverse it."

"He?" I ask.

Daniel smiles. "It's a boy. We know. We already have a name for him. Abraão."

"Abraão," I say, rolling it over my tongue.

Daniel nods. "It's Portuguese for Abraham,"

We both are silent for a moment. Abraham, Bram's full name.

"You'll move in, help, won't you?" He points to the blueprints, the one bedroom that will be made into two, the flat that once housed the two brothers, and for a spell housed all three of them before it was just Daniel all on his own. And then, not even him.

But now we are two here. And soon there will be more. After so much contracting, somehow, inexplicably, my family is growing again.

Thirty-four

Daniel and I are on the way to the plumbing supply shop to pick up a shower body when his bike gets a flat tire.

We stop to inspect. There's a nail lodged deep into the tube. It's four-thirty. The plumbing store closes at five. And then it's closed for the weekend. Daniel frowns and throws his arms in the air like a frustrated child.

"Goddammit!" he curses. "The plumber's coming tomorrow."

We did the bedrooms first, a mess of studs and drywall and plaster, neither of us knowing exactly what we were doing, but between books and some old friends of Bram's, we managed to make a tiny "master" bedroom, with a loft bed, and a tinier nursery, which is where I'm now living.

But the learning curve was high and it took longer than we'd expected, and then the bathroom, which Daniel thought would be simple—swapping out seventy-year-old fixtures for modern ones—turned out to be anything but. All the pipes had to be replaced. Coordinating the arrival of the tub and the sink and the plumber—another of Bram's friends, who is doing the job on the cheap but also on his off hours, nights and weekends—has challenged Daniel's already limited logistical skills, but he soldiers on. He keeps saying that if Bram built a *boat* for his family, dammit, he's going to build a flat for his. And it's such a strange thing to hear, because I'd always thought Bram built the boat for Yael.

The plumber came last night, we thought, to finish the bath and shower installations, only to tell us he couldn't install the new tub that had finally arrived until we had a shower body. And we can't finish tiling the bathroom and move on to the kitchen—which the plumber said will probably also need all new pipes—until we have a shower.

For the most part, Daniel has approached the renovation with the sheer enthusiasm of a child building a sand castle at the beach. Every other night, when he and Fabiola Skype, he lugs his battered laptop around the flat, showing off all the latest modifications, discussing furniture placement (she's big into feng shui) and colors (pale blue for their room; butter yellow for the baby's).

But during those semi-nightly calls, you can see the bump is growing. After the plumber left, Daniel admitted he could almost hear the baby inside, ticking like one of those old alarm clocks. "Ready or not, here he comes," he'd said, shaking his head. "Forty-seven years, you'd think I'd be ready."

"Maybe you're never ready until it's upon you," I'd said.

"Very wise, little man," he'd said. "But goddamn it, if *I'm* not ready, I'm going to have the *flat* ready."

"Go on ahead, take mine," I tell Daniel now, swinging off my bike. It's the same beat-up old workhorse I bought off a junkie when I first came back to Amsterdam last year. It stayed locked up outside Bloemstraat all those months I was in India, no worse for wear. When I started working on the flat, I brought it back to Amsterdam, along with the rest of my things, all of which fit on the bottom two shelves of the bookshelf in the baby's room. I don't have much: Some clothes. A few books. The Ganesha statue Nawal gave me. And Lulu's watch. It still ticks. I hear it in the night sometimes.

Problem solved, Daniel is bright sunshine again. With a gappy grin, he hops onto my bike, and takes off pedaling, waving behind him, almost slamming into an oncoming moto. I wheel his bike off the narrow alley and turn onto the wide canal of the Kloveniersburgwal. I'm in an area sandwiched between the shrinking Red Light District and the university. I head in the direction of the university, more likely to find bike repair shops there. I pass an English-language bookstore I've ridden by a few times before, always somewhat curious. On the stoop is a box of one-euro books. I poke through—it's mostly American paperbacks, the kind of thing I read in a day and traded when I was traveling. But at the bottom of the box, like a displaced refugee, is a copy of *Twelfth Night.*

I know I probably won't read it. But I have a bookshelf now for the first time since college, even if it's only temporary.

I go inside to pay. "Do you know of a bike repair place nearby?" I ask the man behind the counter.

"Two blocks down, on Boerensteeg," he says, without looking up from his book.

"Thanks." I slide over the Shakespeare.

He glances at the cover, then looks up. "You're buying this?" He sounds skeptical.

"Yeah," I say, and then by way of an explanation I don't need to give, I tell him I was in the play last year. "I played Sebastian."

"You did it in English?" he asks, in English, with that strange hybrid accent of someone who's lived abroad a long time.

"Yeah," I say.

"Oh." He goes back to his book. I hand him a euro.

I'm almost out the door when he calls out: "If you do Shakespeare, you should check out the theater down the way. They put on some decent Shakespeare plays in English in Vondelpark in the summer. I saw that they're holding auditions this year."

He says it casually, dropping the suggestion like a piece of litter. I ponder it there, on the ground. Maybe it's worthless, maybe not. I won't know unless I pick it up.

Thirty-five

"Name."

"Willem. De Ruiter." It comes out a whisper.

"Come again."

I clear my throat. Try again. "Willem de Ruiter."

Silence. I can feel my heartbeat, in my chest, my temple, my throat. I can't remember ever being nervous like this before and I don't quite understand it. I've never had stage fright. Not even that first time with the acrobats, not even going on with Guerrilla Will, in French. Not even the first time Faruk shouted action and the cameras rolled and I had to speak Lars Von Gelder's lines, in Hindi.

But now, I can barely say my name out loud. It's as if, unbeknownst to me, there is a volume switch on me and someone has turned it all the way down. I squint my eyes and try to peer into the audience, but the bright lights are rendering whoever is out there invisible.

I wonder what they're doing. Are they looking at the ridiculous headshot I scrambled to put together? Daniel took it of me in the Sarphatipark. And then we'd printed my Guerrilla Will stats on the back. It doesn't look half bad from a distance. I have several plays to my credit, all of them Shakespearian. It's only if you inspect it closely you see that the picture is shitty quality, pixelated to the extreme, taken on a phone and printed at home. And my acting credentials, well, Guerrilla Will isn't exactly repertory theatre. I'd seen some of the headshots of the other actors. They came from all over Europe—the Czech Republic, Germany, France and the UK, as well as here—and had real plays under their belts. Better photos, too.

I take a deep breath. At least I *have* a head shot. Thanks to Kate Roebling. I called her at the last minute for advice because I've never auditioned before. With Guerrilla Will, Tor decided what role you'd play. There was some sniping about this, but I didn't care. The money was split equally, no matter how many lines you had.

"Ahh, yes, Willem," a disembodied voice says. It sounds bored before I've even begun. "What will you be reading for us today?"

The play being produced this summer is *As You Like It*, one I've never seen or heard much about. When I stopped in the theater last week, they told me I could prepare any Shakespearian monologue. In English. Obviously. Kate had told me to take a look at *As You Like It*. That I might find something really meaty in it.

"Sebastian, from *Twelfth Night*," I say. I decided to put together three shorter Sebastian speeches. Easiest to do that.

It was the last part I played. And I still remembered most of the lines.

"Whenever you're ready."

I try to remember Kate's words, but they swirl in my head like a foreign language I barely know. *Choose something you feel? Be who you are, not who they want you to be? Go big or go home?* And there was something else, something she told me before she rang off. It was important. But I can't remember it now. At this point, it'll be enough to remember my lines.

A throat clears. "Whenever you're ready." It's a woman's voice this time, in a tone that says: *Get on with it.*

Breathe. Kate said to breathe. That much I remember. So I breathe. And then I begin:

"By your patience, no. My stars shine darkly over me: the malignancy of my fate might perhaps distemper yours."

The first lines come out. Not too bad. I continue.

"Therefore I shall crave of you your leave that I may bear my evils alone."

The words start to flow out of me. Not as they did last summer in that endless array of parks and squares and plazas. Not haltingly, as they did in Daniel's bathroom, where I practiced them all weekend, to the mirror, to the tiles, and on occasion, to Daniel himself.

"If the heavens had been pleased, would we had so ended!"

The words come differently now. Understood in a fresh way. Sebastian is not just some aimless drifter, going where the wind blows him. He's someone recovering, rubbed raw and unsure by his spate of bad fortune, by the malignancy of his fate.

"She bore a mind that envy could not but call fair," I say and it's Lulu I see, on that hot English night, the last time I spoke these words in front of an audience. The faint smile on her lips.

"She is drowned already sir, with salt water, though I seem to drown her remembrance again with more."

And then it's over. There's no applause, only a loud silence. I can hear my breathing, my heartbeat, still hammering. Aren't the nerves supposed to go away once you are on stage? Once you've finished?

"Thank you," the woman says. Her words are clipped, generic, no actual gratitude in them. For a second, I think perhaps I should thank them.

But I don't. I leave the stage in a bit of a daze wondering what just happened. As I walk up the aisle, I see the director and producer and stage manager (Kate told me whom to expect) already conferring about someone else's headshot. Then I'm squinting in the bright light of the lobby. I rub my eyes. I'm unsure of what to do next.

"Glad that's over?" a skinny guy asks me in English.

"Yeah," I say reflexively. Only it's not true. Already, I'm starting to feel this melancholy set in, like the first cold fall day after a hot summer.

"What brought about the change of mind?" Kate had asked me on the phone. We hadn't been in any kind of contact since Mexico, and when I told her my plans, she sounded surprised.

"Oh, I don't know." I'd explained to her about finding *Twelfth Night* and then being told about the auditions, about being in the right place at the right time.

"So how'd it go?" the skinny guy asks me now. He has a copy of *As You Like It* in his hand, and his knee is thumping, up-down-up-down.

I shrug. I have no idea. Truly. I don't.

"I'm going for Jaques. What about you?"

I look at the play, which I haven't even read. I just figured I'd get what they gave me, as it always was with Tor. With a sinking feeling, I begin to suspect that wasn't the right way to go.

And it's then I remember what Kate said on the phone, after I explained the roundabout way I'd come to audition.

"*Commit*, Willem. You have to *commit*. To something."

Like so many of the important things these days, the memory comes too late.

Thirty-six

———

A week goes by, I hear nothing. The skinny guy I'd spoken to, Vincent, had said there'd be a series of callbacks before final casting. I don't get called. I put it behind me and get back to work on Daniel's flat, channeling so much energy into my tiling that Daniel and I finish the bathroom a couple of days ahead of schedule and get started on the kitchen. We take the metro out to IKEA to pick cabinets. We're in a showcase kitchen with cabinets the color of red nail varnish when my phone rings.

"Willem, this is Linus Felder from the Allerzielentheater."

My heart thuds like I'm on stage all over again.

"I need you to learn Orlando's opening speech and come in tomorrow morning at nine. Can you manage that?" he asks.

Of course I can manage it. I want to tell him that I'll more than manage it. "Sure," I say. And before I have a chance to ask any particulars, Linus hangs up.

"Who was that?" Daniel asks.

"The stage manager from that play I auditioned for. He wants me to come back in. To read for Orlando. The lead."

Daniel jumps up and down like an excited child, knocking over the prop mixer in the show kitchen. "Oh, shit." He pulls us away, whistling innocently.

I leave Daniel in IKEA and spend the rest of the day in the drizzle at the Sarphatipark, memorizing the speech. When it's a decent hour in New York, I call Kate for more advice but I wake her up because it turns out she's in California now. Ruckus is about to start a six-week tour of *Cymbeline* on the West Coast before coming to the UK in August for various festivals. When I hear this, I'm almost embarrassed to ask her for help. But, generous as always, she takes a few minutes to tell me what to expect on a callback. I might read a bunch of scenes and a bunch of parts, opposite several actors, and even though they've asked me to read Orlando, I shouldn't assume that's the role I'm up for. "But it's promising they've asked you to read him," she says. "It's quite a role for you."

"How do you mean?"

She sighs, noisily. "You *still* haven't read the play?"

I'm embarrassed all over again. "I will, I promise. Later today."

We talk a little more. She says she's planning on spending nonfestival weekends traveling out of the UK, so maybe she'll come to Amsterdam. I tell her she's welcome any time. And then she reminds me again to read the play.

Late that night, after I've read the opening monologue so many times I could recite it in my sleep, I start on the rest of the play. I'm falling asleep at this point and it's a little difficult to get into. I try to see what Kate means about Orlando. I suppose it's that he meets a girl and falls in love with her and then meets her again but she's disguised. Except Orlando gets a happy ending.

When I arrive at the theater the next morning, it's almost empty, and dark except for a single lamp burning on the stage. I sit down in the last seat, and a short while later, the house lights flicker on. Linus strolls in, clipboard in hand, and behind him, Petra, the diminutive director.

There are no pleasantries. "Whenever you're ready," Linus says.

This time, I am ready. I'm determined to be.

Except I'm not. I get the lines right, but as I say one, then the next, I can hear myself say them and then I wonder how they sounded, did I hit the right beat? And the more I do that, the stranger the words start to sound, in the way that a perfectly normal word can start to sound like gibberish. I try to focus, but the harder I try, the harder it becomes, and then I hear a cricket chirping somewhere backstage and it sounds like the lobby of the Bombay Royale, and then I'm thinking about Chaudhary and his cot and Yael and Prateek and I'm everywhere in the world except in this theater.

By the time I finish, I'm furious with myself. All that practice, and it was for shit. The Sebastian monologue, which

I didn't even care that much about, was infinitely better than this.

"Can I try that again?" I ask.

"No need," Petra says. I hear her and Linus murmuring.

"Really. I know I could do better." There's a jaunty smile on my face, which may be my finest acting of the day. Because really, I don't know that I could do better. This *was* me trying.

"It was fine," Petra barks. "Come back Monday at nine. Linus will get your paperwork before you leave."

Is that it? Did I just get the part of Orlando?

Maybe I shouldn't be so surprised. After all, it *was* that easy with the acrobats and with Guerrilla Will and even with Lars Von Gelder. I should be elated. I should be relieved. But, weirdly, all I feel is let down. Because this matters to me now. And something tells me if it matters, maybe it shouldn't be easy.

Thirty-seven

"Hey, Willem, how are you feeling today?"

"I'm fine, Jeroen. How are you?"

"Oh, you know, the gout is acting up." Jeroen pounds his chest and heaves a cough.

"Gout is in your leg, you twat," Max says, sliding into the seat next to me.

"Oh, right." Jeroen flashes her his most charming smile as he limps away, laughing.

"What a tosser!" Max says, dropping her bag at my feet. "If I have to kiss him, I swear, I might puke on the stage."

"Pray for Marina's health then."

"Wouldn't mind kissing her though." Max grins and looks at Marina, the actress who plays Rosalind opposite Jeroen's Orlando. "Ahh, lovely Marina, self-serving though it is, wouldn't want her to fall ill. She's so lovely. And, besides if she couldn't go on, I'd have to kiss that git. *He's* the one who I want to get sick."

"But he doesn't get sick," I tell Max, as though she needs reminding. Since being cast as his understudy, I have heard, endlessly, relentlessly, how in his dozen years of doing theater, Jeroen Gosslers has never, ever missed a performance, not even when he was throwing up with the flu, not even when he had lost his voice, not even when his girlfriend went into labor with their daughter hours before curtain. In fact, Jeroen's spotless record is apparently why I was given this shot in the first place, after the actor originally cast as an understudy booked a Mentos ad that would've required him missing three rehearsals to shoot the commercial. Three rehearsals, for an understudy who will never go on. Petra demands everything of her understudies, while at the same time demanding nothing of them.

As required, I've been at the theater every day since that very first table read, when the cast sat around a long wooden scuffed table on the stage, going through the text line by line, parsing meaning, deconstructing what this word meant, how that line should be interpreted. Petra was surprisingly egalitarian, open to almost anyone's opinions about what Sad Lucretia meant or why Rosalind persisted on keeping up her disguise for so long. If one of Duke Frederick's men wanted to interpret an exchange between Celia and Rosalind, Petra would entertain it. "If you are at this table, you have a right to be heard," she said, magnanimously.

Max and I, however, were conspicuously not at the table, but rather seated a few paces away, near enough to hear, but far enough that for us to participate in the discussion made us feel like interlopers. At first, I wondered if this was unintentional. But after hearing Petra repeat, several times, that "performing is so much more than speaking lines. It's about communicating with your audience through every gesture, every word unsaid," I understood it was completely intentional.

It seems almost quaint now, that I worried about it being *too* easy. Though it has turned out to be easy, only not in the way I thought. Max and I are the only understudies who don't have any actual roles in the play. We occupy a strange place in the cast. Semi-cast members. Shadow-cast members. Seat-warmers. Very few people in the cast speak to us. Vincent does. He got his Jaques after all. And Marina, who plays Rosalind, does as well, because she is uniquely gracious. And of course Jeroen makes it a point to talk to me every day, though I wish he wouldn't.

"So, what we got on today?" Max asks in her London cockney. Like me, she's a mutt; her father is Dutch from Surinam and her mother is from London. The cockney gets stronger when she drinks too much, though when she reads Rosalind, her English goes silky as the British Queen's.

"They're going over the fight scene choreography," I tell her.

"Oh, good. Maybe that ponce will actually get hurt." She laughs and runs a hand through her spiky hair. "Wanna run lines later? Won't be much of a chance once we start tech."

Soon, we move the set out of the theater for the final five days of tech rehearsals and dress rehearsals at the amphitheater in Vondelpark where the show will go up for six weekends. In two Fridays, we'll have our soft opening, and then Saturday, the hard opening. For the rest of the cast, this is the payoff for all the work. For Max and me, it's when we cash out, when any semblance of us being in the cast disappears. Linus has told us to make sure we know the entire play, all the blocking, by heart, and we're to trail Jeroen and Marina through the first tech rehearsal. This is as close to the action as we get. Not once has Linus or Petra given us any direction or asked us to run lines or gone over any aspect of the play. Max and I run lines incessantly, the two of us. I think it's how we make ourselves feel like we're actually a part of the production.

"Can we do the Ganymede parts? You know I like those best," Max says.

"Only because you get to be a boy."

"Well, natch. I prefer Rosalind when she's channeling her man. She's such a simp in the beginning."

"She's not a simp. She's in love."

"At first sight." She rolls her eyes. "A simp. She's ballsier when she's pretending to have balls."

"Sometimes it's easier to be someone else," I say.

"I should think so. It's why I became a bleeding actor." And then she looks at me and snorts with laughter. We may memorize the lines. We may know the blocking. We may show up. But neither one of us is an actor. We are seat warmers.

Max sighs and kicks her feet up onto the chair, daring a wordless reprimand from Petra and a follow-up telling off from Linus, or, as Max calls him, the Flunky.

Up on stage, Jeroen is arguing with the choreographer. "That's not really working for me. It doesn't feel authentic," he says. Max rolls her eyes again but I sit up to listen. This happened about every other day during the blocking, Jeroen not "feeling" the movements and Petra changing them, but Jeroen not feeling the new blocking either, so most of the time, she changed it back. My script is a crosshatch of scribbles and erasures, a road map of Jeroen's quest for authenticity.

Marina is sitting on the cement pilings on the stage next to Nikki, the actress playing Celia. They both look bored as they watch the fight choreography. For a second Marina catches my eye and we exchange a sympathetic smile.

"I saw that," Max says.

"Saw what?"

"Marina. She wants you."

"She doesn't even know me."

"That may be the case, but she was giving you fuck-me eyes at the bar last night."

Every night after rehearsal, most of the cast goes to a bar around the corner. Because we are either provocative or masochistic, Max and I go along with them. Usually we wind up sitting at the long wooden bar on our own or at a table with Vincent. There never seems to be room at the big table for Max and me.

"She was not giving me fuck-me eyes."

"She was giving *one* of us fuck-me eyes. I haven't gotten any Sapphic vibes off her, though you never can tell with Dutch girls."

I look at Marina. She's laughing at something Nikki said, as Jeroen and the actor playing Charles the wrestler work some fake punches with the fight choreographer.

"Unless you don't like girls," Max continues, "but I'm not getting that vibe off you either."

"I like girls just fine."

"Then why do you leave the bar with me every night?"

"Are you not a girl?"

Max rolls her eyes. "I am sorry, Willem, but charming as you are, it's not going to happen with us."

I laugh and give Max a wet kiss on the cheek, which she wipes off, with excess drama. Up on stage, Jeroen attempts a false punch at Charles and stumbles over himself. Max claps. "Mind that gout," she calls.

Petra swerves around, her sharp eyes full of disapproval. Max pretends to be absorbed in her script.

"Fuck running lines," Max whispers when Petra's attention is safely returned to the stage. "Let's get drunk."

That night, over drinks at the bar, Max asks me, "So why don't you?"

"Why don't I what?"

"Get off with a girl. If not Marina, one of the civilians at the bar."

"Why don't *you*?" I ask.

"Who's to say I don't?"

"You leave with me every night, Max."

She sighs, a big deep sigh that seems a lot older than Max,

who is only a year older than me. Which is why she doesn't mind seat-warming, she says. *My time will come.* She makes a slash mark over her chest. "Broken heart," she says. "Dykes take dog-years to heal."

I nod.

"So what about you?" Max says. "Broken heart?"

At times, I'd thought it was something like that—after all, I'd never been quite so strung out about a girl. But it's a funny thing because since that day with Lulu in Paris, I've reconnected with Broodje and the boys, I've visited my mother and have been talking to her again, and now I'm living with Uncle Daniel. And I'm acting. Okay, perhaps not acting, exactly. But not accidentally acting, either. And just in general, I'm better. Better than I've been since Bram died, and in some ways, better than I was even before that. No, Lulu didn't break my heart. But I'm beginning to wonder if in some roundabout way, she fixed it.

I shake my head.

"So what are you waiting for?" Max asks me.

"I don't know," I answer.

But one thing I do know: Next time, I'll know it when I find it.

Thirty-eight

Before Daniel leaves, we hang the last of the kitchen cabinets. The kitchen is almost finished. The plumber will come to install the dishwasher and we'll put in the backsplash and then that's that. "We're nearly there," I say.

"Just have to fix the buzzer and tackle your shit in the attic," Daniel says.

"Right. The shit in the attic. How much is there?" I ask. I don't remember putting that many boxes up there.

But Daniel and I lug down at least a dozen boxes with my name on them. "We should just throw it all away," I say. "I've gone this long without."

He shrugs. "Whatever you want."

Curiosity gets me. I open one box, papers and clothes from my dorm, not sure why I kept them. I put them in the garbage. I go through another and do the same. But then I come upon a third box. Inside are colored folders, the kind Yael used to keep patient records in, and I think the box must be mislabeled with my name. But then I see a sheet of paper sticking out of one of the folders. I pick it up.

The wind in my hair
Wheels bounce over cobblestones
As big as the sky

A memory rushes back: "It doesn't rhyme," Bram had said when I'd showed it to him, so full of pride because the teacher had asked me to read it to the entire class.

"It's not supposed to. It's a haiku," Yael had said, rolling her eyes at him and bestowing upon me a rare conspiratorial smile.

I pull out the folder. Inside is some of my old schoolwork, my early writing, math tests. I look in another folder: not schoolwork but drawings of a ship, a star of David that Saba taught me to do with two triangles. Pages and pages of this stuff. Unsentimental Yael and clutter-phobic Bram never displayed things like this. I assumed they threw it away.

In another box, I find a tin full of ticket stubs: airplane tickets, concert tickets, train tickets. An old Israeli passport, Yael's, full of stamps. Beneath that, I uncover a couple of very old black-and-white photos. It takes me a moment to recognize that they're of Saba. I've never seen him this young before. I hadn't realized any of these photos had survived the war. But it's unmistakably him. The eyes, they are Yael's. And mine, too. In one photo, he has his arm slung over a pretty girl, all dark hair and mystery eyes. He looks at her adoringly. She looks vaguely familiar, but it can't be Naomi, whom he didn't meet until after the war.

I look for more old photos of Saba and the girl, but find just an odd newspaper clipping of her in a plastic liner. I peer closer. She's wearing a fancy dress and is flanked by two men in tuxedoes. I hold it up to the light. The faded writing is in Hungarian, but there's a caption with names: Peter Lorre, Fritz Lang—Hollywood names I recognize—and a third name, Olga Szabo, which I don't.

I set the photos aside and keep digging. In another box, there are endless keepsakes. More papers. And then in another box, a large manila envelope. I open it up and out tumbles more photos: me, Yael, and Bram, on holiday in Croatia. I remember again how Bram and I walked to the docks every morning to buy fresh fish that no one really knew how to cook. There's another photo: us bundled up for skating the year the canals froze over and everyone took to their skates. And another: celebrating Bram's fortieth birthday with that massive party that spilled off the boat, onto the pier, onto the street, until all the neighbors came and it became a block party. There are the outtakes from the architectural magazine shoot, the shot of the three of us before I was cropped out. When I get to the bottom of the pile, there's one photo left, stuck to the envelope. I have to gently pry it away.

The breath that comes out of me isn't a sigh or a sob or a shudder. It's something alive, like a bird, wings beating, taking flight. And then it's gone, off into the quiet afternoon.

"Everything okay?" Daniel asks me.

I stare at the shot. The three of us, from my eighteenth birthday, not the photo I lost, but a different picture, taken from a different perspective, from someone else's camera. Another accidental picture.

"I thought I'd lost this," I say, gripping the picture.

Daniel cocks his head to the side and scratches at his temple. "I'm always losing things, and then I find them again in the strangest places."

Thirty-nine

A few days later, I leave for rehearsal and Daniel leaves for the airport. It's strange to think that when I come back that night, Daniel will be gone. Though I won't have the flat to myself for long. Broodje has been in The Hague for most of the summer on an internship, and now he's in Turkey visiting Candace, who's on a two-week trip there with her grandparents. When he comes back, he'll stay here with me until he and Henk move into their new flat in Utrecht in the fall.

Rehearsal today is frenzied and frenetic. The set is being broken down, transported to the park for tomorrow's tech, and the lack of scenery seems to have unhinged everyone. Petra is a whirlwind of terror, yelling at the actors, yelling at the tech guys, yelling at Linus, who looks like he would like to take cover under his clipboard.

"Poor Flunky," Max says. "For someone menopausal,

Petra seems like she's on the rag. She smashed Nikki's mobile."

"Really?" I ask Max, sliding into our usual seats.

"Well you know how she is if you put your phone on in the 'sacred rehearsal room.' But I heard she's extra uppity because Geert said 'Mackers' in the theater earlier."

"Mackers?"

"The Scottish Play," she says. When I fail to understand she mouths *Macbeth*. "Very bad mojo to say it in a theater."

"You believe that?"

"I believe you don't mess with Petra the day before the first tech."

Jeroen walks by. He looks at me and feigns a cough.

"That the best you can do?" Max calls after him. She turns to me. "And he calls himself an actor."

Linus has the cast do an entire run-through. It's a mess. Lines are forgotten. Cues are missed. Blocking is flubbed. "*The curse of Mackers*," Max whispers.

By six o'clock, Petra is in such a state that Linus lets us all go early. "Get a good night's sleep," he says. "Tomorrow is a long day. Call is at ten."

"It's too early to go to the bar," Max says. "Let's go eat and then go dancing or hear a band play. We can see who's on at Paradiso or Melkweg."

We ride over to the Leidseplein. Max is beside herself because some musician who was once in a famous band is playing solo tonight at the Paradiso and there's still tickets left. We buy a pair. Then we wander around the square, which this time of year is ground zero for tourists. There's a crowd of them surrounding some street performers.

"It's probably just those bloody Peruvian musicians," Max says. "Do you know, when I was little, I thought it was the same troupe, following me. Took me ages to work out they were clones." She laughs and knocks her head with her knuckles. "I can be right thick sometimes."

It's not the Peruvians. It's a group of jugglers. They're not bad, juggling all kinds of typically spiked flaming things. We watch for a while, and when the hat passes, I toss in a handful of coins.

We turn to leave and Max pokes me in the side. "Now's the real show," she says. I turn around and see who she's talking about: a woman has her legs wrapped around one of the jugglers' hips, her arms tangled in his hair. "Get a room," Max jokes.

I watch them a moment longer than I ought to. And then the girl drops down and turns around. She spots me and I spot her, and we do a double take.

"Wills?" she calls

"Bex?" I call.

"*Wills?*" Max repeats.

Dragging the juggler behind her, Bex comes up to me and gives me a big theatrical hug and kiss. It's quite a change since the last time I saw her when she would barely shake my hand. She introduces me to Matthias. I introduce her to Max. "Your girlfriend?" Bex asks, sending Max into a theatrical howl of protestation.

After a bit of chit-chat, we run out of things to say, because we never really did have that much to say even when we were sleeping together. "We should go. Matthias needs lots of *rest* before so he can *perform*." Bex gives an obvious wink in case anyone wasn't clear about what kind of resting and what kind of performing she was referring to.

"Okay then." We kiss, kiss, kiss good-bye.

We're walking away when Bex calls out. "Hey, did Tor ever find you?"

I stop. "Tor was looking for me?"

"She was trying to track you down. Apparently some letter came for you at Headingley."

It's like a switch is thrown, the way my body surges. "At Headingley?"

"Tor's place in Leeds," Bex says.

I know where Headingley is. But I rarely gave anyone a mailing address at all, and I don't remember ever giving anyone Tor's home address, which was the occasional Guerrilla Will headquarters, where we'd go to rehearse or recuperate. There's no reason on earth to think she'd send me a letter there, that she'd know to send me a letter there. But still, I walk back toward Bex. "A letter? From whom?"

"Dunno. But Tor was quite keen to get it to you. She said she tried emailing you but you were unresponsive. Imagine that?"

I ignore the dig. "When?"

She scratches her brow, trying to dislodge the memory. "I can't remember. It was a bit ago. Wait, when were we in Belfast?" she asks Matthias.

He shrugs. "Around Easter, wasn't it?"

"No. I think it was earlier. Around Shrove Tuesday," Bex says. She throws up her hands. "Some time around February. I remember pancakes. Or March. Or maybe it was April. Tor said she tried emailing you and got no reply so she wanted to know if *I* knew how to reach you." She widens her eyes, to show the absurdity of such a notion.

March. April. When I was in India, traveling, and my email account got infected with that virus. I switched to a new address after that. I haven't checked the old account in months. Maybe it's right there. Maybe it's been there all along.

"Don't suppose you know who the letter was from?"

Bex looks peeved, bringing back a bunch of memories. When it didn't last between us, and Bex had been nasty the rest of the season, Skev had made fun of me: "Didn't you ever hear? Don't shit where you eat, man."

"No idea," Bex tells me in a bored tone that seems practiced, so I'm unsure whether she doesn't know or does but won't say. "If you're so interested, you can just ask Tor." She laughs then. It's not friendly. "Though good luck getting her before fall."

Part of Tor's "method" was to try to live as close to Shakespearian times as possible while she was on the road. She refused to use a computer or a phone, though she would sometimes borrow someone else's to send an email or make a call if it was important. She didn't watch TV or listen to an iPod. And though she obsessively checked the weather reports, which seemed a rather modern innovation, she checked them in the newspapers, which somehow made it fair game because newspapers were around in seventeenth-century England, so she said.

"Don't suppose you have any idea what she did with it?" My heart has sped up, as if I've been running, and I feel breathless, but I force myself to sound as bored as Bex, for fear that if I make the letter sound important, she won't tell me anything.

"She might've sent it to the boat."

"The boat?"

"The one you used to live on."

"How'd she even know about the boat?"

"Good Christ, Wills, how should I know? Presumably you told someone about it. You did live with everyone for a year, more or less."

I told one person about the boat. Skev. He was going to Amsterdam and asked if I could hook him up with any free places to stay. I mentioned a few squats and also said if the key was still in its hiding place, and no one else was there, he could camp on the boat.

"Yeah, but I haven't lived on that boat for years."

"Well it's obviously not that important," Bex says. "Otherwise whoever wrote it would have known where to find you."

Bex is wrong but she's also right. Because Lulu should've known where to find me. And then I stop myself. Lulu. After all this time? The letter's more likely from a tax collector.

"What was all that about?" Max asks after Bex and Matthias have gone.

I shake my head. "I'm not sure." I look across the square. "Do you mind? I need to duck into an Internet café for a second."

"Okay," she says. "I'll grab a coffee."

I log onto my old email account. There's not much there but junk. I go back to the spring, when it got infected with that virus, and there's a pocket of nothing. Four weeks of messages that have just vanished. I try the bulk bin. Nothing there. Out of habit before I sign off, I scroll back for the emails from Bram and Saba, relieved to find them still there. Tomorrow, I'm going to print them out and also forward them to my new account. In the meantime, I change the settings on my old account to forward all new mail to my current address.

I check my current email account, even though Tor wouldn't have known about it because I only told a handful of people the new address. I search the inbox, the junk mail. There's nothing.

I send Skev a quick note, asking him to ring me. Then I send a note to Tor as well, asking about the letter, what it said, where she sent it. Knowing Tor, I won't get a response until the fall. By that point, it'll have been more than a year since I met Lulu. Any sane person would say it's too late. It already felt too late that first day, when I woke up in the hospital. But even so, I've kept looking.

I'm still looking.

Forty

The tech rehearsal is a monster. Aside from lines, plenty of which get forgotten in the new environment, everything has to be relearned and reblocked on the amphitheater stage. All day long, I stand behind Jeroen, Max behind Marina, as they fumble through their various scenes. Once again we're like their shadows. Except none of us has a shadow because there's no sun today, just a steady drizzle that has put everyone in a sour mood. Jeroen hasn't even made a joke about his malady of the day.

"It makes you wonder whose brilliant idea this was," Max says. "Outdoor bloody Shakespeare. In Holland, where English isn't even the language and it rains all the time."

"You forget, the Dutch are the eternal optimists," I tell her.

"Is that true?" she asks me. "I thought they were the eternal pragmatists."

I don't know. Maybe *I'm* the optimist. I checked my email when I got back from the Paradiso last night and again before I left this morning for rehearsal. There was an email from Yael, and a forwarded joke from Henk, and a bunch of the usual junk, but nothing from Skev or Tor. What exactly did I expect?

I'm not even sure what there is to be optimistic about. If the letter is from her, what's to say it's not a long-distance piss off? She'd have every right.

We break for lunch and I check my phone. Broodje's texted to say he's heading off on some wooden sailing boat and he'll be incommunicado for a few days, but he'll be back in Amsterdam next week. Daniel's also texted to let me know he's arrived safely in Brazil, and forwarded a photo of Fabiola's belly. Tomorrow, I vow, I'm getting a phone that accepts pictures.

Petra forbids mobile phones in rehearsal. But when she's talking to Jeroen, I put my ringer to vibrate and slip my phone into my pocket anyway. Optimist indeed.

Around five o'clock, the drizzle lets up and Linus resumes the rehearsal. We're having trouble with the light cues, which we can't see. Because the show starts at dusk and goes into the night, the lights come up halfway through, so tomorrow's rehearsal will be from two in the afternoon to midnight, so we can make sure the second half, the in-darkness part, is properly lit.

At six, my phone vibrates. I pull it out of my pocket. Max widens her eyes at me. "Cover me," I whisper, and scuttle off to the wings.

It's Skev.

"Hey, thanks for getting back to me," I whisper.

"Where are you?" he asks, his voice dropped to a whisper, too.

"Amsterdam? You?"

"Back in Brighton. Why are we whispering?"

"I'm in a rehearsal."

"For what?"

"Shakespeare."

"In Amsterdam. Fuck, that's cool. I gave that shit up. I'm working at a Starbucks now."

"Oh, shit, sorry."

"Nah, it's all good, man."

"Listen, Skev, I can't talk long but I ran into Bex."

"Bex." He whistles. "How is that sweet thing?"

"Same as always, hooked up with a juggler. She mentioned a letter Tor was trying to get to me. Earlier in the year."

There's a pause. "Victoria. Man. She is something else."

"I know."

"I asked if I could come back and she said no. Just that one time. Off season. Don't shit where you eat."

"I know. I know. About that letter . . ."

"Yeah, man, I don't know anything about it."

"Oh."

"Victoria wouldn't tell me. Said it was personal. You know how she gets." He sighs. "So I just told her to send it you. I gave her the address on the boat. I didn't know if you could get mail on the boat."

"You could. We could. We did."

"So you got the letter?"

"No, Skev. That's why I'm calling."

"Well, it must be at the boat, man."

"But we don't live there anymore. Haven't done for a while."

"Oh, shit. Forgot it was empty. Sorry about that."

"No worries, man."

"Break a leg with your Shakespeare and shit."

"Yeah, you too—with your cappuccinos and all."

He laughs. Then we say good-bye.

I go back to the rehearsal. Max is looking crazed. "I told them you had to puke. The Flunky is mad you didn't ask first. I wonder if he calls Petra for permission before he makes love to his wife."

It's an image I do my best not to conjure. "I owe you. I'll tell Linus it was a false alarm."

"You gonna tell me what this is about?"

I think of Lulu, all the wild-goose chases this year that have led nowhere. Why would this be anything else?

"Probably just what you said: a false alarm," I tell Max.

Except that *probably* becomes a pebble in my shoe, aggravating me for the rest of the day, making it hard to keep from thinking about the letter, where it is, what it says, who it's from. By the time rehearsal ends, I feel this sort of urgency to know; so even though the rain has returned, and even though I'm bone tired, I decide to try Marjolein. She doesn't answer her phone and I don't want to wait until tomorrow. She lives close by, on the ground floor of a wide house in a posh neighborhood at the south end of the park. She's always told me to drop by any time.

"Willem," she says, opening the door. She has a glass of wine in one hand, a cigarette in the other, and she doesn't seem so happy that I've dropped by. I'm dripping wet, and she doesn't invite me in. "What brings you here?"

"Sorry to bother you but I'm trying to find a letter."

"A letter?"

"That was sent to the boat, some time in the spring."

"Why are you still getting mail at the boat?"

"I'm not. Someone just sent it there."

She shakes her head. "If it went to the boat, it would've been forwarded to the office and then on to the address you provided us."

"In Utrecht?"

She sighs. "Probably. Can you call me in the morning?"

"It's important."

She sighs. "Try Sara. She handles the mail."

"Do you have Sara's number?"

"I'd have thought *you'd* have Sara's number," she says.

"Not for a long time now."

She sighs. Then reaches for her mobile. "Don't start anything up with her."

"I won't," I promise.

"Right. You're a changed man." I can't quite get whether she's being sarcastic or not.

Inside, the music changes, from mellow jazz to something

wilder with screaming trumpets. Marjolein looks longingly inside. I realize that she's not alone.

"I'll let you go," I say.

She leans forward to kiss good-bye. "Your mother will be pleased I saw you."

She starts to close the door. "Can I ask you something? About Yael?"

"Sure," she says absently, her attention already back in the warm house and on whomever's waiting in there.

"Did she, I don't know, do things, to help me, that I didn't know about?"

Her face is half hidden in shadows, but her toothy smile shines in the reflected light. "What did she say?"

"She didn't *say* anything."

Marjolein shakes her head. "Then neither can I." She starts to close the door. Then she stops. "But did you consider in all those months you were gone, why your bank account never ever went to zero?"

I hadn't considered it, not really. I rarely used my bank card but when I did, it always worked.

"Someone was always watching," Marjolein says. When she shuts the door, she's still smiling.

Forty-one

Utrecht

Everything takes too long. The train is late. The bike share line is too long. So I catch a bus instead and it stops to pick up every old lady in town. I shouldn't have left so late, but it was already late when I got hold of Sara this morning. Then it took a bit of cajoling before she finally remembered there was a letter. No, she didn't read it. No, she didn't remember where it came from. But she thinks she forwarded to the address on file. The one in Utrecht. Not that long ago.

By the time I get to Bloemstraat, it's almost noon. The second tech rehearsal is at 2:00 back in Amsterdam. I have nothing but time in my life, but never enough of it when I need it.

I ring the eyeball bell. There's no answer. I have no idea who lives here anymore. I texted Broodje on the train over but he didn't answer. Then I remembered that he's in the middle of the Aegean somewhere. With Candace. Whose name he knows, whose telephone number and email address he got before he left Mexico.

The front door is locked but I still have my key and it still works. The first good sign.

"Hello," I call, my voice echoing through the empty house. It no longer looks like the place I lived in. No more lumpy sofa. No more boy smell. Even the Picasso flowers are gone.

There's a dining room table, with the post scattered all over it. I rifle through the stacks as quickly as possible, but I see nothing, so I make myself slow down and methodically go through each piece of mail, dividing it into neat piles: for Broodje, for Henk, for W, even some for Ivo, who's still getting letters here, for a couple of unfamiliar girls who must be living here now. There is some mail for me, mostly dead letters from the university and a travel catalog from the agency I used to book our Mexico tickets.

I look up the stairs. Perhaps the letter is up there. Or in the attic in my old room. Or in one of the cabinets. Or maybe it isn't the one Sara forwarded. Maybe it's still back on the Nieuwe Prinsengracht. Or somewhere in Marjolein's office.

Or maybe there is no letter from her. Maybe it's just another false hope I've conjured for myself.

I hear ticking. On the mantel, where the Picasso used to hang, there's an old-fashioned wooden clock, like the kind Saba once had in his Jerusalem apartment. It was one of the few pieces Yael kept after he died. I wonder where it is now.

It's half past twelve. If I want to get the train back in time for the tech rehearsal, I have to leave now. Otherwise, I'll be late. And being late for tech? The only thing worse in Petra's book would be not showing for a performance. I think of the original understudy, replaced because he had to miss three rehearsals. It's too late for her to replace me, but that's not to say she can't fire me. I'm nothing but a shadow, anyhow.

Being fired won't make any material difference in my life right now. Except I don't *want* to be fired. And more than that, I don't want to hand over that decision to Petra. If I'm late, that's exactly what will happen.

The house seems huge all of a sudden, like it would take years to search all the rooms. The moment seems even bigger.

I've given up on Lulu before. In Utrecht. In Mexico. But that felt like surrendering. Like it was *me* I was really giving up on. This feels different, somehow. Like maybe Lulu brought me to this place, and for the first time in a long time, I'm on the cusp of something real. Maybe *this* is the point of it all. Maybe this is where the road is meant to end.

I think of the postcards I left in her suitcase. I'd written *sorry* on one of them. Only now do I understand what I really should've written was *thank you*.

"Thank you," I say quietly to the empty house. I know she'll never hear it, but somehow that seems besides the point.

Then I drop my mail in the recycling and head back to Amsterdam, closing the door behind me.

PART TWO

One Day

Forty-two

The phone is ringing. And I'm sleeping. Two things that shouldn't be happening at the same time. I open my eyes, fumble for the phone, but the ringing continues, crying out into the still night.

A light flicks on. Broodje, naked as a newborn, stands in front of me squinting in the yellow light of the lamp, and the lemony walls of the nursery. He holds out my phone. "It's for you," he mumbles, and then he flicks off the light and sleep-walks back to bed.

I put the phone to my ear and I hear the exact four words you don't want to hear on the other end of a middle-of-the-night phone call.

"There's been an accident."

My stomach plummets and I hear a whistling my ears as I wait to hear who. Yael. Daniel. Fabiola. The baby. Some subtraction in my family that I can no longer bear.

But the voice continues talking and it takes me a minute to slow my breathing and hear what is being said. *Bicycle* and *moto* and *ankle* and *fracture* and *performance* and *emergency* and it's then that I understand that it's not that kind of accident.

"Jeroen?" I say at last, though who else can it be? I want to laugh. Not because of the irony, but because of the relief.

"Yes, Jeroen," Linus snaps. Jeroen the invincible, felled by a drunken moto driver. Jeroen insistent he can go on anyhow, with his foot in a cast, and maybe he can, for next weekend's performances. But this weekend's? "We might have to cancel," Linus says. "We need you at the theater as soon as possible. Petra wants to see what you can do."

I rub my eyes. Light is peeking through the shades. It's not the middle of the night after all. Linus tells me to be at the theater—the actual theater, not the stage in Vondelpark—at eight.

"It's going to be a long day," he warns.

Petra and Linus hardly look up when I arrive at the theater. A sloe-eyed Marina offers a tired, sympathetic look. She's holding a roll and breaks off half and hands it to me. "Thank you," I say. "I didn't have time to eat."

"I figured as much," she says.

I sit down on the edge of the stage, alongside her. "So what happened?"

She arches her eyebrow. "Karma happened." She tucks

a piece of hair behind her ear. "I know it's his joke to brag about his perfect record, and I've heard him do it many times before and nothing's come of it." She pauses to dust the crumbs off her lap. "But you don't laugh at fate like that without fate eventually having the last laugh. The only problem is, it doesn't just affect him. It might shut down the remaining run."

"Shut it down? I thought it was just tonight's."

"Jeroen won't be able to perform either of this weekend's performances, and even if he can actually manage it in the boot cast he's apparently going to have to wear for the next six weeks, they'll have to reblock the whole thing. Plus, there are questions of insurance." She sighs. "It might be easier to just cancel."

My shoulders slump with the weight of that statement. So it falls to me. "I think I'm starting to believe in the Mackers curse," I tell Marina.

She looks at me, the worry in her eyes mixed with sympathy. She seems about to say something when Petra orders me to the stage.

Linus looks miserable. But Petra, she of the thousand tantrums, is actually calm, cigarette smoke swirling around her like a statue on fire. It takes me a minute to realize she's not calm. She's resigned. She's already written tonight off.

I climb onto the stage. I take a breath. "What can I do?" I ask her.

"We have the cast on standby for a full run-through later," Linus answers. "Right now, we'd like to run your scenes with Marina. See how those go."

Petra stubs out her cigarette. "We'll skip ahead to Act

One, Scene Two with Rosalind. I will read Celia. Linus will read Le Beau and the Duke. Let's start just before the fight with Le Beau's line."

"'Monsieur the challenger, the princesses call for you?'" Linus asks. Petra nods.

"I attend them with all respect and duty," I say, jumping right in with Orlando's next line.

There's a moment of surprise as they all look at me

"Young man, have you challenged Charles the wrestler?" Marina asks as Rosalind.

"No, fair princess; he is the general challenger: I come but in, as others do, to try with him the strength of my youth," I reply, not boastfully, as Jeroen does, but tempering the bravado with a little uncertainty, which I somehow now know is what Orlando must feel.

I've said these words hundreds of times in readings with Max, but they were just lines in a script, and I never stopped to figure out what it all meant because I never really had to. But just as Sebastian's monologue came alive during my audition months ago, the words seem charged with meaning all of a sudden. They become a language I know.

We go back and forth and then I get to Orlando's line: "I shall do my friends no wrong, for I have none to lament me, the world no injury, for in it I have nothing. " As I say the words, I feel a tiny catch of emotion in the back of my throat. Because I know what he means. For a minute, I think to swallow the emotion down, but I don't. I breathe into it, letting it carry me through the scene.

I'm feeling loose and good as we move onto the fight scene, in which I pantomime fighting an invisible opponent.

I know this part well. Orlando wins the fight, but he loses anyway. He is cast out of the duke's kingdom and warned that his brother wants to kill him.

We reach the end of the scene. Petra, Linus, even Marina, they all stare at me, not saying a thing.

"Shall we continue?" I ask. "On to Act Two?" They nod. I run that scene with Linus reading the part of Adam, and when I finish that, Petra clears her throat and asks me to take it from the beginning, Orlando's opening monologue, the one I flubbed so badly during my callback.

I don't flub it this time. When I finish, there is more silence. "So you're off book, that is clear," Linus says finally. "And the blocking?"

"Yes, that too," I say.

They look so incredulous. What do they think I've been doing all this time?

Warming a seat, comes my own answer. And maybe I shouldn't be so surprised by their surprise. Because isn't that exactly what I'd thought I'd been doing, too?

Petra and Linus excuse Marina and me. They have some things to discuss. If they decide to proceed with tonight's performance, there will be an all-cast rehearsal at the theater at noon, and I'll have to do an additional tech run-through at the amphitheater later in the day with just Linus.

"Sit tight. Keep your phone on," Linus says and he pats my back and gives me a look that's almost fatherly. "We'll speak soon."

Marina and I head to a nearby café for coffee. It's raining, and inside the windows are fogged up. We sit down at a table. I rub a circle of condensation off the window. Across the canal is the bookstore where I first found the copy of *Twelfth Night*. It's just opening up for the day. I tell Marina about the flat tire and stopping at the shop, the strange chain of events that led to me being Jeroen's understudy, and now possibly, playing Orlando.

"None of that has anything to do with that performance you just gave." She shakes her head and smiles, a private smile, and it's this, more than anything else, that makes me stop feeling like a member of the shadow cast. "You were holding out on us."

I don't know how to answer. Maybe I've been holding out on myself, too.

"You should tell him," she says, gesturing to the bookstore. "The guy who sold you the book and told you about the play. If you go on, you should tell him it's partly because of him."

If I go on, there are lots of people I'll have to tell.

"Wouldn't you want to know?" Marina continues. "That in some little way, something random you did had such an impact on someone's life? What do they call that? The Butterfly Effect?"

I watch the man open the bookstore. I should tell him. Though the person I really want to tell, the person who is somehow intricately tied up in all this, who has really led me to this, I can't tell.

"While we're confessing," Marina says, "I should tell you that I've been a little intrigued by you from the start, this mysterious actor who keeps to himself, whom no one has ever heard of, but who is good enough to get cast as the understudy."

Good enough? That surprises me. I'd thought it was the opposite.

"I have a strict policy of no showmances," she continues. "Nikki keeps saying you can be an exception because you're an understudy and not in the show, but now that you maybe are I'm even more intrigued." She gives me that private smile again. "Either we close tonight or we close in three weeks, but either way, after it's over maybe we can spend some time together?"

That surge of longing for Lulu is still in my bloodstream, like a drug wearing out its half life. Marina is not Lulu. But Lulu is not even Lulu. And Marina is amazing. Who knows what might happen?

I'm about to tell her yes, after we close, I'd like that, but I'm interrupted by the ringing of my phone. She glances at the number and smiles at me. "That's your fate calling."

Forty-three

So much to do. There's an all-cast rehearsal at noon. Then a tech run-through. I need to run back to the flat, grab some things, tell the boys. And Daniel. Yael.

Broodje is only waking up. Breathlessly, I tell him the news. By the time I've finished, he's already on his phone, calling the boys.

"Did you tell your ma?" he asks when he hangs up.

"I'm calling her now."

I calculate the time difference. It's not quite five o'clock in Mumbai, so Yael will still be working. I send her an email instead. While I'm at it, I send one to Daniel. At the last minute, I send one to Kate, telling her about Jeroen's accident, inviting her to tonight's show if she's at all in the area. I even invite her to stay with me and give her the address of the flat.

I'm about to log off when I do a quick scan of my inbox. There's a new message from an unfamiliar address and I think it's junk. Until I see the subject line: Letter.

My hand's shaking a bit as I click on the message. It's from Tor. Or relayed from Tor via some Guerrilla Will player who doesn't abide by the email ban as she does.

> *Hi Willem:*
>
> *Tor asked me to email you to say that she ran into Bex last week and Bex told her that you hadn't gotten that letter. Tor was pretty upset because the letter was important and she'd gone to a lot of trouble to try to get it to you. She wanted you to know it was from a girl you'd met in Paris who was looking for you because you'd dicked her over and pulled a runner. (Tor's words, not mine.) She said that you ought to know that actions have consequences. Again, Tor's words. Don't shoot the messenger. ☺ You know how she is.*
>
> *Cheers! Josie*

I sink down onto my bed as very different emotions battle it out. *Dicked her over, pulled a runner.* I feel Tor's anger. And Lulu's too. Shame and regret well up but then just stop there, held at bay by some invisible force. Because she's looking for me. Lulu is looking for me, too. Or she was. Maybe just to tell me to piss off. But she was looking for me like I was looking for her.

I don't know what to feel as I wander into the kitchen. It's all just too much for one day.

I find Broodje cracking eggs into a frying pan. "Want an *uitsmijter*?" he asks.

I shake my head.

"You should eat something. Keep your strength up."

"I have to go."

"Now? Henk and W are on their way over. They want to see you. Will you be around at all before your big debut?"

The rehearsal starts at noon and will take at least three hours, and then Linus said I'd have a break before I go for a run-through at the amphitheater at six. "I can probably get back here around four or five?"

"Great. We should have the party plans well under way by then."

"Party plans?"

"Willy, this is big." He pauses to look at me. "After the year you've had—the *years* you've had—we should celebrate this."

"Okay, fine," I say, still half dazed.

I go back into my room to pack up a change of clothes for under the costume, shoes to wear. I'm about to leave when I see Lulu's watch sitting on my shelf. I hold it in my hand. After all this time, it's still ticking. I hold it in my hand a moment longer. Then I slip it into my pocket.

Forty-four

At the theater, the rest of the cast has assembled. Max comes up behind me. *"I've got your back,"* she whispers.

I'm about to ask her what she means, and then I see what she means. For the better part of three months, I have been mostly invisible to many of these people, a shadow-cast member. And now, the spotlight is glaring and there's no safety in the shadows anymore. People are looking at me with a particular mix of suspicion and condescension, a familiar feeling from when I was traveling and walked through certain neighborhoods where my kind didn't tend to wander. As I did when I was traveling, I just act like I don't notice and carry on. Soon enough Petra is clapping her hands, gathering us together.

"We have no time to lose," Linus says. "We will do a modified run-through, skipping over scenes that Orlando is not in."

"So why did you call *all* of us in?" mutters Geert, who plays the swing roles of one of Frederick's men and Silvius; he has almost no scenes with Orlando.

"I know. Sitting around watching other people act is such a bloody waste of time," Max says, her voice so sincere that it takes Geert a few seconds to have the good sense to look chastened.

Max gives me a crooked smile. I'm glad she's here.

"I called everyone in," Petra says, with an exaggerated patience that lets you know she's reaching the end of her supply, "so you could all accustom yourself to the different rhythms of a new actor, and so we could all of us help Willem ensure that the transition between him and Jeroen is as seamless as possible. Ideally, you won't even be able to tell the difference."

Max rolls her eyes at this and once again I'm glad she's here.

"Now from the top, please," Linus says, tapping his clipboard. "There's no set and no marks so just do your best."

As soon as I step onto the stage, I feel relieved. This is where I'm meant to be. In Orlando's head. As we move through the play, I discover more things about Orlando. I discover how key that first scene when he and Rosalind meet is. It's just for a few moments, but they see something in each other, recognize something. And that the spark sustains the passion, for both of them, for the rest of the play. They don't see each other—knowingly see each other—again until the very end.

Such a dance that Shakespeare wrote into a handful of

pages of text. Orlando's about to fight a man far stronger than he is, but he peacocks in front of Rosalind and Celia to impress them. He's scared, he must be, but instead of showing it, he bluffs. He flirts. "Let your fair eyes and gentle wishes go with me to my trial," he says.

The world pivots on moments. And in this play, it's the moment when Rosalind says, "The little strength that I have, I would it were with you."

That one line. It cracks open his facade. It reveals what's underneath. Rosalind sees Orlando. He sees her. That's the whole play, right there.

I feel the lines like I haven't before, like I'm truly understanding Shakespeare's intentions. I feel as if there really was a Rosalind and an Orlando and I'm here to represent them. It isn't acting in a play. It goes back further than that. It's much bigger than me.

"Ten-minute break," Linus calls at the end of Act One. Everyone heads out for a smoke or a coffee. But I am reluctant to leave the stage.

"Willem," Petra calls to me. "A word."

She's smiling, which she rarely does, and at first I read it for pleasure, because isn't that what a smile communicates?

The theater empties out. It's just the two of us now. Not even Linus. "I want to tell you how impressed I am," she begins.

Inside I'm a little boy grinning on a birthday morning, about to get the presents. But I try to keep my face professional.

"With so little experience, to know the language so well.

We were taken with your ease with the language at your audition, but this . . ." She smiles again, only now I notice that it looks a bit like a dog baring its fangs. "And the blocking, you have it cold. Linus tells me that you even learned some of the fight choreography."

"I observed," I tell her. "I paid attention."

"Excellent. That's just what you needed to do." And there's that smile again. Only now do I begin to doubt it reflects any pleasure. "I spoke to Jeroen today," she continues.

I don't say anything but my gut twists. All this, and now Jeroen is going to lumber back with his cast.

"He's terribly embarrassed by what happened, but most of all he's disappointed to have let down his company."

"There's no one to blame. He was in an accident," I say.

"Yes. Of course. An accident. And he very much wants to be back for the last two weeks of the season and we will do our best to adapt to meet his needs, because that is what you do when you are part of a cast. Do you understand?"

I nod, even though I don't really understand what she's on about.

"I understand what you were trying to do up there with your Orlando."

Your Orlando. Something about the way she says that makes me feel like it won't be mine for much longer.

"But the role of the understudy is not to bring his own interpretation to the part," she continues. "It is to play the part as the actor you're replacing played it. So in effect, you aren't playing Orlando. You are playing Jeroen Gosslers playing Orlando."

But Jeroen's Orlando is all wrong, I want to say. It's all machismo and prancing and no revealing; and without vulnerability, Rosalind wouldn't love him, and if Rosalind doesn't love him, why should the audience care? I want to say: *Let me do this. Let me do it right this time.*

But I don't say any of that. And Petra just stares at me. Then, finally she asks: "Do you think you can manage that?"

Petra smiles again. How foolish of me—of all people—not to recognize her smile for what it was. "We can still cancel for this weekend," she says, her voice soft, the threat clear. "Our star has had an accident. No one would fault us."

Something given, something taken away. Does it always have to work like that?

The cast starts to drift back into the theater, the ten-minute break over, ready to get back to work, to make this happen. When they see me and Petra talking, they go quiet.

"Are we understood?" she asks, her voice so friendly it's almost singsong.

I look at the cast again. I look at Petra. I nod. We're understood.

Forty-five

When Linus releases us for the afternoon, I bolt for the door. "Willem," Max calls.

"Willem," Marina calls behind her.

I wave them off. I have to be fitted for my costume and then I have only a couple hours until Linus will meet me to go through my marks on the amphitheater stage. As for what Marina and Max have to say: if it's compliments of my performance, so Jeroen-like even Petra was impressed, I don't want to hear it. If it's questions about why I'm playing it like this, when I played it so differently before, then I really don't want to hear it.

"I have to go," I tell them. "I'll see you tonight."

They look wounded, each in their own way. But I just walk away from them.

Back at the flat, I find W, Henk, and Broodje busy at work, pages of yellow pad on the coffee table. "That's Femke in," Broodje is saying. "Hey, it's the star."

Henk and W start to congratulate me. I just shake my head. "What's all this?" I gesture to the project on the table.

"Your party," W says.

"My party?"

"The one we're throwing tonight," Broodje says.

I sigh. I forgot all about that. "I don't want a party."

"What do you mean you don't want a party?" Broodje asks. "You said it was okay."

"Now it's not. Cancel it."

"Why? Aren't you going on?"

"I'm going on." I go into my room. "No party," I call.

"Willy," Broodje yells after me.

I slam the door, lie down on the bed. I close my eyes and try to sleep, but that's not happening. I sit up and flip through one of Broodje's copies of *Voetbal International* but that's not happening either. I toss it back on my bookshelf. It lands next to a large manila envelope. The package of photos I unearthed from the attic last month.

I open the envelope, thumb through the pictures. I linger on the one of me and Yael and Bram from my eighteenth birthday. It's like an ache, how much I miss them. How much I miss her. I'm so tired of missing things I don't have.

I pick up the phone, not even calculating the time difference.

She answers straight away. And just like that time before, I'm at a loss for words. But not Yael. Not this time.

"What's wrong? Tell me."

"Did you get my email?"

"I haven't checked it. Is something wrong?"

She sounds panicked. I should know better. Out-of-the-blue phone calls. They require reassurance. "It's nothing like that."

"Nothing like what?"

"Like before. I mean, nobody is sick, though someone did break an ankle." I tell her about Jeroen, about my taking on his part.

"But shouldn't this make you happy?" she asks.

I thought it would make me happy. It did make me so happy this morning. Hearing about Lulu's letter made me happy this morning. But now that's worn off and all I feel is her recrimination. How far the pendulum can swing in one day. You'd think I'd know that by now. "It appears not."

She sighs. "But Daniel said you seemed so energized."

"You spoke to Daniel? About me?"

"Several times. I asked his advice."

"You asked *Daniel* for advice?" Somehow this is even more shocking than her asking him about me.

"I wondered if he thought I should ask you to come back here." She pauses. "To live with me."

"You want me to come back to India?"

"If you want to. You might act here. It seemed to go well for you. And we could find a bigger flat. Something big enough for both of us. But Daniel thought I should hold off. He thought you seemed to have found something."

"I haven't found anything. And you might've asked *me*." It comes out so bitter.

She must hear it, too. But her voice stays soft. "I *am* asking you, Willem."

And I realize she is. After all this time. Tears well up in

my eyes. I'm grateful, in that small moment, for the thousands of kilometers that separate us.

"How soon could I come?" I ask.

There's a pause. Then she gives the answer I need: "As soon as you want."

The play. I'll have to do it this weekend, and then Jeroen will come back or I can quit. "Monday?"

"Monday?" She sounds only a little bit surprised. "I'll have to ask Mukesh what he can do."

Monday. It's in three days. But what is there to stay for? The flat is finished. Soon enough Daniel and Fabiola will be back with the baby, and there won't be room for me.

"It's not too soon?" I ask.

"It's not too soon," she says. "I'm just grateful it's not too late."

There's a hitch in my throat and I can't speak. But I don't need to. Because Yael starts speaking. In torrents, apologizing for keeping me at arm's length, telling me what Bram always said, that it wasn't me, it was her, Saba, her childhood. All the things I already knew but just didn't really understand until now.

"Ma, it's okay." I stop her.

"It's not, though," she says.

But it is. Because I understand all the ways of trying to escape, how sometimes you escape one prison only to find you've built yourself a different one.

It's a funny thing, because I think that my mother and I may finally be speaking the same language. But somehow, now words don't seem as necessary.

Forty-six

I hang up the phone with Yael, feeling as though someone has opened a window and let the air in. This is how it is with traveling. One day, it all seems hopeless, lost. And then you take a train or get a phone call, and there's a whole new map of options opening up. Petra, the play, it had seemed like something, but maybe it was just the latest place the wind blew me. And now it's blowing back to India. Back to my mother. Where I belong.

I'm still holding the envelope of photos. Once again, I forgot to ask Yael about them. I look at the one of Saba and mystery girl and realize now why she looked familiar to me the first time I saw her. With her dark hair and playful smile and bobbed hair, she looks quite a bit like Louise Brooks, this . . . I grab the newspaper clipping . . . this Olga Szabo. Who was she? Saba's girlfriend? Was she Saba's one that got away?

I'm not quite sure what to do with them now. The safest thing would be to put them back in the attic, but that feels a little like imprisoning them. I could make copies of them and take the originals with me, but they still might get lost.

I stare at the picture of Saba. I flip to one of Yael. I think of the impossible life those two had together because Saba loved her so much and tried so hard to keep her safe. I'm not sure it's possible to simultaneously love something and keep it safe. Loving someone is such an inherently dangerous act. And yet, love, that's where safety lives.

I wonder if Saba understood this. After all, he's the one who always said: *The truth and its opposite are flip sides of the same coin.*

Forty-seven

It's half past four. I'm not due to meet Linus until six for a quick tech run through before the curtain. Out in the lounge, I hear Broodje and the boys. I don't want to face them. I can't imagine telling them I'm going back to India in three days.

I leave my phone on the bed and slip out the door, saying good-bye to the boys. Broodje gives me such a mournful look. "Do you even want us to go tonight?" he asks.

I don't. Not really. But I can't be that cruel. Not to him. "Sure," I lie.

Downstairs, I bump into my neighbor Mrs. Van Der Meer, who's on her way out to walk her dog. "Looks like we're getting some sun finally," she tells me.

"Great," I say, though this is one time I'd prefer rain. People will stay away in the rain.

But, sure enough, the sun is fighting its way through the

stubborn cloud cover. I make my way over to the little park across the street. I'm almost through the gates when I hear someone calling my name. I keep going. There are a thousand Willems. But the name gets louder. And then it yells in English. "Willem, is that you?"

I stop. I turn around. It can't be.

But it is. Kate.

"Jesus Christ, thank God!" she says, running up to me. "I've been calling you and there's no answer and then I came over but your stupid bell doesn't work. Why didn't you pick up?"

It feels like I sent her that email a year ago. From a different world. I'm embarrassed by it now, to have asked her to come all this way. "I left it in the flat."

"Good thing I saw your dog-walking neighbor and she said she thought you went this way. It's like one of your little accidents." She laughs. "It's a day of them. Because your email came at the most serendipitous moment. David was intent on dragging me to the most hideous sounding avant-garde *Medea* in Berlin tonight and I was desperately trying to find an excuse not to go, and then this morning I got your email so I came here instead. And I was on the plane when I realized I had no idea where you were performing. And you didn't answer your phone and I got a little panicky, so I thought I'd track you down. But now here we are and everything's good." She exaggeratedly wipes a hand across her brow. "Phew!"

"Phew," I say weakly.

Kate's radar goes up. "Or maybe not phew."

"Perhaps not."

"What is it?"

"Can I ask you to do something?" I've asked Kate so much already. But having her there? Broodje and the boys, they may not know any better. But Kate will. She can see through all the bullshit.

"Of course."

"Will you not go tonight?"

She laughs. As if this is a joke. And then she realizes it's not a joke "Oh," she says, turning serious. "Are they not putting you on? Did the other Orlando's ankle mysteriously heal?"

I shake my head. I look down and see that Kate is holding her suitcase. She literally did come straight from the airport. To see me.

"Where are you staying?" I ask Kate.

"The only place I could find at the last minute." She pulls out a slip of paper from her bag. "Major Rug Hotel?" she says. "I have no idea how to pronounce it, let alone where it is." She hands me the paper. "Do you know it?

Hotel Magere Brug. I know exactly where it is. I rode past it almost every day of my life. On weekends they used to serve homemade pastries in the lobby, and Broodje and I would sneak in sometimes to take some. The manager pretended not to notice.

I take her suitcase. "Come on. I'll take you home."

The last time I was at the boat, it was September; I got as far as the pier before I rode away. It looked so empty, so haunted, like it was mourning his loss, too, which made a certain sense because he built it. Even the clematis that Saba had planted—"because even a cloud-soaked country needs shade"—which had once run riot over the deck, had gone shriveled and brown. If Saba had been here, he would've cut it back. It's what he always did when he came back in the summer and found the plants ailing in his absence.

The clematis is back now, bushy and wild, dropping purple petals all over the deck. The deck is full of other blooms, trellises, vines, arbors, pots, viny flowering things.

"This was my home," I tell Kate. "It's where I grew up."

Kate was mostly quiet on the tram ride over. "It's beautiful," she says.

"My father built it." I can see Bram's winked smile, hear him announce as if to no one: *I need a helper this morning.* Yael would hide under the duvet. Ten minutes later, I'd have a drill in my hand. "I helped, though. I haven't been here in a long time. Your hotel is just around the corner."

"What a coincidence," she says.

"Sometimes I think everything is."

"No. Everything isn't." She looks at me. Then she asks, "So what's wrong, Willem? Stage fright?"

"No."

"Then what is it?"

I tell her. About getting the call this morning. About that moment in the first rehearsal, finding something new, finding something real in Orlando, and then having it all go to hell.

"Now I just want to get up there, get through it, get it over with," I tell her. "With as few witnesses as possible."

I expect sympathy. Or Kate's undecipherable yet somehow

resonant acting advice. Instead, I get laughter. Snorts and hiccups of it. Then she says, "You have got to be kidding me."

I am not kidding. I don't say anything.

She attempts to contain herself. "I'm sorry, but the opportunity of a lifetime drops into your lap—you finally get one of your glorious accidents—and you're going to let a lousy piece of direction derail you."

She is making it seem so slight, a bad piece of advice. But it feels like so much more. A wallop in the face, not a piece of bad direction, but a redirection. *This is not the way.* And just when I thought I had really found something. I try to find the words to explain this . . . this betrayal. "It's like finding the girl of your dreams," I begin.

"And realizing you never caught her name?" Kate finishes.

"I was going to say finding out she was actually a guy. That you had it so completely wrong."

"That only happens in movies. Or Shakespeare. Though it's funny you mention the girl of your dreams, because I've been thinking about your girl, the one you were chasing in Mexico."

"Lulu? What does she have to do with this?"

"I was telling David about you and your story and he asked this ridiculously simple question that I've been obsessing about ever since."

"Yes?"

"It's about your backpack."

"You've been obsessing about my *backpack*?" I make it sound like a joke, but all of a sudden, my heart has sped up.

Pulled a runner. Dicked her over. I can hear Tor's disgust, in that Yorkshire accent of hers.

"Here's the thing: If you were just going out for coffee or croissants or to book a hotel room or whatever, why did you take your backpack, with all your things in it, with you?"

"It wasn't a big backpack. You saw it. It was the same one I had in Mexico. I always travel light like that." I'm talking too fast, like someone with something to hide.

"Right. Right. Traveling light. So you can move on. But you were going back to that squat, and you had to climb, if I recall, out of a second-story building. Isn't that right?" I nod. "And you brought a backpack with you? Wouldn't it have been easier to leave most of your things there? Easier to climb. At the very least, it would've been a sure sign that you intended to return."

I was there on that ledge, one leg in, one leg out. A gust of wind, so sharp and cold after all that heat, knifed through me. Inside, I heard rustling as Lulu rolled over and wrapped herself in the tarp. I'd watched her for a moment, and as I did, this feeling had come over me stronger than ever. I'd thought, *Maybe I should just wait for her to wake up.* But I was already out the window and I could see a patisserie down the way.

I'd landed heavily, in a puddle, rainwater sloshing around my feet. When I'd looked back up at the window, the white curtain flapping in the gusty breeze, I'd felt both sadness and relief, the oppositional tug of heaviness and lightness, one lifting me up, one pushing me down. I understood then, Lulu and I had started something, something I'd always wanted, but also something I was scared of getting. Something I wanted more of. And, also, something I wanted to get away from. The truth and its opposite.

I set off for the patisserie not quite knowing what to do, not quite knowing if I should go back, stay another day, but knowing if I did, it would break all this wide open. I bought the croissants, still not knowing what to do. And then I turned a corner and there were the skinheads. And in a twisted way, I was relieved: They would make the decision for me.

Except as soon as I woke up in that hospital, unable to remember Lulu, or her name, or where she was, but desperate to find her, I understood that it was the wrong decision.

"I *was* coming back," I tell Kate. But there's a razor of uncertainty in my voice, and it cuts my deception wide open.

"You know what I think, Willem?" Kate says, her voice gentle. "I think acting, that girl, it's the same thing. You get close to something and you get spooked, so you find a way to distance yourself."

In Paris, the moment when Lulu had made me feel the safest, when she had stood between me and the skinheads, when she had taken care of me, when she became my mountain girl, I'd almost sent her away. That moment, when we'd found safety, I'd looked at her, the determination burning in her eyes, the love already there, improbably after just one day. And I felt it all—the wanting and the needing—but also the fear because I'd seen what losing this kind of thing could do. I wanted to be protected by her love, and to be protected from it.

I didn't understand then. Love is not something you protect. It's something you risk.

"You know the irony about acting?" Kate muses. "We wear a thousand masks, are experts at concealment, but the one place it's impossible to hide is on stage. So no wonder you're freaked out. And Orlando, well now!"

She's right, again. I know she is. Petra didn't do anything today except give me an excuse to pull another runner. But the truth of it is I didn't really want to pull a runner that day with Lulu. And I don't want to pull one now, either.

"What's the worst that happens if you do it your way tonight?" Kate asks.

"She fires me." But if she does, it'll be my action that decides it. Not my inaction. I start to smile. It's tentative, but it's real.

Kate matches mine with a big American version. "You know what I say: Go big or go home."

I look at the boat; it's quiet, but the garden is so lush and well-tended in a way that it never was with us. It is a home, not mine, but someone else's now.

Go big or go home. I heard Kate say that before and didn't quite get it. But I understand it now, though I think on this one, Kate has it wrong. Because for me, it's not go big or go home. It's go big *and* go home.

I need to do one to do the other.

Forty-eight

---

*B*ackstage. It's the usual craziness, only I feel strangely calm. Linus hustles me to the makeshift dressing room where I change out of my street clothes into Orlando's clothes, hastily altered to fit me. I put on my makeup. I fold my clothes into the lockers behind the stage. My jeans, my shirt, Lulu's watch. I hold it in my hand one second longer, feel the ticking vibrate against my palm, and then I put it in the locker.

Linus gathers us into a circle. There are vocal exercises. The musicians tune their guitars. Petra barks last-minute direction, about finding my light and keeping the focus and the other actors supporting me, and just doing my best. She is giving me a piercing, worried look.

Linus calls five minutes and puts on his headset, and Petra walks away. Max has come backstage for tonight's performance and is sitting on a three-legged stool in the wings.

She doesn't say anything, but just looks at me and kisses two fingers and holds them up in the air. I kiss the same two on my hand and hold them up to her.

"*Break a leg*," someone whispers in my ear. It's Marina, come up behind me. Her arms quickly encircle me from behind as she kisses me somewhere between my ear and my neck. Max catches this and smirks.

"Places!" Linus calls. Petra is nowhere to be seen. She disappears before curtain and won't reappear until the show is over. Vincent says she goes somewhere to pace, or smoke, or disembowel kittens.

Linus grabs my wrist. "Willem," he says. I spin to look at him. He gives a small squeeze and nods. I nod back. "Musicians, go!" Linus commands into his headset.

The musicians start to play. I take my place at the side of stage.

"Light cue one, go," Linus says.

The lights go up. The audience hushes.

Linus: "Orlando, go!"

I hesitate a moment. *Breathe*, I hear Kate say. I take a breath.

My heart hammers in my head. *Thud, thud, thud.* I close my eyes and can hear the ticking of Lulu's watch; it's as if I'm still wearing it. I stop and listen to them both before I walk onto the stage.

And then time just stops. It is a year and a day. One hour and twenty-four. It is time, happening, all at once.

The last three years solidify into this one moment, into me, into Orlando. This bereft young man, missing a father, without a family, without a home. This Orlando, who happens upon this Rosalind. And even though these two have known each other only moments, they recognize something in each other.

"The little strength that I have, I would it were with you," Rosalind says, cracking it all wide open.

Who takes care of you? Lulu asked, cracking me wide open.

"Wear this for me," Marina says as Rosalind, handing me the prop chain from around her neck.

I'll be your mountain girl and take care of you, Lulu said, moments before I took the watch from her wrist.

Time is passing. I know it must be. I enter the stage, I exit the stage. I make my cues, hit my marks. The sun dips across the sky and then dances toward the horizon and the stars come out, the floodlights go on, the crickets sing. I sense it happening as I drift above it somehow. I am only here, now. This moment. On this stage. I am Orlando, giving myself to Rosalind. And I am Willem, too, giving myself to Lulu, in a way that I should've done a year ago, but couldn't.

"You should ask me what time o' day: there's no clock in the forest," I say to my Rosalind.

You forget, time doesn't exist anymore. You gave it to me, I said to my Lulu.

I feel the watch on my wrist that day in Paris; I hear it ticking in my head now. I can't tell them apart, last year, this year. They are one and the same. Then is now. Now is then.

"I would not be cured, youth," my Orlando tells Marina's Rosalind.

"I would cure you, if you would but call me Rosalind," Marina replies.

I'll take care of you, Lulu promised.

"By my troth, and in good earnest, and so God mend me, and by all pretty oaths that are not dangerous," Marina's Rosalind says.

I escaped danger, Lulu said.

We both did. Something happened that day. It's still happening. It's happening up here on this stage. It was just one day and it's been just one year. But maybe one day is enough. Maybe one hour is enough. Maybe time has nothing at all to do with it.

"Fair youth, I would I could make thee believe I love," my Orlando tells Rosalind.

Define love, Lulu had demanded. *What would "being stained" look like?*

Like this, Lulu.

It would look like this.

And then it's over. Like a great wave crashing onto a shore, the applause erupts and I'm here, on this stage, surrounded by the shocked and delighted smiles of my castmates. We are grasping hands and bowing and Marina is pulling me out front for our curtain call and then stepping to the side and gesturing for me to walk ahead and I do and the applause grows even louder.

Backstage, it is madness. Max is screaming. And Marina is crying and Linus is smiling, although his eyes keep darting to the side entrance that Petra left from hours ago. People are surrounding me, patting me on the back, offering congratulations and kisses and I'm here but I'm not—I'm still in some strange limbo where the boundaries of time and place and person don't exist where I can be here and in Paris, where it can be now and then, where I'm me and also Orlando.

I try to stay in this place as I change out of my clothes, scrub the makeup off my face. I look at myself in the mirror and try to digest what I just did. It feels completely unreal, and like the truest thing I have ever done. The truth and its opposite. Up on stage, playing a role, revealing myself.

People gather round me. There is talk, of parties, celebration, a cast party tonight, even though the show doesn't wrap for two more weeks and to celebrate now is technically bad luck. But it seems like everyone has given up on luck tonight. We make our own.

Petra comes backstage, stone-faced and not saying a word. She walks right past me. Goes straight to Linus.

I leave the backstage and go out the gate that serves as a stage door. Max is at my side, jumping up and down like an exuberant puppy. "So was Marina a decent kisser?" she asks me.

"I'm sure she was glad not to be kissing Jeroen," Vincent says, and I laugh.

Outside, I scan the area for my friends. I'm not quite sure who will be here. And then I hear her call my name.

"Willem!" she says again.

It's Kate, charging toward me, a blur of gold and red. My heart seems to expand as she leaps into my arms and we spin around.

"You did it. You did it. You did it!" she murmurs in my ear.

"I did it. I did it. I did it." I repeat, laughing with joy and relief and awe at the direction this day has taken.

Someone taps me on the shoulder. "You dropped something."

"Oh, right. Your flowers," Kate says, leaning over to pick up a bouquet of sunflowers. "For your stunning debut."

I take the flowers.

"How do you feel?" she asks.

I have no answer, no words. I just feel full. I try to explain it but then Kate interrupts: "Like you just had the best sex in the world?" And I laugh. Yeah, something like that. I take her hand and kiss it. She twines an arm around my waist.

"Ready to meet your adoring public?" she asks.

I'm not. Right now, I just want to savor this. With the person who helped make it happen. Leading her by the hand, I take us over to a quiet bench under a nearby gazebo and attempt in some way to articulate what just happened.

"How did that happen?" is all I can think to ask.

She holds my hands in hers. "Do you really need to ask that?"

"I think I do. It felt like something otherworldly."

"Oh, no," she says, laughing. "I believe in the muse and all, but don't go attributing that performance to one of your accidents. It was all you up there."

It was. And it wasn't. Because I wasn't alone up there.

We sit there for a little while longer. I feel my whole body buzzing, humming. This night is perfect.

"I think your groupies are waiting," Kate says after a while, gesturing behind me. I turn around and there are Broodje, Henk, W, Lien, and a few other people, watching us curiously. I take Kate by the hand and introduce them to the boys.

"You're coming to our party, aren't you?" Broodje asks.

"*Our* party?" I ask.

Broodje manages to look a tiny bit sheepish. "It's hard to un-throw a party at short notice."

"Especially since he has now invited the cast, and about half the audience," Henk says.

"That's not true!" Broodje says. "Not half. Just a couple of Canadians."

I roll my eyes and laugh. "Fine. Let's go."

Lien laughs and takes my hand. "I'm going to say good-night. One of us should be coherent tomorrow. It's moving day." She kisses W. Then me. "Well done, Willem."

"I'm going to follow her out of the park," Kate says. "This city confounds me."

"You're not coming?" I ask.

"I have some things I need to do first. I'll come later. Prop the door open for me."

"Always," I say. I go to kiss her on the cheek and she whispers into my ear, "I knew you could do it."

"Not without you," I say.

"Don't be silly. You just needed a pep talk."

But I don't mean the pep talk. I know Kate believes that I have to commit, to not rely on the accidents, to take the wheel. But had we not met in Mexico, would I be here now? Was it accidents? Or will?

For the hundredth time tonight, I'm back with Lulu, on Jacques's barge, the improbably named *Viola*. She'd just told me the story of double happiness and we were arguing over the meaning. She'd thought it meant the luck of the boy getting the job and the girl. But I'd disagreed. It was the couplet fitting together, the two halves finding each other. It was love.

But maybe we were both wrong, and both right. It's not either or, not luck *or* love. Not fate *or* will.

Maybe for double happiness, you need both.

Forty-nine

*I*nside the flat, it is complete mayhem. More than fifty people, from the cast, from Utrecht, even old school friends from my Amsterdam days. I have no idea how Broodje dug everyone up so fast.

Max pounces on me as soon as she comes in the door, followed by Vincent. "Holy. Shit," Max says.

"You might've mentioned you could act!" Vincent adds.

I smile. "I like to preserve a bit of mystery."

"Yeah, well, everyone in the cast is bloody delighted," says Max. "Except Petra. She's pissy as ever."

"Only because her understudy just completely cock-blocked her star. And now she has to decide whether to put up a lame, and I mean that both literally and figuratively, star, or let you carry us home," Vincent says.

"Decisions, decisions," Max adds. "Don't look now but Marina is giving you the fuck-me eyes again."

We all look. Marina is staring right at me and smiling.

"And don't even deny it, unless it's *me* she wants to shag," Max says.

"I'll be right back," I tell Max. I go over to her to where Marina's standing by the table Broodje has turned into the bar. She has a jug of something in her hand. "What do you have there?" I ask.

"Not entirely sure. One of your mates gave it to me, promised me no hangover. I'm taking him at his word."

"That's your first mistake right there."

She runs a finger along the top of the rim. "I have a feeling I'm long past making my first mistake." She takes a gulp of her drink. "Aren't you drinking?"

"I already feel drunk."

"Here. Catch up with yourself."

She hands me her glass and I take a sip. I taste the sour tequila that Broodje now favors, mixed with some other orange-flavored booze. "Yeah. No hangover from this. Definitely not."

She laughs, touches my arm. "I'm not going to tell you how fantastic you were tonight. You're probably sick of hearing it."

"Do you *ever* get sick of hearing it?"

She grins. "No." She looks away. "I know what I said earlier today, about after the show, but all the rules seem to be getting broken today. . . ." She trails off. "So really, can three weeks make much of a difference?"

Marina is sexy and gorgeous and smart. And she's also wrong. Three weeks can make all the difference. I know that because one day can make all the difference.

"Yes," I tell Marina. "They can."

"Oh," she says, sounding surprised, a little hurt. Then: "Are you with someone else?"

Tonight on that stage, it felt like I was. But that *was* a ghost. Shakespeare's full of them. "No," I tell her.

"Oh, I just saw you, with that woman. After the show. I wasn't sure."

Kate. The need to see her feels urgent. Because what I want is so clear to me now.

I excuse myself from Marina and poke through the flat, but there's no sign of Kate. I go downstairs to see if the door is still propped open. It is. I bump into Mrs. Van der Meer again, out walking her dog. "Sorry about all the noise," I tell her.

"It's okay," she says. She looks upstairs. "We used to have some wild parties here."

"You lived here back when it was a squat?" I ask, trying to reconcile the middle-aged *vrouw* with the young anarchists I've seen in pictures.

"Oh, yes. I knew your father."

"What was he like then?" I don't know why I'm asking that. Bram was never the hard one to crack.

But Mrs. Van der Meer's answer surprises me. "He was a bit of a melancholy young man," she says. And then her eyes flicker up to the flat, like she's seeing him there. "Until that mother of yours showed up."

Her dog yanks on the leash and she sets off, leaving me to ponder how much I know, and don't know, about my parents.

Fifty

The phone is ringing. And I'm sleeping.

I fumble for it. It's next to my pillow.

"Hello," I mumble.

"Willem!" Yael says in a breathless gulp. "Did I wake you?"

"Ma?" I ask. I wait to feel the usual panic but none comes. Instead, there's something else, a residue of something good. I rub my eyes and it's still there, floating like a mist: a dream I was having.

"I talked to Mukesh. And he worked his magic. He can get you out Monday but we have to book now. We'll do an open-ended ticket this time. Come for a year. Then decide what to do."

My head is hazy with lack of sleep. The party went until four. I fell asleep around five. The sun was already up. Slowly, yesterday's conversation with my mother comes back to me. The offer she made. How much I wanted it. Or thought I did. Some things you don't know you want until they're gone. Other things you think want, but don't understand you already have them.

"Ma," I say. "I'm not coming back to India."

"You're not?" There's curiosity in her voice, and disappointment, too.

"I don't belong there."

"You belong where I belong."

It's a relief, after all this time, to hear her say so. But I don't think it's true. I'm grateful that she has made a new home for herself in India, but it's not where I'm meant to be.

Go big and go home.

"I'm going to act, Ma," I say. And I feel it. The idea, the plan, fully formed since last night, maybe since much longer. The urgency to see Kate, who never did show up at the party, courses through me. This is one chance I'm not going to let slip through my fingers. This *is* something I need. "I'm going to act," I repeat. "Because I'm an actor."

Yael laughs. "Of course you are. It's in your blood. Just like Olga."

The name is instantly familiar. "Olga Szabo, you mean?"

There's a pause. I can feel her surprise crackle through the line. "Saba told you about her?"

"No. I found the pictures. In the attic. I meant to ask you about them but I didn't, because I've been busy . . ." I trail off. "And because we never really talked about these things."

"No. We never did, did we?"

"Who was she? Saba's girlfriend?"

"She was his sister," she replies. And I should be surprised, but I'm not. Not at all. It's like the pieces of a puzzle slotting together.

"She would have been your great aunt," Yael continues. "He always said she was an incredible actress. She was meant to go to Hollywood. But then the war came and she didn't survive."

She didn't survive. Only Saba did.

"Was Szabo her stage name?" I ask.

"No. Szabo was Saba's surname before he emigrated to Israel and Hebreified it. Lots of Europeans did that."

To distance himself, I think. I understand that. Though he couldn't really distance himself. All those silent films he took me to. The ghosts he held at bay, and held close.

Olga Szabo, my great aunt. Sister to my grandfather, Oskar Szabo, who became Oskar Shiloh, father of Yael Shiloh, wife of Bram de Ruiter, brother of Daniel de Ruiter, soon to be father of Abraão de Ruiter.

And just like that, my family grows again.

Fifty-one

When I emerge from my bedroom, Broodje and Henk are just waking up and are surveying the wreckage like army generals who have lost a major ground battle.

Broodje turns to me, his face twisted in apology. "I'm sorry. I can clean it all later. But we promised we'd meet W at ten to help him move. And we're already late."

"I think I'm going to be sick," Henk says.

Broodje picks up a beer bottle, two-thirds full of cigarette butts. "You can be sick *later*," he says. "We made a promise to W." Broodje looks at me. "And to Willy. I'll clean the flat later. And Henk's vomit, which he's going to keep corked for now."

"Don't worry about it," I say. "I'll clean it all. I'll fix everything!"

"You don't have to be so cheerful about it," Henk says, wincing and touching his temples.

I grab the keys from the counter. "Sorry," I say, not sorry at all. I head to the door.

"Where are you going?" Broodje.

"To take the wheel!"

I'm unlocking my bike downstairs when my phone rings. It's her. Kate.

"I've been calling you for the last hour," I say. "I'm coming to your hotel."

"My hotel, huh?" she says. I can hear the smile in her voice.

"I was worried you'd leave. And I have a proposition for you."

"Well, propositions *are* best proposed in person. But sit tight because I'm actually on my way to you. That's why I'm calling. Are you home?"

I think of the flat, Broodje and Henk in their boxers, the unbelievable mess. The sun is out, really out, for the first time in days. I suggest we meet at the Sarphatipark instead. "Across the street. Where we were yesterday," I remind her.

"Proposition downgraded from a hotel to a park, Willem?" she teases. "I'm not sure whether to be flattered or insulted."

"Yeah, me neither."

I go straight to the park and wait, sitting down on one of the benches near the sandpit. A little boy and girl are discussing their plans for a fort.

"Can it have one hundred towers?" the little boy asks. The girl says, "I think twenty is better." Then the boy asks,

"Can we live there forever?" The girl considers the sky a moment and says, "Until it rains."

By the time Kate shows up, they've made significant progress, digging a moat and constructing two towers.

"Sorry it took so long," Kate says, breathless. "I got lost. This city of yours, it runs in circles."

I start to explain about the concentric canals, the Ceintuurbaan being a belt that goes around the waist of the city. She waves me off. "Don't bother. I'm hopeless." She sits down next to me. "Any word from Frau Directeur?"

"Total silence."

"That sounds ominous."

I shrug. "Maybe. Nothing I can do. Anyway, I have a new plan."

"Oh," Kate says, widening her already big green eyes. "You do?"

"I do. In fact, that's what my proposition is about."

"The thick plottens."

"What?"

She shakes her head. "Never mind." She crosses her legs, leans in toward me. "I'm ready. Proposition me."

I take her hand. "I want you." I pause. "To be my director."

"Isn't that a little like shaking hands after making love?" she asks.

"What happened last night," I begin, "it happened because of you. And I want to work with you. I want to come study with Ruckus. Be an apprentice."

Kate's eyes slit into smiles. "How do you know about our apprenticeships?" she drawls.

"I may have looked at your website one or a hundred

times. And I know you mostly work with Americans, but I grew up speaking English, I act in English. Most of the time, I dream in English. I want to do Shakespeare. In English. I want to do it. With you."

The grin has disappeared from Kate's face. "It wouldn't be like last night—Orlando on a main stage. Our apprentices do everything. They build sets. They work tech. They study. They act in the ensemble. I'm not saying you wouldn't play principal roles one day—I would not rule that out, not after last night. But it would take a while. And, there are visa issues to consider, not to mention the union, so you couldn't come over expecting the spotlight. And I've told David he needs to meet you."

I look at Kate and am about to say that I wouldn't expect that, that I'd be patient, that I know how to build things. But I stop myself because it occurs to me that I don't need to convince *her* of anything.

"Where do you think I was last night?" she asks. "I was waiting for David to get back from his *Medea*, so I could tell him about you. Then I arranged for him to get his ass on a plane so he could see you tonight before that invalid comes back. He's on his way, and in fact, I have to leave soon to go to the airport to meet him. After all this trouble, they'd better put you on again, otherwise, you're going to have to do it solo for him."

She laughs. "I'm kidding. But Ruckus is a small operation so we make decisions like this communally. That's another thing you have to be prepared for, how dysfunctionally co-dependent we all are." She throws up her arms. "But every family is like that."

"So, wait? You were going to ask me?"

The grin is back. "Was there any doubt? But it pleases me no end, Willem, that *you* asked *me*. It shows you've been paying attention, which is what a director wants in an actor." She taps her temple. "Also, very clever of you to move to the States. Good for your career but also it's where your Lulu is from."

I think of Tor's letter, only today the regret and recrimination is gone. She looked for me. I looked for her. And last night, in some strange way, we found each other.

"That's not why I want to go," I tell Kate.

She smiles. "I know. I'm just teasing. Though I think you'll really take to Brooklyn. It has a lot in common with Amsterdam. The brownstones and the rowhouses, the loving tolerance of eccentricity. I think you'll feel right at home."

When she says that a feeling comes over me. Of pausing, of resting, of all the clocks in the world going quiet.

Home.

Fifty-two

But Daniel's home. That is a mess.

When I get back, the boys have left, and there is crap everywhere. It looks like how Bram used to describe it in the old days, before Yael arrived and asserted her brand of order.

There are bottles and ashtrays and plates and pizza boxes and every dish seems dirty and out. The whole place smells like cigarettes. It's certainly not a place that a baby should live. I'm momentarily paralyzed, not sure where to start.

I put on a CD of Adam Wilde, that singer-songwriter Max and I went to see a few weeks ago. And then I just go. I empty out the beer and wine bottles and put them in a box for recycling. Next, I dump the ashtrays and rinse them out. Even though there's a dishwasher now, I fill the sink with hot, soapy water and clean all the dirty dishes, then dry them. I throw open the windows to air our the place, and sunshine and fresh air come blowing in.

By noon, I've collected the bottles, tossed the cigarette butts, washed and dried the dishes, dusted and vacuumed. It's about as clean as it was on its best day with Daniel, though when he comes home with Abraão and Fabiola, I'll have it spotless. Ready.

I make a coffee. I check my phone to see if there's any word from Linus, but it's sitting on my bed, dead. I plug it in to charge, setting the coffee on my shelf. The envelope is still there, with the photos of me Yael, Bram, Saba, Olga. I run my finger along the crease of the envelope, feel the weight of history inside. Wherever I'm going next, these are coming with me.

I glance at my phone. It's still dead, but soon there will be some word from Linus and Petra. Part of me thinks that I must be fired. That has to be the price to pay for last night's triumph, and it's okay because it's a price I'm willing to pay. But another part of me is losing faith that the universal law of equilibrium operates that way.

I go back into the lounge. The Adam Wilde CD has been repeating and the songs are starting to become familiar enough that I know I will be able to hear them when I'm not listening to them.

I look around the room. I fluff the cushions and lie down on the sofa. I should be in suspense, waiting for word about tonight, but I feel the opposite. It's like that moment of pause when I step out of a train station or bus station or airport into a new city and it's nothing but possibility.

Through the open window, the dissonant sounds of the city—of tram chimes and bicycle bells and the occasional jet roaring overhead—drift in and mingle with the music and lull me to sleep.

For the third time in one day, I'm woken up by the ringing of a phone. Like this morning when Yael called, I have that same feeling, of being somewhere else, somewhere right.

The ringing stops. But I know it must be Linus. *My fate*, Marina had called it. But it's not my fate; it's just about tonight. My fate is up to me.

I go into my room and pick up the phone. Out the window, climbing through the clouds I make out the blue-and-white underbelly of a KLM jet. I picture myself on a plane, flying out of Amsterdam, over the North Sea, over England and Ireland, past Iceland and Greenland and down Newfoundland and along the Eastern Seaboard, into New York. I feel the jerk, hear the skid of the tires touching down, the explosion of applause from the passengers. Because we are all of us, so grateful for having at last arrived.

I glance at my phone. It's full of congratulatory texts from last night, and a voicemail from Linus. "Willem, can you please call in as soon as possible," he says.

I take a deep breath, prepare myself for whatever he has to say. It doesn't really matter. I went big and now I'm going home.

Just as Linus answers there's a faint knock at the front door.

"Hello, hello . . ." Linus's voice echoes.

There's another knock, louder this time. Kate? Broodje?

I tell Linus I'll call him right back. I put the phone down. I open the door. And once again, time stops.

I'm shocked. And I'm not. She is just as I remember her. And completely transformed. A stranger. And someone I know. *The truth and its opposite are flip sides of the same coin*, I hear Saba say.

"Hello Willem," she says. "My name is Allyson."

Allyson. I say the name in my head and a year's worth of memories and fantasies and one-sided conversations are revised and updated. Not Lulu. Allyson. A strong name. A solid name. And somehow, a familiar name. Everything about her seems familiar. I know this person. I'm known to this person. It's then I understand what I was dreaming about this morning, who it is that's been sitting next to me on that plane all this time.

Allyson walks in.

The door clicks shut behind her. And for a minute, they're in the room with us too. Yael and Bram, thirty years ago. Their entire story rushes through my head, because it's our story, too. Only now, I realize, it was an incomplete story. Because so matter how many times he told it, Bram never told me the important part. What happened during those first three hours together in the car.

Or maybe he did, only without words. With his action.

"And so I kissed her. Like I'd been expecting her all that time," my previously melancholy father would say, always with wonder in his voice.

I'd thought the wonder was for the accidents. But maybe it wasn't. Maybe the wonder was for the stain. Three hours in a car, that was all it took. And two years later, there she was.

Maybe he was overwhelmed, like I am overwhelmed, by

that mysterious intersection where love meets luck, where fate meets will. Because he'd been waiting for her. And there she was.

So he'd kissed her.

I kiss Allyson.

I complete the history that came before us, and in doing so, begin one all of our own.

Double happiness: I get it now.

Acknowledgments

A novelist is a thief by necessity. I would first like to apologize to and then thank all of the people I've met over the years in my travels and in my life, whose bits and pieces I've stolen, disguised, and put in this book. There are too many of you to list, and I don't even know if I remember everyone's names. But I remember them just the same. People you meet for a day really can inspire you in ways you might not recognize until, decades later, a tiny piece of them gets plunked into a novel.

For all those who knowingly helped me with this great big hodgepodge of an internationally globetrotting book, a heartfelt thank you, merci, bedankt, gracias, הדות, धन्यवाद, köszönöm, and obrigada. Specifically to: Jessie Austrian, Fabiola Bergi, Michael Bourret, Libba Bray, Sarah Burnes, Heleen Buth, Mitali Dave (and parents), Danielle Delaney, Céline Faure, Fiasco Theater Company, Greg Forman, Lee and Ruth Forman, Rebecca Gardner, Logan Garrison, Tamara Glenny, Marie-Elisa Gramain, Tori Hill, Ben Hoffman, Marjorie Ingall, Anna Jarzab, Maureen Johnson, Deborah Kaplan, Isabel Kyriacou, E. Lockhart, Elyse Marshall, Tali Meas, Stephanie Perkins, Mukesh Prasad, Will Roberts, Philippe Robinet, Leila Sales, Tamar and Robert Schamhart,

William Shakespeare, Deb Shapiro, Courtney Sheinmel, *Slings & Arrows*, Andreas Sonju, Emke Spauwen, Margaret Stohl, Julie Strauss-Gabel, Alex Ulyett, Robin Wasserman, Cameron and Jackie Wilson, Ken Wright, and the whole team at Penguin Young Readers Group. It takes a village—in this case, a global one.

And finally, thank you to Nick, Willa, and Denbele: My family. My home.